AT THE YELLOW
MINE SALOON

Piles of gold and greenbacks littered the roulette and faro tables. Hard-faced gamblers, bearded mountain men, lean cowpunchers—all bent with intent gaze over their cards or chips. Drunken miners stamped to and from the long mahogany bar. An odor of whiskey mingled with the thick tobacco haze.

In one corner, a slender girl with bare shoulders stood beside a poker table. She looked up and caught Panhandle's eyes. She gave him the lazy, come-on smile she had used on a thousand other cowboys.

Suddenly, one of the gamblers turned, and Smith recognized Dick Hardman, the desperado he had followed a thousand miles—to kill!

Books by Zane Grey

The Arizona Clan
Black Mesa
The Border Legion
Boulder Dam
The Call of the Canyon
Drift Fence
The Dude Ranger
Fighting Caravans
Forlorn River
The Fugitive Trail
The Hash Knife Outfit
The Heritage of the Desert
Lone Star Ranger
Lost Pueblo
The Lost Wagon Train
Majesty's Rancho

Raiders of Spanish Peaks
The Rainbow Trail
Riders of the Purple Sage
Rogue River Feud
Stairs of Sand
Stranger from the Tonto
Thunder Mountain
Twin Sombreros
Under the Tonto Rim
The U.P. Trail
Valley of Wild Horses
Western Union
West of the Pecos
Wilderness Trek
Wildfire
Wyoming

Published by POCKET BOOKS

ZANE GREY

VALLEY OF WILD HORSES

PUBLISHED BY POCKET BOOKS NEW YORK

POCKET BOOKS, a Simon & Schuster division of
GULF & WESTERN CORPORATION
1230 Avenue of the Americas, New York, N.Y. 10020

ISBN: 0-671-43948-2

First Pocket Books printing September, 1959

20   19   18   17   16   15   14   13

POCKET and colophon are trademarks of Simon & Schuster.

Printed in the U.S.A.

1

◈

THE PANHANDLE was a lonely purple range land, unfenced and wind swept. Bill Smith, cattleman, threw up a cabin and looked at the future with hopeful eyes. One day while plowing almost out of sight of his little home—which that morning he had left apprehensively owing to an impending event—he espied his wife Margaret coming along the edge of the plowed field. She had brought his lunch this day, despite his order to the contrary. Bill dropped the loop of his driving reins over the plow handle and strode toward her. Presently she halted wearily and sat down where the dark rich overturned earth met the line of bleached grass. Bill meant to scold Margaret for bringing his lunch, but it developed she had brought him something more. A son!

This boy was born on the fragrant fresh soil, out on the open prairie, under the steely sun and the cool wind from off the Llano Estacado. He came into the world protesting against this primitive manner of birth. Bill often related that the youngster arrived squalling and showed that his lung capacity fitted his unusual size. Despite the mother's protestations, Bill insisted on calling the lad Panhandle.

Panhandle's first memory was of climbing into the big cupboard in the cabin, falling upon his head and getting blood all over his white dress. His next adventurous experience was that of chewing tobacco he found in his father's coat. This made him very sick. His mother thought he was poisoned, and as Bill was away, she ran to the nearest neighbors for help. By the time she returned with the experienced neighbor woman Panhandle had gotten rid of the tobacco and was bent upon further conquest.

Another day Panhandle manifested a growing tendency toward self-assertion. He ran away from home. Owing to his short legs and scant breath he did not get very far down over the slope. His will and intention were tremendous. Did the dim desert call to the child? His parents had often seen him stand gazing into the purple distance. But Panhandle on this runaway occasion fell asleep on the dry grassy bottom of an irrigation ditch. Bye and bye he was missed, and father and mother and the farm hands ran hither and thither in wild search for him. No one, however, found him. In the haste of the search someone left his work at the irrigation dam, and the water running down rudely awoke the child out of his dreams. Wet and bedraggled, squalling at the top of his lungs, Panhandle trudged back home to the relief of a distracted mother.

"Doggone it." ejaculated Bill to his neighbors. "That kid's goin' to be just like me. I never could stay home."

A year later Bill Smith sold his farm and moved farther west in Texas, where he took up a homestead, and divided his time between that and work on a big irrigating canal which was being constructed.

Panhandle now lived on a ranch and it was far lonelier than his first home, because his father was away so much of the time. At first the nearest neighbor was Panhandle's uncle, who lived two long prairie miles away. His house was a black dot on the horizon, not unattainable. it seemed to Panhandle, but very far away. He would have risked the distance, save for his mother, who was very timid in this country so new to her. Panhandle would never forget how she was frightened at a crazy wanderer who happened to come along, and another time by some drunken Mexican laborers.

Panhandle undoubtedly had an adventuring soul. One day he discovered that a skunk had dug a hole under the front porch and had given birth to her kittens there. Panhandle was not afraid of them, and neither hurt nor frightened them After a time he made playmates of them, and was one day hugely enjoying himself with them when his mother found him. She was frightened, enraged and horrified all at once. She entreated Panhandle to let the dirty little skunks alone. Panhandle would promise and then

2

forget. His mother punished him, all to no avail. Then she adopted harsher measures.

Homesteaders had located near by and Mrs. Smith called on them, in the hope that she could hire a cowboy or ranch hand to come over and destroy the skunks. It chanced there was no one but a Mrs. Hardman and her only boy. His name was Dick. He was seven years old, large for his age, a bold handsome lad with red hair. Mrs. Smith made a bargain with Dick, and led him back with her.

Here Panhandle took violent exception to having his pets killed or routed out by this boy he had never before seen. He did not like his looks anyway. But Dick paid little heed to Panhandle, except once when Mrs. Smith went into the house, and then he knocked Panhandle down. For once Panhandle did not squall. He got up, round eyed, pale, with his hands clenched. He never said a word. Something was born in the depths of his gentle soul then.

Dick tore a hole in the little wall of rocks that supported the porch, and with a lighted torch on a stick he wormed his way in to rout out the skunks.

Panhandle suddenly was thrilled and frightened by a bellowing from Dick. The boy came hurriedly backing out of the hole. He fetched an odor with him that nearly suffocated Panhandle, so strange and raw and terrible was it. Dick's eyes were shut. For the time being he had been blinded. He bounced around like a chicken with its head cut off, bawling wildly.

What had happened Panhandle did not know, but it certainly suited him. "Goody! Goody!" he shouted, holding his nose, and edging away from the lad.

Then Panhandle saw smoke issuing from the hole under the porch. The mother skunk and her kittens scampered out into the weeds. He heard the crackle of flames. That boy had dropped his torch under the porch. Screaming, Panhandle ran to alarm his mother. But it was too late. There were no men near at hand, so nothing could be done. Panhandle stood crying beside his mother, watching their little home burn to the ground. Somehow in his mind the boy, Dick, had been to blame. Panhandle peered round to find him, but he was gone. Never would Panhandle forget that boy.

They walked to the uncle's house and spent the night

3

there. Soon another home was under construction on the same site. It was more of a shack than a house, for building materials were scarce, and the near approach of winter made hasty construction imperative. Winter came soon, and Panhandle and his mother were alone. It was cold and they huddled over the little wood fire. They had plenty to eat, but were very uncomfortable in the one-room shack. Bill Smith came home but seldom. That fall the valley had been over-run with homesteaders, "nesters," they were called, and these newcomers passed by often from the town drunk and rough.

Panhandle used to lie awake a good deal. During these lonely hours the moan of the prairie wind, the mourn of wolves and yelp of coyotes became part of his existence. He understood why his mother barred and blocked the one door, placed the ax by the bed and the gun under her pillow. Even then he longed for the time when he would be old and big enough to protect her.

The lonely winter, with its innumerable hours of solitude for Mrs. Smith and the boy, had incalculable influence upon his character. She taught him much, ways and things, words and feelings that became an integral part of his life.

At last the long winter ended. With spring came the gales of wind which, though no longer cold, were terrible in their violence. Many a night Panhandle lay awake, shrinking beside his mother, fearing the shack would blow away over their heads. Many a day the sun was obscured, and nothing could be cooked, no work done while the dust storm raged.

As spring advanced, with a lessening of the tornadoes, a new and fascinating game came into Panhandle's life. It was to sit at the one little window and watch the cowboys ride by. How he came to worship them! They were on their way to the spring roundups. His father had told him all about them. Panhandle would strain his eyes to get a first glimpse of them, to count the shaggy prancing horses, the lithe supple riders with their great sombreros, their bright scarfs, guns and chaps, and boots and spurs. Their lassos! How they fascinated Panhandle! Ropes to whirl and throw at a running steer! That was a game he resolved to play when he grew up. And his mother, discovering his interest, made him a little *reata* and taught him how to throw it, how to make

4

loops and knots. She told him how her people had owned horses, thrown lassos, run cattle.

Panhandle was always watching for the cowboys. When they passed by he would run to the other side of the shack where there was a knothole stuffed with a rag, and through this he would peep until he was blinded by dust. These were full days for the lad, rousing in him wonder and awe, eagerness and fear—strange longings for he knew not what.

Then one day his father brought home a black pony with three white feet and a white spot on his face. Panhandle was in rapture. For him! He could have burst for very joy, but he could not speak. It developed that his mother would not let him ride the pony except when she led it. This roused as great a grief as possession was joy. A beautiful little pony he could not ride! Ideas formed in his mind, scintillated and grew into dark purpose.

One day he stole Curly, and led him out of sight behind the barn, and mounting him rode down to the spring. Panhandle found himself alone. He was free. He was on the back of a horse. Mighty and incalculable fact!

Curly felt the spirit of that occasion. After drinking at the spring he broke into a lope. Panhandle stuck on somehow and turned the pony toward the house. Curly loped faster. Panhandle felt the wind in his hair. He bounced up and down. Squealing with delight he twisted his hands in the flowing mane and held on. At the top of the hill his joy became divided by fear. Curly kept on loping down the hill toward the house. Faster and faster! Panhandle bounced higher and higher, up on his neck, back on his haunches, until suddenly his hold broke and he was thrown. Down he went with a thud. It jarred him so he could hardly get up, and he reeled dizzily. There stood his mother, white of face, reproachful of eye. "Oh, Mama—I ain't hurt!" he cried.

Bill Smith was approached about this and listened, stroking his lean chin, while the mother eloquently enlarged upon the lad's guilt.

"Wal, wife, let the boy ride," he replied. "He's a nervy kid. I named him well. He'll make a great cowboy. Panhandle Smith. Pan, for short!"

Pan heard that and his heart beat high. How he loved his dad then! "Cowboy" meant one of the great riders of the range. He would be one. Thereafter he lived on the back of Curly. He learned to ride, to stick on like a burr, to keep his seat on the bare back of the pony, to move with him as he moved. One day Pan was riding home from his uncle's, and coming to a level stretch of ground he urged Curly to his topmost speed. The wind stung him, the motion exhilarated him, controlling the pony awoke and fixed some strange feeling in him. He was a cowboy. Suddenly Curly put a speeding foot into a prairie-dog hole. Something happened. Pan felt himself jerked loose and shot through the air. He struck the ground and all went black. When he came to, he found he had plowed the soft earth with his face, skinned nose and chin, but was not badly hurt. That was his first great spill. It sobered him. Curly waited for him a little way farther on and he was lame. Pan knew he could not hide the evidences of his rashness, so he decided to tell the truth.

Pan encountered his father at the barn.

"Say, you bloody cowpuncher," demanded his parent, "did he pitch with you?"

"No, Dad," replied Pan, with effort. "I runned him fast."

"Ah-huh, so I see," went on the father; and after a searching look over the boy he fell to examining the pony.

Pan emboldened by what his father had called him went straight to his mother. She screamed at sight of him, and that struck Pan to the heart. "Aw, Mama, it ain't nuthin'. I'm just a bloody cowpuncher."

Pan was not quite six years old when he rode to his first roundup, which occurred that summer early in June. His glory in the experience was marred by shame because he had to appear before all these cowboys without a saddle on his horse. He had feared just exactly what happened.

"Wal, heah comes the Ridin' Kid from Loco Range," said one, edging near to Pan, with a smile on his shining red face.

"Sonny, yo're forkin' a grand hoss, but you forgot to saddle him," remarked another, with a twinkle of gray eyes.

"Fellars, this heah is Panhandle Smith, kid of the homesteader, over by the river. I heerd Pan's a trick bareback rider."

These genial fiery young men, lithe and tall and round limbed, breathing the life and spirit of the range, crowded round Pan, proving that there never was a cowboy who did not like youngsters.

"Say, kid, I'll swap saddles with you," spoke up the one who had first addressed him.

Pan's heart was palpitating. How could they know how beautiful and wonderful they looked to him? If it had not been that he was riding Curly bareback! They were making fun of him. Tears were not far from his eyes.

"Young fellar, I'll bet this nag of yourn can't run fast enough to ketch cold," spoke up another.

"I'll bet he kin," added a third.

"Pan, do this to them," put in the cowboy who appeared to know him, and suiting act to word he placed his thumb to his nose and twiddled his finger. "Do that, Pan. That'll shore shut them up."

Pan found himself impelled to do as he was bidden, which action raised a howl of mirth from the cowboys.

And so at that early age Panhandle Smith was initiated into the hilarity and trickery and spirit common to these carefree riders of the ranges.

When the roundup began he found that he was far from forgotten.

"Come on, Pan," shouted one. "Ride in heah an' help me. . . . Turn 'em back, kid."

Pan rode like the wind, breathless and radiant, beside himself with bliss.

Then another rider would yell to him: "Charge him, cowboy. Fetch him back."

And Pan, scarcely knowing what he was doing, saw with wild eyes how the yearling or calf would seem to be driven by him. There was always a cowboy near him, riding fast, yet close, yelling to him, making him a part of the roundup.

At the noon hour an older man, no doubt the rancher who owned the cattle, called off the work. A lusty voice from somewhere yelled: "Come an' git it!"

The rancher, espying Pan, rode over to him and said: "Stranger, did you fetch your chuck with you?"

"No—sir," faltered Pan. "My mama—said for me to hurry back."

"Wal, you stay an' eat with me," replied the man, kindly.

7

"Shore them varmints might stampede an' we'd need you powerful bad."

Pan sat next this big black-eyed man, in the circle of hungry cowboys. They made no more fun of Pan. He was one of them. Hard indeed was it for him to sit cross-legged, after the fashion of cowboys, with a steady plate upon his knees. But he had no trouble disposing of the juicy beefsteak and boiled potatoes and beans and hot biscuits that Tex, the boss, piled upon his plate.

After dinner the cowboys resumed work.

"Stand heah by the fire, kid," said Tex.

Then Pan saw a calf being dragged across the ground. A mounted cowboy held the rope.

"The brand!" he yelled.

Pan stood there trembling while one of the flankers went down the tight rope to catch the bawling, leaping calf. It's eyes stood out, it foamed at the mouth. The flanker threw it over his leg on its back with feet sticking up. A brander with a white iron leaped closed. The calf bellowed. There was a sizzling of hair, a white smoke, the odor of burned hide, all of which sickened Pan.

Then one of the cowboys came to him: "Reckon thet's yore mammy come for you."

He lifted Pan up on Curly and led the pony away from the roundup, out in the open where Pan espied his mother, eager and anxious with her big dark eyes strained.

"Beg pardon, lady," spoke up the cowboy, touching his sombrero. "It's our fault yore boy stayed so long. We're sorry if you worried. Please don't blame him. He's shore a game kid an' will make a grand cowboy some day."

2

◆

So this was how Panhandle Smith, at the mature age of five, received the stimulus that set the current of his life in one strong channel. He called himself "Tex." If his mother forgot to use this thrilling name he was offended. He adopted Tex's way of walking, riding, talking. And all the hours of daylight, outdoors or indoors, he played roundup. Stones, chips, nails—anything served for cattle—and he had a special wooden image of himself and horse. Much of this time he spent on the back of Curly, in the corral or the field, rounding up an imaginary herd. At night his dreams were full of cowboys, chuck wagons, pitching horses and bawling steers.

Every new sight of a snaky slim cowpuncher on a racy horse intensified this impression in Pan's mind, stamped the future more vividly on his heart. It was what he had been born to.

One by one pioneers came in their covered wagons to this promising range and took up homesteads of one hundred and sixty acres each. Some of these men, like Pan's father, had to work part of the time away from home, to earn much-needed money.

Jim Blake, the latest of these incoming settlers, had chosen a site down in a deep swale that Pan always crossed when he went to visit his uncle. It was a pretty place, with grass and cottonwoods, and a thin stream of water, a lonesome and hidden spot which other homesteaders had passed by.

Pan met Jim one day and rode with him. He was a young

9

man, pleasant and jolly, a farmer and would-be rancher, without any of the signs of cowboy about him. Pan thought this a great detriment, but he managed to like Jim and loftily acquainted him with his achievements on Curly.

One day Pan saw Jim's wife, a pretty blonde girl, strong and healthy and rosy cheeked. Her sleeves were rolled up showing round bare arms. Her smile won Pan, yet he was too shy to go in and take the cookies she offered.

Autumn days came, dull and gray, with cold wind sweeping the plain, and threatening clouds lodging against the mountain peaks. Another winter was coming. Pan hated the thought. Snow, ice, piercing winds would prevent him from riding Curly. With this fact pressing closer he rode as much as his mother would let him and some more besides.

His father and mother wanted him to go with them to the settlement one Saturday. They were taking the wagon in for winter supplies. Pan's yearning for adventure almost persuaded him, but he preferred to stay with Curly. His mother demurred, but his father said he might remain at home.

"Pan, you can ride over to Uncle George's with some things. But be careful not to get caught in a storm."

Thus it came about that Pan found himself alone for the first time in his life, master of himself, free to act as he chose. And he did not choose to go at once to Uncle George's. His uncle was nice, but did not accord Pan the freedom that he craved. So what with one and another of his important cowboy tasks the hours flew and it was late before he got started across the prairie toward his uncle's homestead.

Pan never needed an excuse to ride fast, but now he had one that justified him. The two miles would not take long. He would have to hurry back, for indeed it looked as if a storm were sweeping down from the black peaks. Pan realized that he should have gotten his errand done earlier in the day.

The cold wind stung his face and made his eyes water. Curly loped at his easy swift stride over the well-trodden trail. The bleached grass waved, the tumbleweeds rolled along the brown ground. There was no sun. All the west was draped in drab clouds. Soon Pan was riding down into the swale where Blake lived. The cottonwoods were almost

bare. Only a few yellow leaves clung to the branches, and
every moment a leaf fluttered down. Here in this swale Pan
caught the autumn smells, dank and woody.

Once across the swale he put his pony to a gallop and
soon reached Uncle George's homestead. No one at home!
The horse and wagon were gone. Pan left his package and
turned back. As he trotted past the Blake gate Pan heard a
faint call. It startled him. Reining in Curly he listened and
looked. Blake's cabin stood back out of sight among the cottonwoods. The barn, however, with its low open-sided shed,
stood just inside the gate. The cows had been brought in for
milking. A lusty calf was trying to steal milk from its mother.
Chickens were going to roost. Pan did not believe that any
of these had made the call. He was about to ride on by when
suddenly he again caught a strange cry that appeared to
come from the barn or shed. It excited rather than frightened him. Sliding off Curly he pushed open the big board
gate and ran in.

Under the open shed he found Mrs. Blake lying on some
hay which evidently she had just pulled down from the
loft. When she saw Pan her pale convulsed face changed
somehow. "Oh—thank God!" she cried.

"Are you hurted?" asked Pan in hurried sympathy. "Did
you fall out of the haymow?"

"No, but I'm in terrible pain."

"Aw—you're sick?"

"Yes. And I'm alone. Will you please—go for your
mother?"

"Mama an' Daddy went to town," replied Pan in distress. "An' nobody's home at Uncle George's."

"Then you must be a brave little boy and help me."

Hurrying homeward, Bill Smith and his wife, and Jim
Blake, were belated by the storm. It was midnight when
they arrived at Bill's house. They found Curly with bridle
hanging, standing in the snow beside the barn. Mrs. Smith
was distracted. Bill and Jim, though worried, did not fear
the worst. But with lanterns they set out upon the tracks
Curly had left in the snow. Bill's wife would not remain
behind.

Soon they arrived at Blake's homestead, though the pony

11

tracks became difficult to follow and found Pan wide awake, huddled beside the cow, true to the trust that had been given him. Mrs. Blake was not in bad condition, considering the circumstances, nor was the baby. It was a girl, whom Jim named Lucy right then and there, after his wife.

The men carried the mother and her babe up to the house, while Mrs. Smith followed with the now sleepy Pan. They built fires in the open grate, and in the kitchen stove, and left Mrs. Smith to attend to the mother. Both women heard the men talking. But Pan never heard, for he had been put to bed in a corner, rolled in blankets.

"Doggone my hide!" exclaimed Bill. "Never seen the beat of that kid of mine!"

"Mebbe Pan saved both their lives, God bless him," replied Blake with emotion.

"*Quien sabe?* It might be. . . . Wal, strange things happen. Jim, that kid of mine was born right out on the plowed field. An' here comes your kid—born in the cowshed on the hay!"

"It is strange," mused Blake, "though we ought to look for such happenin's out in this great west."

"Wal, Pan an' Lucy couldn't have a better birthright. It ought to settle them two kids for life."

"You mean grow up an' marry some day? Now that would be fine. Shake on it, Bill."

Pan asleep in the corner of the room and Lucy wailing at her mother's breast were pledged to each other by their fathers.

The winter passed for Pan much as had the preceding one, except that he had more comfort to play his everlasting game of roundup.

"When will Lucy be big enough to play with me?" he often asked. The strange little baby girl had never passed from his mind, though he had never seen her. She seemed to form the third link in his memory of the forging of his life. Curly—the cowboys—and Lucy! He did not know how to reconcile her with the other two. But those three events stood out above the blur of the past.

At last the snow melted, the prairie took on a sheen of green, the trees burst into bud, and birds returned to sing once more. All of this was beautiful, but insignificant beside Curly. He was fatter and friskier than ever.

Pan's father came home once or twice a month that spring, always arriving late and leaving at any early hour. How Pan longed for his father's coming!

Then there came the fourth epoch in Pan's life. His father brought him a saddle. It was far from new, of Mexican make, covered with rawhide, and had an enormous shiny horn. Pan loved it almost as much as he loved Curly; and when it was not on the pony it adorned the fence or a chair, always with Pan astride it, acting like Tex.

The fifth, and surely the greatest event in Pan's rapidly developing career, though he did not know it then, was when his mother took him over to see his baby, Lucy Blake. It appeared that the parents in both homesteads playfully called her "Pan's baby." That did not displease Pan, but it made him singularly shy. So it was long before his mother could get him to make the acquaintance of his protégée.

Pan's first sight of Lucy was when she crawled over the floor to get to him. How vastly different she really was from the picture he recalled of a moving bundle wrapped in a towel! She was quite big and very wonderful. She was dressed in a little white dress. Her feet and legs were chubby. She had tiny pink hands. Her face was like a wild rose dotted with two violets for eyes. And her hair was spun gold. Marvelous as were all these things they were as nothing to the light of her smile. Pan's shyness vanished, and he sat on the floor to play with her. He produced little chips and pebbles, and stones, with which he played roundup. Lucy grew most gratifyingly interested in Pan's game, but she made it hard for him to play it, and also embarrassing, by clinging with most tenacious and unshakable grip to his finger.

Every Sunday that summer the Smiths visited at the homestead of the Blakes. They became fast friends. Bill and Jim discussed the cattle business. The mothers sewed and talked hopefully of the future. Pan never missed one of these Sunday visits, and the time came when he rode over on his own account. Lucy was the most satisfactory cowgirl in all the world. She did not object to his being Tex. She tried her best to call him Tex. And she crawled after him and toddled after him with unfailing worship. The grown folks looked on and smiled.

Meanwhile the weeks and months passed, the number of homesteaders increased, more and more cattle dotted the range. When winter came some of the homesteaders, including Pan and his mother, moved into Littleton to send their children to school.

Pan's first teacher was Emma Jones. He liked her immediately which was when she called to take him to school. Pan was not used to strangers. The men in the streets, the grown boys all bother him. Cowboys were scarce, and that was a big disappointment to Pan. It lowered Littleton in his estimation.

It developed that Pan was left handed. Now Miss Jones considered it wrong for anyone to write with his left hand so she tied Pan's fast to the desk, and made him practice letters with his right. What a dreary unprofitable time Pan had of it! So many little boys and girls confused him, though he was not backward in making acquaintance. But he wanted Curly and the prairie. He would rather be with Lucy. Most of all he wanted the cowboys.

Dick Hardman came again into Pan's life, fatefully, inevitably, as if the future had settled something inscrutable and sinister, and childhood days, school days, days of youth and manhood had been inextricably planned before they were born. Dick was in a higher grade and made the fact known to Pan. He had grown into a large boy, handsomer, bolder, with a mop of red hair that shone like a flame. He called Pan "the little skunk tamer," and incited other boys to ridicule. So the buried resentment in Pan's depths smoldered and burst into blaze again, and found fuel to burn it into hate. He told his mother what Dick had got the boys to call him. Then he was indeed surprised to see his sweet soft-eyed mother give way to quick-flashing passion. Somehow this leap of her temper strengthened Pan in his resentment. He had her blood, her fire, her pride, though he was only a child.

Then the endless school days were over for a while. Summer had come. Pan moved back to the beloved homestead, to the open ranges, to Curly and Lucy. Only she had changed. She could stand at his knee and call him Tex. He

14

resumed his old games with her, and in time graduated her to a seat on the back of Curly. If she had not already consciously filled his heart that picture of her laughing and unafraid would have done so.

Another uncle had moved into the country to take up a homestead. Pan now had a second place to ride to, farther away, over a wilder bit of range, and much to his liking. He saw cowboys every time he rode there.

One day while Pan was at this new uncle's, a dreadful thing happened—his first real tragedy. Some cowboy left the slide door of the granary open. Curly got in there at the wheat. Before it became known he ate enormously and then drank copiously. It foundered him. It killed him.

When Pan came out of his stupefaction to realize his actual loss he was heartbroken. He could not be consoled. Hours he spent crying over his saddle. Not for a long time did he go to see little Lucy. His father could not afford to buy him another horse then and indeed it was a long time before he did get one.

Days and weeks passed, and fall came, then winter with more school, tedious and wearing, and again spring and summer. Cowboys were plentiful now in the growing range, but Pan avoided them, ashamed and sick because he could not approach them without Curly. He never got over grieving for his pony, though he reached a stage where any horse would have freed him from his melancholy. He played alone, or with Lucy. She was the one bright spot in all that gray prairie. Lucy was growing up fast now; her golden curly head seemed to spring up at him.

That autumn the homesteaders erected a schoolhouse of their own. It was scarcely three miles from Pan's home.

"Pan, can you walk it?" asked Bill Smith with his keen eye on the lad.

"Yes, Daddy—but—but," replied Pan, unable to finish with the thought so dear to his heart.

"Ah—huh. An' before long Lucy will be old enough to go too," added his father. "Reckon you'll take her?"

"Yes, Daddy." And for Pan there was real gladness in that promise.

"Wal, you're a good boy," declared the father. "An' you

15

won't have to walk to school. I've traded for two horses for you."

"Two!" screamed Pan, wild with joy. "Oh! Oh! Oh!"

In due time the new horses arrived at the Smith homestead. Their names were Pelter and Pilldarlick. Pelter was a pinto, snappy and pretty, though he had a wicked eye. Pilldarlick was not showy, but he was small and strong, easy gaited and gentle. Pan thought he was going to like Pelter best, although Pilldarlick was surely a cowboy name and therefore all satisfying. It turned out, however, that Pan could not ride Pelter. He was locoed. He bucked Pan off every time. Pilldarlick was really much better than he looked, and soon filled the void in Pan's heart.

The first time he rode Pilldarlick to the new school marked another red-letter day in the life of Panhandle Smith, cowboy. There were many boys and a few girls who had come to attend the school, only a few of whom had horses to ride. Pan was the proud cynosure of all eyes as he rode Pilldarlick round the yard for the edification of his schoolmates. It was the happiest day of Pan's life—up until Dick Hardman arrived on a spirited little black mustang.

"Hey, where'd you git that nag?" yelled Dick, when he sighted Pan. "An' say, your saddle ain't nothin' but rawhide on a stump."

"You're a liar!" shouted Pan, fiercely tumbling off Pilldarlick.

The red-headed lad pitched out of his saddle and made for Pan.

They began to fight. Instinct was Pan's guide. He hit and scratched and kicked. But Dick being the larger began to get the better of the battle, and soon was beating Pan badly when the new teacher came out to his rescue.

"Stop it," she ordered, separating the belligerents. "Only cats and dogs fight."

"So—do—cowboys!" panted Pan.

"Not nice ones. Only bad cowboys," she replied, leading Pan away.

"I'll lick you next time," yelled Dick, evilly. "You stuck-up little snot!"

3

❖

Miss Amanda Hill, the teacher, rang the bell, calling all her scholars in, and school began once more.

Dick Hardman sat across the room from Pan and behind the teacher's back he made ugly faces at Pan and, more than that, put his nose to his thumb. Pan understood that, and quick as a flash, he returned the compliment.

Recess came. Before half the scholars were out of the room Dick and Pan had run to the barn, out of the teacher's sight, and here they fell upon each other like wildcats. It did not take Dick long to give Pan the first real beating of his life. Cut lip, bloody nose, black eye, dirty face, torn blouse—these things betrayed Pan at least to Miss Hill. She kept him in after school, and instead of scolding she talked sweetly and kindly. Pan came out of his sullenness, and felt love for her rouse in him. But somehow he could not promise not to fight again.

"S'pose Dick Hardman does that all over again!" expostulated Pan in despair. He did not realize what he felt. He wanted to please and obey this sweet little woman, but there was a revolt in him. "What'll my—my daddy—say when he hears I got licked!" he sobbed.

She compromised finally by accepting Pan's willing promise not to pick a fight with Dick.

Despite the unpleasant proximity of Dick Hardman, that winter at school promised to be happy and helpful to Pan. There were three large boys, already cowboys, who attended Miss Hill's school. Pan gravitated at once to them, and to his great satisfaction they accepted him.

17

Later his old cowboy friends of the roundup arrived on the range with a trail herd of cattle from Texas. Their brand was an O X, a new one to Pan. He kept a record of all the brands he had seen, and practiced drawing them on a paper. Moore and three of his cowboys came to board at Pan's home, and kept their horses there. Pan's cup was full. The days flew by. Snow and cold were nothing to him. Not even study, and the ever-malicious Dick Hardman could daunt his spirit. Moore meant to winter his herd there, and wait for spring before he drove it farther north.

The cowboys' nickname for Moore was Pug, and another fellow whose real name Pan never heard was called Slats. They taught Pan all the cowboy songs from "Ti Yi Oop Oop Ya Ya" to "Bury Me on the Lone Prairie." Every night Pan listened to them sing by the fire in their bunkhouse, and many times he had to be called to do his chores.

Another of the cowboys was called Hookey. His nose resembled that of a parrot and he had the disposition of a locoed coyote, according to Pug and Slats. Hookey took a dislike to Pan, and always sought to arouse the boy's temper. These cowboys were always gone in the morning before Pan got up, but by the time he arrived home from school on Pilldarlick they were usually there.

Slats, who wanted to be a lady killer, would say: "Wal, Button, what did your school marm say about me today?" And Hookey would make fun of Pilldarlick, which ridicule had more power to hurt Pan than anything else. One day Pan gave way to fury, and with flying rocks he chased Hookey into the cellar, and every time Hookey poked up his head Pan would fling a stone with menacing accuracy. That time his mother came to the rescue of the cowboy. After that Hookey bought a new saddle and gave Pan his old one. That settled hostilities. Pan had a change of heart. No matter how Hookey teased or tormented him he could never again make him angry. Pan saw Hookey with different eyes.

He was unutterably happy now with a horse and saddle too, and went about singing: "My trade is cinchin' saddles an' pullin' bridle reins."

One day two strange men arrived at the Smith homestead. They had still hard faces, intent gray eyes; they packed guns, and one of them wore a bright star on his vest.

These men took Hookey away with them. And after they were gone the cowboys told Pan that Hookey was wanted for horse stealing. Young as Pan was he understood the enormity of that crime in the eyes of cowboys. He felt terribly hurt and betrayed. Long indeed was it before he forgot Hookey.

Swiftly that winter passed. Pan had a happy growing time of it. Study had not seemed so irksome, perhaps owing to the fact that he had a horse and saddle; he could ride to and fro; he often stopped to see Lucy who was now big enough to want to go to school herself; and the teacher had won his love. Pan kept out of fights with Dick Hardman until one recess when Dick called him "teacher's pet." That inflamed Pan, as much because of the truth of it as the shame. So this time, though he had hardly picked a fight, he was the first to strike. With surprising suddenness he hit the big Dick square on the nose. When Dick got up howling and swearing, his face was hideous with dirt and blood. Then began a battle that dwarfed the one in the barn. Pan had grown considerably. He was quick and strong, and when once his mother's fighting blood burned in him he was as fierce as a young savage. But again Dick whipped him.

Miss Hill, grieved and sorrowful, sent Pan home with a note. It chanced that both his father and mother were at home when he arrived. They stood aghast at his appearance.

"You dirty ragged bloody boy!" cried his mother, horrified.

"Huh! You oughta see Dick Hardman!" ejaculated Pan.

The lad thought he had ruined himself forever with Miss Amanda Hill. But to his amaze and joy he had not. Next day she kept him in after school, cried over him, kissed him, and talked long and earnestly. All that Pan remembered was: "Something terrible will come of your hate for Dick Hardman if you don't root it out of your heart."

"Teacher—why don't you—talk to Dick this way?" faltered Pan, always won by her tenderness.

"Because Dick is a different kind of boy," she replied, but never explained what she meant.

At Christmas time the parents of the school children gave a party at the schoolhouse. Every one on the range for miles

19

around was there. Pan for once had his fill of seeing cowboys. Miss Amanda was an attraction no cowboys could resist. That night Pan spoke his first piece entitled: "Sugar-Tooth Dick for Sweeties Was Sick."

To Pan it seemed a silly piece, but he spoke it to please Miss Amanda, and because it was a hit at Dick Hardman. To his surprise he received a roar of applause. After the supper, dancing began. Some of the cowboys got drunk. There were fights. two of which Pan saw, to his thrilling fear and awe. It was long past midnight when he yielded to the intense drowsiness that overcame him. When he awoke at dawn they were still dancing.

Winter passed. Spring came with roundups too numerous for Pan to keep track of. And a swift happy summer sped by.

That fall a third uncle settled in the valley. He was an older brother of Pan's father, whom they called Old Uncle Ike. He was a queer old bachelor, lived alone. and did not invite friendliness. Pan was told to stay away from him. Old Uncle Ike was crabby and hard; when a boy, his heart had been broken by an unfaithful sweetheart; he had shot her lover and run away to war. After serving through the Civil War he fought Indians, and had lived an otherwise wild life.

But Pan was only the keener to see and know Old Uncle Ike. He went boldly to make his acquaintance. He found a sad-faced. gray old man. sitting alone.

Pan said bravely: "Uncle, I'm Pan Smith, your brother Bill's boy, an' I've come to see you because I'm sure I'll like you."

He did not find the old man unfriendly. Pan was welcome, and soon they became fast friends. Every Saturday Pan rode over to Uncle Ike's place, stealing some of the time he was supposed to be spending with Lucy. The little girl pouted and cried and railed at Pan for such base desertion, but he only laughed at her Any time he wanted he could have Lucy. She grew sweeter and more lovable as she grew older, facts Pan took to his heart. but he chose the old man's stories of war and Indians in preference to Lucy's society.

Months passed, and Pan grew tall and supple, with promise of developing the true horseman's build. Then the spring when he was twelve years old arrived and his father consented to let him ride for wages at the roundup.

He joined a big outfit. There were over fifty cowboys, two bed wagons, two chuck wagons, and strings of horses too numerous to count. A new horse to ride twice a day! This work was as near paradise as Pan felt he had ever been. But for one circumstance, it would have been absolutely perfect, and that was that he had no boots. A fast-riding cowboy without boots!

In the heat of action, amid the whirling loop of bawling calves and cows, when the dry dust rose to stop up Pan's nostrils and cake on his hot sweaty face, when the ropes were whistling, the cowboys yelling, the brand iron sizzling, all he felt was the wild delight of it, the thrill of the risk, the excitement, the constant stirring of life and motion. During leisure hours, however, he was always confronted with his lack of rider's equipment.

"Say, kid, who built them top boots of yourn?" asked one cowboy.

"Shore, I'll trade spurs with you," drawled another.

"Whar's yore fur chaps there, cowboy?" queried a third.

And so it went always and forever. The cowboys could not help that. It was born in them, born of the atmosphere and spirit of the singular life they lived. Nevertheless Pan loved them, and they were good to him.

His best friends in this outfit were Si and Slick, both horse wranglers, whose real names Pan never learned.

That roundup was prolific of wonderful experience. One night when a storm threatened, the foreman called to the cowboys not on duty: "Talk to 'em low, boys, fer they're gettin' ready."

He meant that the herd of cattle was likely to stampede. And when the thunder and rain burst the herd broke away with a trampling roar. Pan got soaked to the skin and lost in the rain. When he returned to camp only the cook and wagons were there. Next morning the cowboys straggled in in bunches, each driving part of the stampeded herd.

At breakfast one morning Pan heard a yell. "Ride him, cowboy!"

"Whoopee! Look at that outlaw comin' high, wide an' handsome!"

21

Pan just had time to see a terribly pitching red horse come tearing into the circle of cowboys. His rider went shooting over his head to alight among them. Then what a scattering! That red fiend spoiled the breakfast and cleaned out the camp. How the cowboys reviled the poor fellow who had been thrown!

"Huh! Broke yore collar bone?" yelled one. "Why you dod-blasted son of a sea cook, he oughta hev broke yore neck!"

And Si, the horse wrangler, said: "Charlie, I reckon it's onconsiderate of you to exercise yore pet hoss on our stummicks."

One of the amazing things that happened during the winter was the elopement of Miss Amanda Hill with a cowboy. Pan did not like this fellow very well, but the incident heightened his already magnificent opinion of cowboys.

Pan never forgot Lucy's first day of school when he rode over with her sitting astride behind him, "wringin' his neck," as a cowboy remarked. Pan had not particularly been aware of that part of the performance for he was used to having Lucy cling to him. That embarrassed him. He dropped her off rather unceremoniously at the door, and went to put his horse in the corral. She was little and he was big, which fact further bore upon his consciousness, through the giggles of the girls and gibes of the boys. But they did not make any change in his attitude toward Lucy. All winter he took her to and from school on his horse. The summer following, he worked for his Uncle Ike.

As Pan grew older time seemed so much shorter than when he was little. There was so much to do. And all at once he was fifteen years old. His mother gave him a party on that birthday, which was marked on his memory by the attention his boy friends paid to Lucy. She was by far the prettiest girl in the valley. He did not know exactly what to make of his resentment, nor of the queer attitude of proprietorship he had assumed over her.

He was destined to learn more abut his state of mind. It happened the next day at school during the noon hour. That late November, a spell of Indian summer weather had lingered, and the pupils ate their lunches out under the trees.

Suddenly Lucy came running up to Pan, who as usual

22

was having a care for his horse. Her golden hair was flying disheveled. She was weeping. Her big violet eyes streamed with tears. She was wiping her face with most expressive disgust.

"Pan—you go right off—and thrash Dick Hardman," she cried, passionately.

"Lucy!—What's he done?" queried Pan, after a sudden sense of inward shock.

"He's always worrying me—when you're not around. I never told 'cause I knew you'd fight. . . . But now he's done it. He grabbed me and kissed me! Before all the boys!"

Pan looked steadily at her tear-wet face, seeing Lucy differently. She was not a baby any more. For some strange reason beyond his understanding he was furious with her. Pushing her aside he strode toward the group of boys, leering close by.

Dick Hardman, a strapping big lad now, edged back into the crowd. Pan violently burst into it, forcing the boys back, until he confronted his adversary. On Dick's sallow face the brown freckles stood out prominently. Something in the look and advance of Pan had intimidated him. But he blustered, he snarled.

"You're a skunk," said Pan fiercely, and struck out with all his might.

One hour from that moment they were still fighting. They had fought from the grove to the schoolyard, from there down the road and back again. Bloody, ragged, black, they beat, tore, hit, bit and clawed each other. The teacher, wringing her hands, called upon the other boys to separate the belligerents. They had tried, but in vain, and only got kicked for their pains. The girls, most of them, screamed and cried. But not Lucy! White faced and with dilated eyes she watched that struggle. All the spectators, even the youngest, seemed to recognize it as a different kind of a fight from any that had ever occurred before. At last the teacher sent some of the children for help from the nearest farmhouse.

Dick would lower his head and lunge at Pan, trying to butt him in the abdomen. Twice he had bowled Pan over, to his distinct advantage. But the crafty Pan, timing another and last attack of this kind, swung up his knee with terrific force, square into Dick's face.

23

Down Dick plumped, rolled over on his back, yelling loudly. Suddenly he ceased, he raised up on one elbow, he spat blood, and something that rattled on the gravel. A tooth! His grimy hand went trembling to his blood-stained mouth. He felt of his front teeth. One was gone, others were loose. Vanity, Dick's distinguishing characteristic, suffered a terrible blow. Staggering to his feet, fetching a stone with him, he glared at Pan: "I'll—kill—you!"

He flung the stone with deadly intent. But Pan dodged it and leaped at him. Dick ran hard toward the schoolhouse, stooping to snatch up stones, and turning to fling them at Pan. The yelling boys scattered, the frightened girls fled. Pan was not to be outdone at any kind of fight. He returned stone for stone, the last of which struck Dick low down in the leg. Like a crippled beast Dick shrieked and plunged into the schoolhouse, slamming shut the door. But Pan, rushing after, grabbed up a rock and flung it so powerfully that it split the door and knocked it off the hinges.

Pan rushed in to receive full in the face a long, thick teacher's ruler thrown by Dick. It knocked him flat. Picking it up Pan brandished it and charged his enemy. Dick ran along the blackboard, and jerking up one eraser after another he threw them. His aim was poor. His strength waning. His courage had gone. As for Pan it was as if the long fight had only inspired him to renewed ferocity and might. The truth was that a hot dancing fire in Pan's blood had burned to white intensity, unquenchable and devastating.

Suddenly Dick made for the teacher's table. An idea, an inspiration showed in his renewed speed. Pan divined its purpose. Leaping upon the desks he endeavored to head Dick off. Too late! When Pan sprang off the last desk to the platform Dick had turned—with the teacher's long paper knife in his hand and baleful hate in his prominent eyes.

Later, when the children outside dared to peep into the schoolroom they neither saw nor heard anything of the fighters. But fearing they were just hiding behind the benches, ready for a renewed fusillade, not one of the pupils dared go in. The teacher had hurried down the road to meet the men some of the boys had fetched.

And these men were Jim Blake and Bill Smith who had been riding home from the range. When they entered the

24

schoolroom with the teacher fearfully following, and only Lucy of all the scholars daring to come too, they found the fight was over.

Dick lay unconscious on the floor with a bloody forehead. Pan sat crouched on the platform, haggard and sullen, with face, shirt, hands all bloody.

"Ah-uh! Reckon you've been fightin' like a cowboy for shore this time," said Pan's father in his matter of fact way. "Stand up. Let's look at you. . . . Jim, take a look at that lad on the floor."

While Pan painfully endeavored to get up, Blake knelt beside Dick.

"Bill, this heah rooster has had a wallop," said Blake.

"You little cowpunchin' ruffian," exploded Smith angrily, reaching a large arm for Pan. "Now then. . . . What the hell? . . . Boy, you've been *stabbed!*"

"Yes—Dad—he stuck me—with teacher's knife," replied Pan faintly. He tottered on his feet, and his right hand was pressed tight to his left shoulder, high up, where the broken haft of the paper knife showed between his red-stained fingers.

Bill Smith's anger vanished in alarm, and something stern and grim took its place. Just then Lucy broke away from the teacher and confronted him.

"Oh—please don't punish him, Mr. Smith." she burst out poignantly. "It was all my fault. I—I stuck up my nose at Dick. He said things that—that weren't nice. . . . I slapped him. Then he grabbed me, kissed me. . . . I ran to Pan—and—and told him. . . . Oh, that made Pan fight."

Smith looked gravely down into the white little face with the distended violet eyes, slowly losing their passion. He seemed to be struck with something that he had never seen before.

"Wal, Lucy, I'll not punish Pan," he said, slowly. "I think more of him for fightin' for you."

4

❖

THEY did not meet again during the winter. It was a hard winter. Pan left school and stayed close to home, working for his mother, and playing less than any time before.

"I heard Dick say he'd kill you someday," said one cowboy seriously. "An' take it from me, kid, he's a bad hombre."

"Ah-uh!" was all the reply Pan vouchsafed, as he walked away. He did not like to be reminded of Dick. It sent an electric spark to the deep-seated smoldering mine in his breast.

When springtime came Pan joined the roundup in earnest, for part of the cattle and outfit now belonged to his father. Out on the range the forty riders waited for the wagons. There were five cowboys from Big Sandy in Pan's bunch and several more arrived from the Crow Roost country. Old Dutch John, a famous range character, was driving the chuck wagon. At one time he had been a crony of Pan's father, and that attracted Pan to the profane old grizzled cook. He could not talk without swearing and if he replied to a question that needed only yes or no, he would supplement it with a string of oaths.

Next day the outfit rode the west side of Dobe Creek, rounding up perhaps a thousand cattle. Pete Blaine and Hooley roped calves while Pan helped hold up.

On the following day the riders circled Blue Lakes, where cattle swarmed. Old John had yelled to the boys: "Hey, punchers, heave at them today. You gotta throw an awful mess of 'em heah."

26

These two lakes were always dry, except during the spring; and now they were full, with green grass blanketing the range as far as eye could see. By Monday long lines of cattle moved with flying dust down to the spot chosen for the roundup. As the herds closed in, the green range itself seemed to be moving. When thrown together all these cattle formed a sea of red and white, from which roared an incessant bawling. It looked impossible to separate cows and calves from the others. But dozens of fearless cowboys, riding in here and in there, soon began to cut out the cows and calves.

It was a spectacle that inspired Pan as never before. The wagons were lined up near the lake, their big white canvas tops shining in the afternoon sun, and higher on a bench stood the "hoodelum" or bed wagon, so stocked with bed-rolls that it resembled a haystack. Beyond the margin of the lake, four hundred fine saddle horses grazed and kicked and bit at one another. Beyond the saddle horses grazed the day herd of cattle. And over on the other side dinned the melee over the main herd, the incessant riding, yelling of the cowboys and the bawling of the cows.

When all the cows and calves were cut out, a rider of each outfit owning cattle on that range would go through to claim those belonging to his brand. Next the herd of bulls and steers, old cows and yearlings, would be driven back out upon the range.

Fires were started, and as there was no wood on that range, buffalo chips were used instead. It took many cowboys to collect sufficient for their needs.

At sunset, when the branding of calves was finished, each cowboy caught a horse for night duty. Pan got one he called Old Paint.

"Say, kid," called one of the Crow Nest cowboys, "ain't you tyin' up a pretty fancy hoss fer night work?"

"Oh, I guess not," laughed Pan.

"Come heah, Blowy," called the cowboy to another. "See what I found."

A long lanky red-faced rider detached himself from the others, and strode with jingling spurs over to look at Pan's horse.

"Wal, I'll go to hell, Ben Bolt, if it ain't Ol' Calico!" he ejaculated, in amaze and pleasure. "Kid, whar'd you ever git him?"

"Dad made a trade," replied Pan.

"Kid, look a heah. Don't ever tie that hoss to a stake pin. He's the best cow hoss I ever slung a leg over. The puncher who broke him an' teached him all he knows was my pard, long ago. An' he's daid. Kid, he'd roll over in his grave if he knowed Ol' Cal was tied to a picket pin."

"Aw, is that so?" replied Pan. "Fact is, I don't know much about him. We called him Old Paint. Haven't forked him yet. Dad got him from a lady last winter. She was trying to work him to a cart. But he balked. She said she poured some hot water on. . . ."

"Lady, hell!" shouted the cowboy, growing redder of face. "She wasn't no lady if she treated that grand hoss that way. . . . See heah, kid, I'll stake you to a good night hoss. Turn Ol' Cal loose, an' whenever you need to do some real fancy separatin' jest set your frusky on Ol' Cal. Better tie to your stirrups if you're perticler about keepin' your seat, 'cause 'at ol' pony can sure git from under a cowhand."

"All right, I'll turn Old Calico loose," replied Pan. "And I'll remember what you said about him."

Blowy pointed out one of his horses. "Kid, screw your wood to thet jasper, an' you'll never be walkin'."

"Thanks, but I got lots of horses," said Pan.

"Aw go on—lots of horses. Why, bunkie, I got more mean horses than I can start to keep gentle. I just fetched thet one to stake my friends."

Pan saddled up the horse indicated, and found him the best he had ever mounted. That experience led to his acquaintance with Blowy. He was a ceaseless talker, hence his name, but beloved by all the outfit. Pan learned something from every cowboy he met and it was not all for the best.

That roundup was Pan's real introduction to the raw range. When the time came for the outfit to break up, with each unit taking its own cattle, the boss said to Pan, "Come ride fer me."

Pan, flushed and pleased, mumbled his thanks, but he had to work for his father. Then he and the boy with him, Joe Crawley, bade their comrades good-by, especially loath to part with Old Dutch, and started home with their cows and calves. They crossed the old Indian battlefield where Colonel Shivington gave the famous order to his soldiers: "Kill 'em all. Nits make lice!"

Pan and Joe set out from there for Limestone Creek with their small herd and extra horses. Pan wanted to bring Old Calico, but he had drifted off to the range.

"Heel flies are workin', kid," said Joe, who was older and more experienced. "We're shore goin' to be on the mud fer the next month."

There was something in the air, storm perhaps, or such conditions that have strange effect upon beasts. Pan and Joe fought their cattle and horses all that day, and most of the night. They could not make them travel. Halting where they were they kept guard till dawn, then tried to drive their outfit on. But not for several hours could they move them. At length, however, the stock began to get dry, and string out and travel.

Late in the afternoon the boys reached Limestone. They found three old cows stuck in the mud, up to their eyes, with only their horns and faces showing. It took long hard work to get them out. They made camp there, turning the cows and calves loose, as this was their range.

The following morning Pan and Joe rode up to the next boghole. They found seventeen mired cattle.

"Nice an' deep," said Joe. "Damn these heah cows, allus pickin' out quicksand!"

It took until noon to pull them out. Another boghole showed twenty-four more in deep.

"How many more bogholes on Limestone?" asked Pan.

"Only four an' the wust ones," replied Joe, groaning. "If they're boggin' as good up there in them big holes, your dad will sure have to ship more cattle in soon."

There were six thousand cattle watering along that stream. When the water was low, as it was then, the cattle mired by the hundreds.

"Looks bad, Pan," remarked the older cowboy. "We're goin' to need help."

They returned to camp, got their supper, took fresh horses, and worked half the night pulling cows out of the mud.

By sunrise the next morning the boys were at work again.

Some of the mired cattle had died, others had kinks in their necks and had to be killed. Farther up the creek conditions grew worse, and the biggest pool on the range looked from a distance like a small lake dotted with ducks.

"I'm cussin' the world by sections," growled Joe. "Wal, kid, you g'on up the crick, and get as near a count as you can. I'm ridin' in after men an' wagons. We'll move the camp up heah. It's the wust I ever seen, an' we'll lose a heap of stock. There's a loblolly of blue gumbo mud an' no bottom. An' by thunder we're stuck heah for Lord knows how long."

That fall Jim Blake sold his farm, and took his family to New Mexico. He had not been prospering in the valley, and things had gone from bad to worse. Pan did not get home in time to say good-by to Lucy—something that hurt in an indefinable way. He had not forgotten Lucy for in his mind she had become a steadfast factor in his home life. She left a little note of farewell, simple and loyal, hopeful, yet somehow stultified. Not so childish as former notes! Time flew by and Lucy might be growing up.

The Hardmans had also moved away from the valley, where, none of the neighbors appeared to know. But Pan was assured of two facts concerning them; firstly that Dick had gotten into a serious shooting scrape in which he had wounded a rancher's son, and secondly that from some unexpected and unknown source the Hardmans had acquired or been left some money.

Pan promptly forgot his boyhood enemy. This winter was the last that he spent at home. He rode the Limestone range that summer, and according to cowboys' gossip was fast developing all the qualities that pertained to the best riders of the day.

Upon returning home he found that his father had made unwise deals and was not getting along very well. Grasping settlers had closed in on the range. Rustlers had ridden down from the north, raiding the valley. During Pan's absence a little sister was born, which was indeed joyful news for him. And as he played with the baby he was reminded of Lucy. What had become of her? It occurred to Pan that sooner or later he must hunt her up.

Pan decided that he could not remain idle during the winter. He could have had plenty to do at home, working without wages, but that was no longer to be thought of. So he decided to join two other adventurous cowboys who had planned to go south, and in the spring come back with some of the great herds being driven north.

But Pan liked the vast ranges of the Lone Star State, and he rode there for two years, inevitably drifting into the wild free life of the cowboys. Sometimes he sent money home to his mother, but that was seldom, because he was always in debt. She wrote him regularly, which fact was the only link between him and the old home memories. Thought of Lucy returned now and then, on the lonely rides on night watches, and it seemed like a sweet melancholy dream. Never a word did he hear of her.

Spring had come again when he rode into the Panhandle, and as luck would have it he fell in with an outfit who were driving cattle to Montana, a job that would take until late fall. To his chagrin stories of his wildness had preceded him. Ill rumor travels swiftly. Pan was the more liked and respected by these riders. But he feared that gossip of the southern ranges would reach his mother. He would go home that fall to reassure her of his well-being, and that he was not one of those "bad, gun-throwing cowboys."

But late fall found him cheated of his long summer's wages, without money and job. He would not ride a "grub line" home, so he found a place with a rancher in Montana. He learned to hate the bleak ranges of that northern state, the piercing blasts of wind, the ice and snow. Spring saw him riding south toward his old stamping grounds. But always he was drifting, with the swift months flying by as fleet as the mustangs he rode, and he did not reach home. The Cimarron, the Platte, the Arkansas ranges came to know the tracks of his horses; and after he had drifted on, to remember him as few cowboys were remembered.

At twenty years of age Panhandle Smith looked older—looked the hard life, the hard fare, the hard companionship that had been his lot as an American cowboy He had absorbed all the virtues of that remarkable character, and most of the vices. But he had always kept aloof from women. His comrades gave many forceful and humorous reasons for his apparent fear of the sex, but they never understood him. Pan never lost the reverence for women his mother had instilled in him, or his first and only love for Lucy Blake.

One summer night Pan was standing night-guard duty for his cowboy comrade, who was enamored of the daughter of the rancher for whom they worked. Jim was terribly in love, and closely pressed by a rival from another outfit. This night was to be the crucial one.

Pan had to laugh at his friend. He was funny, he was pathetic, so prone to be cast down one moment and the next raised aloft to the skies, according to the whim of the capricious young lady. Many times Pan had ridden and worked with a boy afflicted with a similar malady.

This night, however, Pan had been conscious of encroaching melancholy. Perhaps it was a yearning for something he did not know how to define.

The night was strange, a sultry oppressive one, silent except for the uneasy lowing of the herd, a rumble of thunder from the dark rolling clouds. A weird yellow moon hung just above the horizon. The range spread away dark, lonely and wild. No wind stirred. The wolves and coyotes were quiet. All at once to Pan the whole world seemed empty. It was an unaccountable feeling. The open range, the solitude, the herd of cattle in his charge, the comrades asleep, the horses grazing round their pickets—these always sufficient things suddenly lost their magic potency. He divined at length that he was homesick. And by the time the day watch was ended he had determined to quit his job and ride home.

5

◈

ON HIS way home Panhandle Smith rode across the old Limestone range that had been the scene of his first cowboy activities. It had not changed, although the cattle were not so numerous. Familiar as yesterday were the bogholes, where he and his partner—what was that cowpuncher's name?—had spent so many toilsome days and nights.

Pan made camp on the rocky ford where a brook joined the Limestone. It was thirty miles to Littleton, farther to Las Animas, and his pack horse was tired. He cooked his meager meal, and unrolled his bed, and as on many a hundred other nights he lay down under the open sky. But his wakefulness was new. He could not get to sleep for long. The nearer he got to home the stranger and deeper his thoughts.

Moving on next day he kept sharp lookout among the cattle for his father's brand. But he saw no sign of it. At length, toward sunset, after passing thousands of cattle, he concluded in surprise that his father's stock no longer ran this range. Too many homesteads and fences! He reached Littleton at dark. It had grown to be a sizable settlement. Pan treated himself to a room at the new hotel, and after supper went out to find somebody he knew. It was Saturday night and the town was full of riders and ranchers. He expected to meet an old acquaintance any moment, but to his further surprise he did not. Finally he went to Campbell's store, long a fixture in the settlement of that country. John Campbell, huge of build, with his long beard and ruddy face, appeared exactly the same as when he used to give Pan a stick of candy. It did seem a long time, now. Campbell did not recognize him.

"Howdy, stranger, reckon you've got the best of me," he replied to Pan's question, and he sized up the tall lithe rider with curious and appreciating eyes.

"Now, John, you used to give me a stick of candy, every time I came to town," said Pan, with a laugh.

"Wal, I done that for every Tom, Dick an' Harry of a kid in this heah country," returned the old man, stroking his beard. "But durn if I recollect you."

"Panhandle Smith," announced Pan, with just a little diffidence. Perhaps if he was not remembered personally he might have the good luck to be unknown in reputation.

"Wal—Pan, if 't ain't you, by gosh!" ejaculated Campbell, cordially, and there was unmistakable welcome in his grip. "But no one here will ever recognize you. Say, you've sprung up. We've heerd a lot about you—nothin' of late years, though, now I tax myself . . . Cowboy, you've seen some range life, if talk is true."

"You mustn't believe all you hear, Mr. Campbell," replied Pan, with a smile. "I'd like to know about my dad and mother."

"Wal, haven't you heerd?" queried Campbell, hesitatingly.

"What?" flashed Pan, noting the other's sudden change to gravity. "It's two years and more since I got a letter from Mother. I wrote a couple of times, but she never answered."

"You ought to have come home long ago," said Campbell. "Your father lost his cattle. Old deal with Hardman that stood for years. Mebbe you never knowed about it. There are ranchers around here who swear Hardman drove sharp deals. Wal, your father sold the homestead an' left. Reckon it's been over a year."

"Where'd they go?"

"Your pa never told me where, but I heerd afterward that he hit Hardman's trail an' went to western New Mexico. Marco is the name of the place. New country up there. Gold an' silver minin', some cattle outfits goin' in, an' lately I heerd of some big wild-hoss deals on."

"Well," exclaimed Pan, in profound amaze and sorrow at this news.

"It's a wide-open frontier place, all right," declared Campbell. "Some cowpuncher rode through here an' talked about Marco. He said they stepped high, wide an' handsome up there."

"Why did Dad go?" asked Pan in wonder.

"Reckon I couldn't say fer sure. But he was sore at Hardman, an' the funny thing is he wasn't sore till some time after Hardman left these parts. Mebbe he learned somethin'. An' you can learn whatever it was if you hunt up them ranchers who once got stung by Hardman."

"Ah-uh!" muttered Pan, thoughtfully. "Don't know as I care to learn. Dad will tell me. . . . Jim Blake, now, what become of him?"

"Jim, a while back, I reckon some years though after you left home, was foreman for Hardman's outfit. An' he went

34

to Marco first. Reckon Hardman sent him up there to scout around."

"Did Jim take his family along?" inquired Pan, pondering.

"No. But they left soon after. In fact, now I tax myself, several homesteaders from hereabouts went. There's a boom over west, Pan, an' this here country is gettin' crowded."

"Marco. How do you get there?"

"Wal, it's on the old road to Californy."

Pan went to the seclusion of his room, and there in the dark, sleepless, he knew the pangs of remorse. Without realizing the flight of years, always meaning to return home, to help father, mother, little sister, to take up again with his never-forgotten Lucy—he had allowed the wild life of the range to hold him too long. Excuses were futile. Suppose he had failed to save money—suppose he had become numbered among those whom his old schoolteacher had called "bad cowboys"! Pride, neglect, love of the range and new country, new adventure had kept him from doing his duty by his parents. That hour was indeed dark and shameful for Panhandle Smith. Instead of drowning his grief in drink, as would have been natural for a cowboy, he let it work its will upon him. He deserved the pangs of self-reproach, the futile wondering, the revived memories that roused longings stronger than that which had turned him on the homeward trail.

Next day Pan sold his outfit except the few belongings he cherished, and boarded a west-bound stage. Once on the way he recovered from his brooding mood and gradually awakened to the fact that he was riding to a new country, a new adventure—the biggest of his life—in which he must make amends to his mother, and to Lucy. Quite naturally he included Lucy in the little circle of beloved ones—Lucy, whom he had deserted for the open range, for pitching horses and running steers, for the dust and turmoil of the roundup, for the long day ride and the lonely night watch, for the gaming table, the bottle, the gun—for all that made life so thrilling to the American cowboy.

Riding by stage was not new to Pan, though he had never before taken more than a day's journey The stage driver,

Jim Wells, was an oldtimer. He had been a pony-express rider, miner, teamster and freighter, and now, grizzled and scarred he liked to perch upon the driver's seat of the stage, chew tobacco and talk. His keen eyes took Pan's measure in one glance.

"Pitch your bag up, cowboy, an' climb aboard," he said. "An' what might your handle be?"

"Panhandle Smith," replied Pan nonchalantly, "late of Sycamore Bend."

"Wal, now, whar'd I hear thet name? I got a plumb good memory fer names an' faces. 'Pears I heerd thet name in Cheyenne, last summer. . . . I got it. Cowpuncher named Panhandle rode down street draggin' a bolt of red calico thet unwound an' stampeded all the hosses. Might thet lad have happened to be you?"

"I reckon it might," replied Pan, with a grin. "But if you know any more about me keep it under your sombrero, old-timer."

"Haw! Haw!" roared Wells, slapping his knee. "By golly, I will if I can. There's a funny old lady inside what's powerful afeerd of bandits, an' there's a gurl. I seen her takin' in your size an' spurs, an' thet gun you pack sort of comfortable like. An' there's a gambler, too, if I ever seen one. Reckon I'm agoin' to enjoy this ride."

After the next stop, where the travelers got dinner, Pan returned to the stage to find a young lady perched upon the driver's seat. She had serious gray eyes and pale cheeks.

"I took your seat," she said, shyly, "but there's enough room."

"Thanks, I'll ride inside," replied Pan.

"But if you don't sit here—someone else might—and I—he—" she faltered, flushing a little.

"Oh, in that case, I'll be glad to," interrupted Pan, and climbed to the seat beside her. He had become aware of the appearance of a flashily dressed, hawk-eyed individual about to enter the stage. "Are you traveling alone?"

"No, thank you. Father is with me, but he never sees anything. I have been annoyed," she replied.

The stage driver arrived, and surveyed the couple on the seat with a wink and a grin and a knowing look that quite embarrassed the young lady.

"Wal, now, this here stage drivin' is gettin' to be mighty fine," he said, as he clambered up to the seat, and unwound the reins from the brake handle. "Lady, I reckon I seen you didn't like ridin' inside. Wal, you'll shore be all right ridin' between me an' my young friend Panhandle Smith."

"I think I will," replied the girl, dimpling prettily. "My name is Emily Newman. I'm on my way with my father to visit relatives in California."

Pan soon found it needful to make conversation, in order to keep the loquacious old stage driver from talking too much. He had told Miss Newman about Pan's escapade with the red calico, and had launched upon another story about him, not funny at all to Pan but one calculated to make conquest of a romancing young girl. Pan managed to shut Wells up, but too late. Miss Newman turned bright eyes upon Pan.

"Oh, of course, I saw you were a cowboy," she said, dimpling again. "Those enormous spurs you wear! I wondered how you could walk."

"These spurs? They're nothing. I sleep in them," replied Pan.

"Indeed. You're not serious. . . . Was that true about your riding round Cheyenne dragging yards and yards of red calico behind your horse?"

"Yes. It was silly of me. I fear I had been looking upon something beside calico that was red."

"Oh, you mean red liquor? . . . You were—under its influence!"

"A little," replied Pan laughing, yet not liking the turn of the conversation.

"I wouldn't have guessed that you—" she added, without concluding what she meant to say. But her tone, her look, and the intimation conveyed a subtle flattery to Pan. It seemed that whenever he approached young women he always received similar impressions. That was seldom, for his encounters with girls were few and far between. He could not help feeling pleased, somehow embarrassed, and rather vaguely elated. He divined danger for him in these potent impressions. Without ever understanding why he had avoided friendships with girls.

"Miss Newman, cowboys as a rule aren't worth much,"

rejoined Pan, submerging his annoyance in good humor. "But at that they are not terrible liars like most of the stage drivers you meet."

"Haw! Haw!" roared Jim Wells, cracking his long whip, as the stage bowled over the road. "He's a modest young fellar, Miss, a most extraordinary kind of a cowboy."

And so they bandied words and laughs from one to another, while the long white road stretched ahead, and rolled behind under the wheels. The girl was plainly curious, interested, fascinated. Old Jim, after the manner of westerners, was bent on making a conquest for Pan. And Pan, trying hard to make himself appear only an ordinary and quite worthless cowboy, succeeded only in giving an opposite impression.

The little lady rode three whole days on the driver's seat between Pan and Wells. She made the hours flee. When the stage reached Las Vegas, she got off with her father and turned in the crowd to wave good-by. Her eyes were wistful with what might have been. They haunted Pan for days, over the mountain uplands and on and on. Pan cherished the experience. To him it had been just a chance meeting with a nice girl, but somehow it opened his eyes to what he had missed. The way of cowboys with girls was the one way in which he had been totally unfamiliar. What he had missed was not the dancing and flirting and courting that cowboys loved so well, but something he could not quite grasp. It belonged to the never-fading influence of his mother; and likewise it had some inscrutable association with little Lucy Blake. Little? Surely she could not be little now. She was a grown girl, a young woman like this Emily Newman, beautiful perhaps, with all the nameless charms women had for men. Pan grew conscious of a mounting eagerness to see Lucy, and each day during the ride across the desert the feeling augmented, and with it a bewilderment equally incomprehensible to him.

New Mexico was strange and new. He saw the desert through eyes intensified by emotion. He knew the plains from Montana to Texas. But this was different country, with its stretches of valley, its walls of red and yellow, its strange shafts of rock, its amber ranges, and far away on every horizon the dim purple and white of great peaks were magnificent.

The Mormon ranches were scattered along the few green valleys. Cattle were scarce, only a few herds dotting the endless sweeps of green sage and bleached grass. As he traveled farther westward, however, the numbers of wild horses increased until they ran into the thousands.

Horses had meant more to Pan than anything. In his wanderings up and down the western slope of the prairie land east of the Rockies he had often encountered wild horses, and had enjoyed many a chase after them. Every cowboy was a wild horse hunter, on occasions. If he had ridden these desert ranges, he would inevitably have become permanently a hunter and lover of wild horses. Moreover, Pan did not see why there would not be vastly more money in it than in punching cows. He grew charmed with the idea.

Western New Mexico at last! It appeared a continuation and a magnifying of all the color and wildness and vastness. Sand dunes and wastes of black lava, dry lake beds and cone-shaped extinct volcanoes, with the ragged crater mouths gaping, low ranges of yellow cedar-dotted hills, valleys of purple, and green forests on the mountain slopes—all these in endless variety were new to the cowboy of the plains. Water was conspicuous for its absence, though at long intervals of travel he crossed a stream. The homesteader, that hopeful and lonely pioneer, was as scarce as the streams.

One night, hours after dark, the stage rolled into Marco, with Pan one of five passengers. Sunset had overtaken them miles from their destination. At that time Pan thought the country wild and beautiful in the extreme. Darkness had soon blotted out the strange formations of colored rocks, the endless sweep of valley, the cold white peaks in the far distance.

Marco! How unusual the swelling of his heart! The long three-week ride had ended. The stage had rolled down a main street the like of which Pan had never even imagined. It was crude, rough, garish with lights and stark board fronts of buildings, and a motley jostling crowd of men; women, too, were not wanting in the throngs streaming up and down. Again it was Saturday night. Always it appeared Pan hit town on this of all nights. Noise and dust filled the air. Pan pulled down his bag, and mounted the board steps of the hotel the stage driver had announced.

If Pan had not been keenly strung, after long weeks, with the thought of soon seeing his mother, father, his little sister and Lucy, he would yet have been excited over this adventure beyond the Rockies.

Contrary to his usual habit of throwing his money to the winds like most cowboys, he had exercised rigid economy on this trip. Indeed, it was the first time he had ever done such a thing. He had between four and five hundred dollars, consisting of wages he had saved and the proceeds from the sale of his horses and outfit. There was no telling in what difficulties he might find his father and what need there might be for his money. So Pan took cheap lodgings, and patronized a restaurant kept by a Chinaman.

He chose a table at which sat a young man whose face and hands and clothes told of rough life in the open in contact with elemental things. Pan could catch such significance as quickly as he could the points of a horse. He belonged to that fraternity himself.

"Mind if I sit here?" he asked, indicating the vacant chair.

"Help yourself, stranger," was the reply, accompanied by an appraising glance from level quiet eyes.

"I'm sure hungry. How's the chuck here?" went on Pan, seating himself.

"The Chink is a first-rate cook an' clean. . . . Just come to town?"

"Yes," replied Pan, and after giving his order to a boy waiter he turned to his companion across the table and continued. "And it took a darn long ride to get here. From Texas."

"That so? Well, I come from western Kansas, just across the Texas line."

"Been here long?"

"Reckon a matter of six months."

"What's your work, if you'll excuse curiosity. I'm green, you see, and want to know."

"I've been workin' a minin' claim. Gold."

"Ah-huh!" replied Pan with quickened interest. "Sounds

awful good to me. I never saw any gold but a few gold eagles, and they've sure been scarce enough."

Pan's frankness, and that something simple and careless about him, combined with his appearance, always created the best of impressions upon men.

His companion grinned across the table, as if he had shared Pan's experience. "Reckon you needn't tell me you're a cowpuncher. I heard you comin' before I saw you. . . . My name's Brown."

"Howdy, glad to meet you," replied Pan, and then with evident hesitation: "Mine is Smith."

"Panhandle Smith?" queried the other quickly.

"Why, sure," returned Pan with a laugh.

"Shake," was all the reply Brown made, except to extend a lean strong hand.

"I'm most as lucky as I am unlucky," said Pan warmly. "It's a small world. . . . Now tell me, Brown, have you seen or heard anything of my dad, Bill Smith?"

"No, sorry to say. But I haven't mingled much. Been layin' pretty low, because the fact is I think I've struck a rich claim. An' it's made me cautious."

"Ah-uh. Pretty wide open town, I'll bet. I appreciate your confidence in me."

"To tell you the truth I'm darn glad to run into some one from near home. Lord, I wish you could have brought word from my wife an' baby."

"Married, and got a kid. That's fine. Boy or girl?"

"It's a girl. I never saw her, as she was born after I left home. My wife wasn't very well when she wrote last. She wants to come out here, but I can't see that yet a while."

"Well, wish I could have brought you news. It must be tough to be separated from your family. I'm not married, but I know what a little girl means. . . . Say, Brown, did you ever run into a man out here named Jim Blake?"

"No."

"Or a man named Hardman? Jard Hardman?"

"Hardman! Now you're talkin', Panhandle. I should smile I have," replied Brown, with a flash of quiet eyes that Pan had learned to recognize as dangerous in men. His own pulse heightened. It was like coming suddenly on a track for which he had long been searching. The one word Hardman had struck fire from this young miner.

"What's Hardman doing?" asked Pan quietly.

"Everythin' an' between you an' me, he's doin' everybody. Jard Hardman is in everythin'. Minin', ranchin', an' I've heard he's gone in for this wild horse chasin'. That's the newest boom around Marco. But Hardman has big interests here in town. It's rumored he's back of the Yellow Mine, the biggest saloon an' gamblin' hell in town."

"Well, I'll be doggoned," ejaculated Pan thoughtfully. "Things turn out funny. You can show me that place presently. Does Hardman hang out here in Marco?"

"Part of the time. He travels to Frisco, Salt Lake, an' St. Louis where he sells cattle an' horses. He has a big ranch out here in the valley, an' stays there some. His son runs the outfit."

"His son?" queried Pan, suddenly hot with a flash of memory.

"Yes, his son," declared Brown, eyeing Pan earnestly. "Reckon you must know Dick Hardman?"

"I used to—long ago," replied Pan, pondering. How far in the past that seemed! How vivid now in memory!

"Old Hardman makes the money an' Dick blows it in," went on Brown, with something of contempt in his voice. "Dick plays, an' they say he's a rotten gambler. He drinks like a fish, too. I don't run around much in this burg, believe me, but I see Dick often. I heard he'd fetched a girl here from Frisco."

"Ah-uh! Well, that's enough about my old schoolmate, thank you," rejoined Pan. "Tell me, Brown, what's this Marco town anyway?"

"Well, it's both old an' new," replied the other. "That's about all, I reckon. Findin' gold an' silver out in the hills has made a boom this last year or so. That's what fetched me. The town is twice the size it was when I saw it first, an' many times more people. There's a lot of these people, riffraff, that work these minin' towns. Gamblers, sharks, claim jumpers, outlaws, adventurers, tramps, an' of course the kind of women that go along with them. A good many cow outfits make this their headquarters now. An' last, this horse tradin', an' wild horse catchin'. Sellin' an' shippin' has attracted lots of men. Every day or so a new fellar, like you, drops in from east of the Rockies. There are some big mining men investigatin' the claims. An' if good mineral is found Marco will be solid, an' not just a mushroom town."

"Any law?" inquired Pan thoughtfully.

"Not so you'd notice it much, especially when you need it," asserted Brown grimly. "Matthews is the town marshal. Self-elected so far as I could see. An' he's hand an' glove with Hardman. He's mayor, magistrate, sheriff, an' the whole caboodle, includin' the court. But there are substantial men here, who sooner or later will organize an' do things. They're too darned busy now workin', gettin' on their feet."

"Ah-uh. I savvy. I reckon you're giving me a hunch that in your private opinion Matthews isn't exactly straight where some interests are concerned. Hardman's for instance. I've run across that sort of deal in half a dozen towns."

"You got me," replied Brown, soberly. "But please regard that as my confidential opinion. I couldn't prove it. This town hasn't grown up to political corruption an' graft. But it's headed that way."

"Well, I was lucky to run into you," said Pan with satisfaction. "I'll tell you why some other time. I'm pretty sure to stick here. . . . Now let's go out and see the town, especially the Yellow Mine."

Pan had not strolled the length of the main street before he realized that there was an atmosphere here strangely unfamiliar to him. Yet he had visited some fairly wild and wide-open towns. But they had owed their wildness and excitement and atmosphere to the range and the omnipresent cowboy. Old-timers had told him stories of Abilene and Dodge, when they were in their heyday. He had gambled in the hells of Juárez, across the Texas border where there was no law. Some of the Montana cattle towns were far from slow, in cowboy vernacular. But here he sensed a new element. And soon he grasped it as the fever of the rush for gold. The excitement of it took hold of him, so that he had to reason with himself to shake it off.

The town appeared about a mile long, spread out on two sides of the main street, graduating from the big buildings of stone and wood in the center to flimsy frame structures and tents along the outskirts. Pan estimated that he must have passed three thousand people during his stroll, up one side of the street and down the other. Even if these made up the whole population it was enough to insure a good-sized town. There were no street lamps. And the many yellow lights from open doors and windows fell upon the throngs moving to and fro, in the street as well as on the sidewalks.

Pan's guide eventually led him into the Yellow Mine.

He saw a long wide room full of moving figures, thin wreaths of blue smoke that floated in the glaring yellow lights. A bar ran the whole length of this room, and drinkers were crowded in front of it. The clink of glass, the clink of gold, the incessant murmur of hoarse voices almost drowned faint strains of music from another room that opened from this one.

The thousand and one saloons and gambling dives that Pan had seen could not in any sense compare with this one. This was on a big scale without restraint of law or order. Piles of gold and greenbacks littered the tables where roulette, faro, poker were in progress. Black garbed, pale hardfaced gamblers sat with long mobile hands on the tables. Bearded men, lean-faced youths bent with intent gaze over their cards. Sloe-eyed Mexicans in their high-peaked sombreros and gaudy trappings lounged here and there, watching, waiting—for what did not seem clear to Pan. Drunken miners in their shirt sleeves stamped through the open door, to or from the bar. An odor of whisky mingled with that of tobacco smoke. Young women with bare arms and necks and painted faces were in evidence, some alone, most of them attended by men.

The gambling games attracted Pan. Like all cowboys he had felt the fascination of games of chance. He watched the roulette wheel, then the faro games. In one corner of the big room, almost an alcove, Pan espied a large round table at which were seated six players engrossed in a game of poker. He saw thousands of dollars in gold and notes on that table. A pretty flashy girl with bold eyes and a lazy sleepy smile hung over the shoulder of one of the gamblers.

Pan's comrade nudged him in the side.

"What? Where?" whispered Pan answering quickly to the suggestion and his glance swept everywhere.

Brown was gazing with gleaming eyes at the young card player over whose shoulder the white-armed girl hung.

Then Pan saw a face that was strangely familiar—a handsome face of a complexion between red and white, with large sensual mouth, bold eyes, and a broad low brow. The young gambler was Dick Hardman.

Pan knew him. The recognition meant nothing, yet it gave Pan a start, a twinge, and then sent a slow heat along his veins. He laughed to find the boyishness of old still alive in him. After eight years of hard life on the ranges! By that sudden resurging of long forgotten emotion Pan judged the nature of what the years had made him. It would be interesting to see how Dick Hardman met him.

But it was the girl who first seemed drawn by Pan's piercing gaze. She caught it—then looked a second time. Sliding off the arms of Hardman's chair she moved with undulating motion of her slender form, and with bright eyes, round the table toward Pan. And at that moment Dick Hardman looked up from his cards and watched her.

6

"HELLO, cowboy. How'd I ever miss you?" she queried roguishly, running her bright eyes from his face down to his spurs and back again.

"Good evening, lady," replied Pan, removing his sombrero and bowing, with his genial smile. "I just come to town."

She hesitated as if struck by a deference she was not accustomed to. Then she took his hands in hers and dragged

45

him out a little away from Brown, whom she gave a curt nod. Again she looked Pan up and down.

"Did you take off that big hat because you know you're mighty good to look at?" she asked archly.

"Well, no, hardly," answered Pan.

"What for then?"

"It's a habit I have when I meet a pretty girl."

"Thank you. Does she have to be *pretty?*"

"Reckon not. Any girl, miss."

"You are a stranger in Marco. Look out somebody doesn't shoot a hole in that hat when you doff it."

While she smiled up at him, losing something of the hawklike, possession-taking manner that had at first characterized her, Pan could see Dick Hardman staring hard across the table. Before Pan could find a reply for the girl one of the gamesters, an unshaven scowling fellow, addressed Hardman.

"Say, air you playin' cairds or watchin' your dame make up to that big hat an' high boots?"

Pan grasped the opportunity, though he never would have let that remark pass under any circumstances. He disengaged his right hand from the girl's, and stepping up to the table, drawing her with him, he bent a glance upon the disgruntled gambler.

"Excuse me, mister," he began in the slow easy cool speech of a cowboy, "but did you mean me?"

His tone, his presence, drew the attention of all at the table, especially the one he addressed, and Hardman. The former laid down his cards. Shrewd eyes took Pan's measure, surely not missing the gun at his hip.

"Suppose I did mean you?" demanded the gambler curiously.

"Well, if you did I'd have to break up your game," replied Pan, apologetically. "You see, mister, it hurts my feelings to have anyone make fun of my clothes."

"All right, cowboy, no offense meant," returned the other, at which everyone except Hardman, let out a laugh. "But you'll break up our game anyhow, if you don't trot off with Louise there."

His further remark, dryly sarcastic, mostly directed at Hardman did not help the situation, so far as Pan was concerned. It was, however, exactly what Pan wanted. Dick stared insolently and fixedly at Pan. He appeared as much puzzled as annoyed. Manifestly he was trying to place Pan, and did not succeed. Pan had hardly expected to be recognized, though he stood there a moment, head uncovered, under the light, giving his old enemy eye for eye. In fact his steady gaze disconcerted Dick, who turned his glance on the amused girl. Then his face darkened and he spat out his cigar to utter harshly: "Go on, you cat! And don't purr round me any more!"

Insolently she laughed in his face. "You forget I can scratch." Then she drew Pan away from the table, beckoning for Brown to come also.

Halting presently near the wide opening into the dance hall she said: "I'm always starting fights. What might your name be, cowboy?"

"Well, it might be Tinkerdam, but it isn't," replied Pan nonchalantly.

"Aren't you funny?" she queried, half-inclined to be affronted. But she thought better of it, and turned to Brown. "I know your face."

"Sure you do, Miss Louise," said Brown easily. "I'm a miner. Was here when you came to town, an' I often drop in to see the fun."

"What's your name?" she asked.

"Charley Brown, an' that's straight."

"Thanks, Charley. Now tell me who's this big good-looking pard of yours? I just want to know. You can't fool me about men. He doffs his hat to *me*. He talks nice and low, and smiles as no men smile at me. Then he bluffs the toughest nut in this town. . . . Who *is* he?"

"All right, I'll introduce you," drawled Brown. "Meet Panhandle Smith, from Texas."

"Well," she mused, fastening her hands in the lapels of his coat. "I thought you'd have a high-sounding handle. . . . Will you dance with me?"

"Sure, but I'm afraid I step pretty high and wide."

They entered another garish room, around which a throng of couples spun and wagged and tramped and romped. Pan danced with the girl, and despite the jostling of the heavy-footed miners acquitted himself in a manner he

47

thought was creditable for him. He had not been one of the dancing cowboys.

"That was a treat after those clodhoppers," she said, when the dance ended. "You're a modest boy, Panhandle. You've got me guessing. I'm not used to your kind—out here. . . . Let's go have a drink. I've got to have whisky."

That jarred somewhat upon Pan and, as she led him back to Brown and then both of them to an empty table, he began to grasp the significance of these bare-armed white-faced girls with their dark-hollowed eyes and scarlet lips.

She drank straight whisky, and it was liquor that burned Pan like fire. Brown, too, made a wry face.

"Panhandle, are you going to stay here in Marco?" she inquired, leaning on her white round arms.

"Yes, if I find my folks," he replied simply. "They lost all they had—ranch, cattle, horses—and moved out here. I never knew until I went back home. Makes me feel pretty mean. But Dad was doing well when I left home."

"Mother—sister, too?"

"Yes. And my sister Alice must be quite a girl now," mused Pan.

"And you're going to help them?" she asked softly.

"I should smile," said Pan feelingly.

"Then, you mustn't buy drinks for me—or run after me—as I was going to make you do."

Pan was at a loss for a reply to that frank statement. And as he gazed at her, conscious of a subtle change, someone pounded him on the back and then fell on his neck.

"My Gawd—if heah ain't Panhandle!" burst out a husky voice.

Pan got up as best he could, and pulled free from the fellow. The voice had prepared Pan for an old acquaintance, and when he saw that lean red face and blue eyes he knew them.

"Well, I'll be darned. Blinky Moran! You son of a gun! Drunk—the same as when I saw you last."

"Aw, Pan, I ain't jes drunk," he replied. "Mebbe I was—but shein' you—ole pard—my Gawd! It's like cold sweet water on my hot face."

"Blink, I'm sure glad to see you, drunk or sober," replied Pan warmly. "What're you doing out here?"

48

Moran braced himself, not without the help of his hold upon Pan, and it was evident that this meeting had roused him.

"Pan, meet my pard heah," he began, indicating a stalwart young man in overalls and high boots. "Gus Hans, puncher of Montana."

Pan shook hands with the grinning cowboy.

"Pard, yore shakin' the paw of Panhandle Smith," announced Moran in solemn emotion. "This heah's the boy, frens. You've heerd me rave many's the time. He was my pard, my bunkmate, my brother. We rode the Cimarron together, an' the Arkansaw, an' we was the only straight punchers in the Long Bar C outfit that was drove out of Wyomin'. . . . His beat never forked a hoss or coiled a rope. An' shorer'n hell, pard, I'd been a rustler but fer Panhandle. More'n onct he throwed his gun fer me an—"

"Say, Blink, I'll have to choke you," interrupted Pan, laughing. "Now, you meet my friends here, Miss Louise—and Charley Brown."

Pan did not miss the effect the bright-eyed red-lipped girl made upon the cowboys, especially Moran who, he remembered, had always succumbed easily to feminine charms.

"Blinky, you've been drinking too much to dance with a lady," presently remarked Louise.

"Wal, now, miss, I'm as sober as Panhandle there," replied Moran ardently.

She shook her curly head smilingly and, rising from the table, went round to Pan and leaned up to him with both wistfulness and recklessness in her face.

"Panhandle Smith, I'll leave you to your friends," she said. "But don't you drift in here again—for if you do—I'll forget my sacrifice for little Alice. . . . There!"

She kissed him square on the lips and ran off without a backward glance.

Blinky fell into a chair, overcome with some unusual kind of emotion. He stared comically at Pan.

"Say, ole pard, you used to be shy of skirts!" he expostulated.

"Reckon I am yet, for all the evidence," retorted Pan, half amused and half angry at the unexpected move of the girl.

Charley Brown joined in the mirth at Pan's expense.

"Guess the drinks are on me," he said. "And they'll be the last."

"Pan, that there girl is Louie Melliss!" ejaculated Moran.

"Is it? Well, who in the deuce is she?"

"Say, cowboy, quit your foolin'!"

"Honest, I never saw or heard of the young lady till a few minutes ago. Ask Brown."

"That's a fact," corroborated Brown, thus appealed to. "She's the belle of this hell. Sure, Smith, you savvy that?"

"No," rejoined Pan bluntly. He began to fear he had been rather thickheaded. "I've holed up in a few gambling hells where drinks and scraps went pretty lively. But this is the first one for me where there were a lot of half-naked girls."

"You're west of the Rockies, now," replied Brown grimly. "An' you'll soon find that out in more ways than one. . . . Louie Melliss is straight from Frisco, an' chain-lightnin' to her fingertips, so they say. Been some bad messes over her. But they say too, she's as white an' square as any good woman."

"Aw! . . . Reckon I'm pretty much of a tenderfoot," returned Pan. His regret was for the pretty audacious girl whose boldness of approach he had not understood.

"For Gawd's sake, pard," began Moran, recovering from his shock. "Don't you come ridin' around heah fer thet little devil to get stuck on you. She's shore agoin' to give young Hardman a bootiful trimmin'. An' let her do it!"

"Oh. So you don't care much about young Hardman?" inquired Pan with interest. He certainly felt that he was falling into news.

"I'd like to throw a gun on him an' onct I damn near done it," declared Moran.

"What for?"

"He an' another fellar jumped the only claim I ever struck thet showed any color," went on the cowboy with earnestness that showed excitement had sobered him. "I went back one mawnin' an' there was Hardman an' a miner named Purcell. They ran me off, swore it was their claim. Purcell said he'd worked it before an' sold it to Jard Hardman. Thet's young Hardman's dad, an' he wouldn't fit in any square hole. I went to Matthews an' raised a holler.

But I couldn't prove nothin'. . . . An' by Gawd, Pan, thet claim is a mine now, payin' well."

"Tough luck, Blink. You always did have the darndest luck. . . . Say, Brown, is that sort of deal worked often?"

"Common as dirt, in the early days of a find," replied Brown. "I haven't heard of any claim jumpin' just lately, though. It's somethin' like rustlin' cattle. You know most every cowman now and then picks up some unbranded stock that he knows isn't his. But he takes it along. Now claim jumpin' is somethin' like that. If a fellar leaves his claim for a day or a week he's liable to come back an' find some one has jumped it. I never leave mine in the daytime, an' I have witnesses to that."

"Blinky, I came out here to find my dad," said Pan. "Have you ever run across him?"

"Nope. Never heerd of him. I'd shore have asked aboot you."

"How am I going to find out quick if Dad is here, and where?"

"Easy as pie. Go to the stage office, where they get the mail an' express. Matty Smith has been handlin' thet since this heah burg was a kid in short dresses."

"Good. I'll go the first thing in the morning. . . . Now, you little knock-kneed, bow-legged two-bit cowpuncher! What're you doing with those things on your boots?"

"Huh! What things?" queried Moran.

"Why, those long shiny things that jingle when you walk."

"Haw! Haw! . . . Say, Pan, I might ask you the same. What you travel with them spurs on your boots fer?"

"I tried traveling without them, but I couldn't feel that I was moving."

"Wal, by gum, I been needin' mine. Ask Gus there. We've been wranglin' wild hosses. Broomtails they calls them heah. We've been doin' pretty good. Hardman an' Wiggate pay twelve dollars an' four bits a hoss on the hoof. Right heah in Marco. We could get more if we could risk shippin' to St. Louis. But thet's a hell of a job. Long ways to the railroad, an' say, mebbe drivin' them broomies isn't tough! Then two of us anyhow would have to go on the freight train with the hosses. Shore we cain't figger it thet way now. But later when we ketch a thousand haid we may try it."

"A thousand head! Blinky, are you still on the ground? You're talkin' fifteen thousand dollars."

"Shore. An' I'm tellin' you, Pan, thet we can make it. But ketchin' these wild hosses in any number hasn't been done yet. Hardman has an outfit ridin'. But them fellars couldn't get away from their own dust. We're not so blame swift, either. S'pose you throw in with us, Pan. You've chased wild hosses."

"Not such an awful lot, Blink. That game depends on the lay of the land."

"Shore. An' it lays bad in these parts. Will you throw in with us? An' have you got any money?"

"Yes to both questions, old-timer. But I've got to find Dad before I get careless with my money. Where are you boys staying?"

"We got a camp just out of town. We eat at the Chink's when we're heah, an' thet's every few days. We got lots of room an' welcome for you, but no bedroll."

"I'll buy an outfit in the morning and throw in with you. . . . Hello, there's shooting. Gun play. Let's get out of this place where there's more room and air."

With that they, and many others left the hall and joined the moving crowd in the street. The night was delightfully cool. Stars shone white in a velvet sky. The dry wind from mountain and desert blew in their faces. Pan halted at the steps of the hotel.

"Blink, I'm going to turn in. Call for me in the morning. I can't tell you how glad I am that I ran into you boys. And you, too, Brown. I'd like to see more of you."

They shook hands and parted. Pan entered the hotel, and sat a while in the bare smoky lobby, where sharp-eyed men and women passed him by with one look at his cowboy attire. They were seeking bigger game. Pan experienced a strange excitation in the hour, in the place.

When he went to his room he was not sleepy. "Lucky to meet those boys," he soliloquized, as he undressed. "Now to find Dad—Mother—Alice! Lord, I hope all's well with them. But I've a feeling it isn't. . . . And Lucy! I wonder will she be here too. Will *she* recognize me? I'll bet a million she does. Funny about Dick Hardman. Never knew me. Didn't he look, though? . . . And that girl Louise. She had to laugh and talk all the time to hide the sadness of her face. . . . At that, she's too good for Dick Hardman. . . . I'll bet another million he and I clash again."

Pan was up bright and early, enjoying the keen desert air, and the vast difference between Marco at night and at dawn. The little spell of morbid doubt and worry that had settled upon him did not abide in the clear rosy light of day. Hope and thrill resurged in him.

Blinky and his partner soon appeared, and quarreled over which should carry Pan's baggage out to their quarters. Pan decidedly preferred the locality to that he had just left. The boys had a big tent set up on a framework of wood, an open shed which they used as a kitchen, and a big corral. The site was up on a gradual slope, somewhat above the town, and rendered attractive by a small brook and straggling cedars. They had a Mexican cook who was known everywhere as Lying Juan. Pan grasped at once that he would have a lot of fun with Juan.

The boys talked so fast they almost neglected to eat their breakfast. They were full of enthusiasm, which fact Pan could not but see was owing to his arrival. It amused him. Moran, like many other cowboys, had always attributed to Pan a prowess and character he felt sure were undeserved. Yet it touched him.

"Wal, ole-timer, we'll rustle now," finally said Moran. "We've got aboot fifty broomies out heah in a canyon. We'll drive 'em in today, an' also some saddle hosses for you."

"I'll buy a horse," interposed Pan.

"You'll do nothin' of the sort," declared Blinky stoutly. "Ain't we got a string of hosses, an' there shore might be *one* of them good enough even for Panhandle Smith. But you want a saddle. There's one in Black's store. It's Mexican, an' a blamed good one. Cheap, too."

Gus came trotting up on a spirited sorrel, leading two other well-pointed horses, saddled, champing their bits. Sight of them was good for Pan's eyes. He would never long have been happy away from horses. Moran leaped astride one of them, and then said, hesitatingly:

"Pard, shore hope you hev good luck findin' your dad."

Pan watched them ride away down the slope to the road, and around a bend out of sight. It was wonderful country that faced him, cedar, piñon and sage, colored hills and flats, walls of yellow rock stretching away, and dim purple mountains all around. If his keen eyes did not deceive him there was a bunch of wild horses grazing on top of the first hill.

"Juan, are there lots of wild horses?" he asked the Mexican cook. And presently he came into knowledge of the justice of the name "Lying Juan." Pan had met some great liars in his life on the range, but if Juan could do any better than this he would be the champion of them all.

Pan shaved, put on a clean flannel shirt and new scarf, and leaving his coat behind he strode off toward the town. The business of the day had begun, and there was considerable bustle. Certainly Marco showed no similarity to a cattle town. Somebody directed him to the stage and express office, a plain board building off the main street. There men lounged before it, one on the steps, and the others against the hitching-rail. Pan took them in before they paid any particular attention to him.

"Morning, gents," he said easily. "Is the agent Smith around?"

"Howdy, stranger," replied one of them, looking Pan over. "Smith just stepped over to the bank. He'll be back pronto."

Another of the group straightened up to run a hard gray eye from Pan's spurs to his sombrero, and back for a second glance at his low hanging gun. He was a tall man, in loose tan garments, trousers stuffed in his boots. He had a big sandy mustache. He moved to face Pan, and either by accident or design the flap of his coat fell back to expose a bright silver shield on his vest.

"Reckon you're new in these parts?" he queried.

"Yep. Just rode in," replied Pan cheerfully.

"See you're packin' hardware," went on the other, with a significant glance at Pan's gun.

Pan at once took this man to be Matthews, the town marshal mentioned by Charley Brown. He had not needed Brown's hint; he had encountered many sheriffs of like stripe. Pan, usually the kindliest and most genial of cowboys, returned the sheriff's curious scrutiny with a cool stare.

"Am I packing a gun?" rejoined Pan, with pretended surprise, as he looked down at his hip. "Sure, so I am. Clean forgot it, Mister Habit of mine."

"What's a habit?" snapped the other.

Pan now shot a straight level gaze into the hard gray eyes of the sheriff. He knew he was going to have dealings with this man, and the sooner they began the better.

"Why, my packing a gun—when I'm in bad company," said Pan.

"Pretty strong talk, cowboy, west of the Rockies. . . . I'm Matthews, the town marshal."

"I knew that, and I'm right glad to meet you," rejoined Pan pertly. He made no move to meet the half-proffered hand, and his steady gaze disconcerted the marshal.

Another man came briskly up, carrying papers in his hand.

"Are you the agent, Mr. Smith?" asked Pan.

"I am thet air, young fellar."

"Can I see you a moment, on business?"

"Come right in." He ushered Pan into his office and shut the door.

"My name's Smith," began Pan hurriedly. "I'm hunting for my dad . . . Bill Smith. Do you know him—if he's in Marco?"

"Bill Smith's cowboy! Wal, put her thar," burst out the other, heartily, shoving out a big hand. His surprise and pleasure were marked. "Know Bill? Wal, I should smile. We're neighbors an' good friends."

Pan was so overcome by relief and sudden joy that he could not speak for a moment, but he wrung the agent's hand.

"Wal, now, sort of hit you in the gizzard, hey?" he queried, with humor and sympathy. He released his hand and put it on Pan's shoulder. "I've heard all about you, cowboy. Bill always talked a lot—until lately. Reckon he's deep hurt thet you never wrote."

"I've been pretty low-down," replied Pan with agitation. "But I never meant to be. . . . I just drifted along. . . . Always I was going back home soon. But I didn't. And I haven't written home for two years."

"Wal, forget thet now, son," said the agent kindly. "Boys will be boys, especially cowboys. You've been a wild one, if reports comin' to Bill was true. . . . But you've come home to make up to him. Lord knows he needs you, boy."

"Yes—I'll make it—up," replied Pan, trying to swallow his emotion. "Tell me."

"Wal, I wish I had better news to tell," replied Smith, gravely shaking his head. "Your dad's had tough luck. He lost his ranch in Texas, as I reckon you know, an' he follered—the man who'd done him out here to try to make him square up. Bill only got a worse deal. Then he got started again pretty good an' lost out because of a dry year. Now he's workin' in Carter's Wagon Shop. He's a first-rate carpenter. But his wages are small, an' he can't never get nowhere. He's talked some of wild-hoss wranglin'. But thet takes an outfit, which he ain't got. I'll give you a hunch, son. If you can stake your dad to an outfit an' throw in with him you might give him another start."

Pan had on his tongue an enthusiastic reply to that, but the entrance of the curious Matthews halted him.

"Thank you, Mr. Smith," he said eagerly. "Where'll I find Carter's Wagon Shop?"

"Other end of town. Right down Main Street. You can't miss it."

Pan hurried out, and through the door he heard Matthews' loud voice: "Carter's Wagon Shop! . . . By thunder, I've got the hunch! That cowboy is Panhandle Smith!"

Pan smiled grimly to himself, as he passed on out of hearing. The name and fame that had meant so little to him back on the prairie ranges might stand him in good stead out here west of the Rockies. He strode swiftly, his thought reverting to his father. He wanted to run. Remorse knocked at his heart. Desertion! He had gone off, like so many cowboys, forgetting home, father, mother, duty. They had suffered. Never a word of it had come to him.

The way appeared long, and the line of stone houses and board shacks, never ending. At last he reached the outskirts of Marco and espied the building and sign he was so eagerly seeking. Resounding hammer strokes came from the shop. Outward coolness, an achievement habitual with him when excitement mounted to a certain stage, came with effort and he paused a moment to gaze at the sweeping country, green and purple, dotted by gray rocks, rising to hills gold with autumn colors. His long journey was at an end. In a moment more anxiety would be a thing of the past. Let him only see his father actually in the flesh!

Pan entered the shop. It was open, like any other wagon shop with wood scattered about, shavings everywhere, a long bench laden with tools, a forge. Then he espied a man wielding a hammer on a wheel. His back was turned. But Pan knew him. Knew that back, that shaggy head beginning to turn gray, knew even the swing of arm! He approached leisurely. The moment seemed big, splendid.

"Howdy, Dad," he called, at the end of one of the hammer strokes.

His father's lax figure stiffened. He dropped the wheel, then the hammer. But not on the instant did he turn. His posture was strained, doubtful. Then he sprang erect, and whirled. Pan saw his father greatly changed; but how it was impossible to grasp because his seamed face was suddenly transformed.

"For the good—Lord's sake—if it ain't Pan!" he gasped.

"It sure is, Dad. Are you glad to see me?"

"*Glad!* . . . Reckon this'll save your mother's life!" and to Pan's amaze he felt himself crushed in his father's arms. That sort of thing had never been Bill Smith's way. He thrilled to it, and tried again to beat back the remorse mounting higher. His father released him, and drew back, as if suddenly ashamed of his emotion. His face, which he had been trying to control, smoothed out.

"Wal, Pan, you come back now—after long ago I gave up hopin'?" he queried, haltingly.

"Yes, Dad," began Pan with swift rush of words. "I'm sorry. I always meant to come home. But one thing and another prevented. Then I never heard of your troubles. I never knew you needed me. You didn't write. Why didn't you *tell* me? . . . But forget that. I rode the ranges—drifted with the cowboys—till I got homesick. Now I've found you—and well, I want to make up to you and Mother."

"Ah-huh! Sounds like music to me," replied Smith, growing slow and cool. He eyed Pan up and down, walked round him twice. Then he suddenly burst out, "Wal, you long-legged strappin' son of a gun! If sight of you ain't good for sore eyes! . . . Ah-huh! Look where he packs that gun!"

With slow strange action he reached down to draw Pan's gun from its holster. It was long and heavy, blue, with a deadly look. The father's intent gaze moved from it up to the face of the son. Pan realized what his father knew, what he thought. The moment was sickening for Pan. A cold shadow, forgotten for long, seemed to pass through his mind.

"Pan, I've kept tab on you for years," spoke his father slowly, "but I'd have heard, even if I hadn't took pains to learn. . . . Panhandle Smith! You damned hard-ridin', gun-throwin' son of mine! . . . Once my heart broke because you drifted with the wild cowpunchers—but now—by God, I believe I'm glad."

"Dad, never mind range talk. You know how cowboys brag and blow. . . . I'm not ashamed to face you and Mother. I've come clean, Dad."

"But, son, you've—you've used that gun!" whispered Smith, hoarsely.

"Sure I have. On some two-legged coyotes an' skunks. . . . And maybe greasers. I forget."

"Panhandle Smith!" ejaculated his father, refusing to take the matter in Pan's light vein. "They know here in Marco. . . . You're known, Pan, here west of the Rockies."

"Well, what of it?" flashed Pan, suddenly gripped again by that strange cold emotion in the depths of him. "I should think you'd be glad. Reckon it was all good practice for what I'll have to do out here."

"Don't talk that way. You've read my mind," replied Smith, huskily. "I'm afraid. I'm almost sorry you came. Yet, right now I feel more of a man than for years."

"Dad, you can tell me everything some other time," rejoined Pan, throwing off the sinister spell. "Now, I only want to know about Mother and Alice."

"They're well an' fine, son, though your mother grieves

for you. She never got over that. An' Alice, she's a big girl, goin' to school an' helpin' with work. . . . An' Pan, you've got a baby brother nearly two years old."

"Jumping cowbells!" shouted Pan, in delight. "Where are they? Tell me quick."

"We live on a farm a mile or so out. I rent it for most nothin'. Hall, who owns it, has a big ranch. I've got an option on this farm, an' it shore is a bargain. Hundred an' ten acres, most of it cultivated. Good water, pasture, barn, an' nice little cabin. I work here mornin's, an' out there afternoons. You'll—"

"Stop talking about it. I'll buy the farm," interrupted Pan. "But *where* is it?"

"Keep right out this road. Second farmhouse," said his father, pointing to the west. "I'd go with you, but I promised some work. But I'll be home at noon. . . . Hey, hold on. There's more to tell. You'll get a—a jolt. Wait."

But Pan rushed on out of the shop, and took to the road with the stride of a giant. To be compelled to walk, when if he had had his horse he could ride that mile in two minutes! His heart was beating high. Mother! Grieving for me. Alice a big girl. And a baby boy! This is too good for a prodigal like me.

All else he had forgotten for the moment. Shadows of memories overhung his consciousness, striving for entrance, but he denied them. How shaken his father had been at sight of him! Poor old Dad! And then what was the significance of all that talk about his range name, Panhandle Smith, and his father's strange fascinated handling of Pan's gun? Would his mother know him at first glance? Oh! no doubt of that! But Alice would not; she had been a child; and he had grown, changed.

While his thoughts raced he kept gazing near and far. The farm land showed a fair degree of cultivation. Grassy hills shone in the bright morning sun; high up, flares of gold spoke eloquently of aspen thickets tinged by the frost; purple belts crossing the mountains told of forests. The wall of rock that he had observed from Moran's camp wound away over the eastern horizon. A new country it was, a fair and wild country, rugged and hard on the uplands, suitable for pasture and cultivation in the lowlands.

Pan passed the first farmhouse. Beyond that he could make out only a green patch, where he judged lay the home he was hunting. His buoyant step swallowed up the rods. Cattle and horses grazed in a pasture. The road turned to the right, round the slope of a low hill. Pan's quick eye caught a column of curling blue smoke that rose from a grove of trees. The house would be in there. Pasture, orchard, cornfield, ragged and uncut, a grove of low trees with thick foliage, barns and corrals he noted with appreciative enthusiasm. The place did not have the bareness characteristic of a ranch.

At last Pan reached the wagon gate that led into the farm. It bordered an orchard of fair-sized trees, the leaves of which were colored. He cut across the orchard so as to reach the house more quickly. It was still mostly hidden among the trees. Smell of hay, of fruit, of the barnyard assailed his nostrils. And then the fragrance of wood smoke and burning leaves! His heart swelled full high in his breast. He could never meet his mother with his usual cool easy nonchalance.

Suddenly he espied a woman through the trees. She was quite close. He almost ran. No, it could not be his mother. This was a girl, lithe, tall, swift stepping. His mother had been rather short and stout. Could this girl be his sister Alice? The swift supposition was absurd, because Alice was only about ten, and this girl was grown. She had a grace of motion that struck Pan. He hurried around some trees to intercept her, losing sight of her for a moment.

Suddenly he came out of the shade to confront her, face to face in the open sunlight. She uttered a cry and dropped something she had been carrying.

"Don't be scared, miss," he said, happily. "I'm no tramp, though I did rant in like a trespasser. I want to find Mrs. Bill Smith. I'm—"

But Pan got no farther. The girl had reason to be scared, but should her hands fly to her bosom like that, and press there as if she had been hurt? He must have frightened her. And he was about to stammer his apologies and make himself known, when the expression on her face struck him mute. Her healthy golden skin turned white. Her lips quivered, opened. Then her eyes—their color was violet and something about them seemed to stab Pan. His mind went into a deadlock—seemed to whirl—and to flash again into magnified thoughts.

"*Pan! Pan!*" she cried, and moved toward him, her eyes widening, shining with a light he had never seen in another woman's.

"Pan! Don't you—know me?"

"Sure—but I don't know *who* you are," Pan muttered in bewilderment.

"I'm Lucy! . . . Oh, Pan—you've come back," she burst out, huskily, with a deep break in her voice.

She seemed to leap toward him—into the arms he flung wide, as with tremendous shock he recognized her name, her voice, her eyes. It was a moment beyond reason. . . . He was crushing her to his breast, kissing her in a frenzy of sudden realization of love. Lucy! Lucy! Little Lucy Blake, his baby, his child sweetheart, his schoolmate! And the hunger of the long lonely years, never realized, leaped to his lips now.

She flung her arms round his neck, and for a few moments gave him kiss for kiss. Then suddenly she shivered and her head fell forward on his breast.

Pan held her closely, striving for self-control. And he gazed out into the trees with blurred eyes. What a homecoming! Lucy, grown into a tall beautiful girl who had never forgotten him. He was shaken to his depths by the revelation that now came to him. He had always loved Lucy! Never anyone else, never knowing until this precious moment! What a glorious trick for life to play him. He held her, wrapped her closer, bent his face to her fragrant hair. It was dull gold now. Once it had been bright, shiny, light as the color of grass on the hill. He kissed it, conscious of unutterable gratitude and exaltation.

She stirred, put her hands to his breast and broke away from him, tragic eyed, strange.

"Pan, I—I was beside myself," she whispered. "Forgive me. . . . Oh, the joy of seeing you. It was too much. . . . Go to your mother. She—will—"

"Yes, presently, but Lucy, don't feel badly about this—about my not recognizing you at once," he interrupted, in glad swift eagerness. "How you have grown!

61

Changed! . . . Lucy, your hair is gold now. My little white-headed kid! Oh, I remember. I never forgot you that way. But you're so changed—so—so—Lucy, you're beautiful. . . . I've come back to you. I always loved you. I didn't know it as I do now, but I've been true to you. Lucy, I swear. . . . I'm Panhandle Smith and as wild as any of that prairie outfit. But, darling, I've been *true* to you—*true*. . . . And I've come back to love you, to make up for absence, to take care of you—marry you. Oh, darling, I know you've been true to me—you've waited for me."

Rapture and agony both seemed to be struggling for the mastery over Lucy. Pan suddenly divined that this was the meaning of her emotion.

"My God!" she whispered, finally, warding him off. "Don't you know—haven't you heard?"

"Nothing. Dad didn't mention you," replied Pan hoarsely, fighting an icy sickening fear. "What's wrong?"

"Go to your mother. Don't let her wait. I'll see you later."

"But, Lucy—"

"Go. Give me a little while to—to get hold of myself."

"Are—are you married?" he faltered.

"No—no—but—"

"Don't you love me?"

She made no reply, except to cover her face with shaking hands. They could not hide the betraying scarlet.

"Lucy, you *must* love me," he rushed on, almost incoherently. "You gave yourself away. . . . It lifted me—changed me. All my life I've loved you, though I never realized it. . . . Your kisses—they made me know myself. . . . But, my God, *say* that you love me!"

"Yes, Pan, I do love you," she replied, quietly, lifting her eyes to his. Again the rich color fled.

"Then, nothing else matters," cried Pan. "Whatever's wrong, I'll make right. Don't forget that. I've much to make up for. . . . Forgive me for this—this—whatever has hurt you so. I'll go now to Mother and see you later. You'll stay?"

"I live here with your people," replied Lucy and walked away through the trees.

"Something wrong!" muttered Pan, as he watched her go. But the black fear of he knew not what could not stand before his consciousness of finding Lucy, of seeing her betray her love. Doubt lingered, but his glad heart downed that too. He was home. What surprise and joy to learn that it was also Lucy's home! He stifled his intense curiosity and longing. He composed himself. He walked a little under the trees. He thought of the happiness he would bring his mother, and Alice. In a few moments he would make the acquaintance of his baby brother.

Flowers that he recognized as the favorites of his mother bordered the sandy path around the cabin. The house had been constructed of logs and later improved with a frame addition, unpainted, weather stained, covered with vines. A cozy little porch, with wide eaves and a windbreak of vines, faced the south. A rude homemade rocking chair sat on the porch; a child's wooden toys also attested to a carpenter's skill Pan well remembered. He heard a child singing, then a woman's mellow voice.

Pan drew a long breath and took off his sombrero. It had come—the moment he had long dreamed of. He stepped loudly upon the porch, so that his spurs jangled musically, and he knocked upon the door frame.

"Who's there?" called the voice again. It made Pan's heart beat fast. In deep husky tones he replied:

"Just a poor starved cowboy, ma'am, beggin' a little grub."

"Gracious me!" she exclaimed, and her footsteps thudded on the floor inside.

Pan knew his words would fetch her. Then he saw her come to the door. Years, trouble, pain had wrought their havoc, but he would have known her at first sight among a thousand women.

"Mother!" he called, poignantly, and stepped toward her, with his arms out.

She seemed stricken. The kindly eyes changed, rolled. Her mouth opened wide. She gasped and fainted in his arms.

A little while later, when she had recovered from the shock and the rapture of Pan's return, they sat in the neat little room.

"Bobby, don't you know your big brother?" Pan was repeating to the big-eyed boy who regarded him so solemnly. Bobby was fascinated by this stranger, and at last was induced to approach his knee.

"Mother, I reckon you'll never let Bobby be a cowboy," teased Pan, with a smile.

"Never," she murmured fervently.

"Well, he might do worse," went on Pan thoughtfully. "But we'll make a plain rancher of him, with a leaning to horses. How's that?"

"I'd like it, but not in a wild country like this," she replied.

"Reckon we'd do well to figure on a permanent home in Arizona, where both summers and winters are pleasant. I've heard a lot about Arizona. It's a land of wonderful grass and sage ranges, fine forests, canyons. We'll go there, some day."

"Then, Pan, you've come home to stay?" she asked, with agitation.

"Yes, Mother," he assured her, squeezing the worn hand that kept reaching to touch him, as if to see if he were real. Then Bobby engaged his attention. "Hey, you rascal, let go. That's my gun. . . . Bad sign, Mother. Bobby's as keen about a gun as I was over a horse. . . . There, Bobby, now it's safe to play with. . . . Mother, there's a million things to talk about. But we'll let most of them go for the present. You say Alice is in school. When will she be home?"

"Late this afternoon. Pan," she went on, hesitatingly, "Lucy Blake lives with us now."

"Yes, I met Lucy outside," replied Pan, drawing a deep breath. "But first about Dad. I didn't take time to talk much with him. I wanted to see you. . . . Is Dad well in health?"

"He's well enough. Really he does two men's work. Worry drags him down."

"We'll cheer him up. At Littleton I heard a little about Dad's bad luck. Now you tell me everything."

"There's little to tell," she replied, sadly. "Your father made foolish deals back in Texas, the last and biggest of which was with Jard Hardman. There came a bad year—año seco, the Mexicans call it. Failure of crops left your father ruined. He lost the farm. He found later that Hardman had cheated him out of his cattle. We followed

64

Hardman out here. Our neighbors, the Blakes, had come ahead of us. Hardman not only wouldn't be square about the cattle deal but he knocked your father out again, just as he had another start. In my mind it was worse than the cattle deal. We bought a homestead from a man named Sprague. His wife wanted to go home to Missouri. This homestead had water, good soil, some timber, and an undeveloped mining claim that turned out well. Then along comes Jard Hardman with claims, papers, witnesses, and law back of him. He claimed to have gotten possession of the homestead from the original owner. It was all a lie. But they put us off. . . . Then your father tried several things that did not pan out. Now we're here—and he has to work in the wagon shop to pay the rent."

"Ah-huh!" replied Pan, relieving his oppressed breast with an effort. "And now about Lucy. How does it come she's living with you?"

"She had no home, poor girl," replied his mother, hastily. "She came out here with her father and uncle. Her mother died soon after you left us. Jim Blake had interests with Hardman back in Texas. He talked big—and drank a good deal. He and Hardman quarreled. It was the same big deal that ruined your father. But Jim came to New Mexico with Hardman. They were getting along all right when we arrived. But trouble soon arose—and that over Lucy. . . . Young Dick Hardman—you certainly ought to remember him, Pan—fell madly in love with Lucy. Dick always was a wild boy. Here in Marco he went the pace. Well, bad as Jard Hardman is he loves that boy and would move heaven and earth for him. Lucy despised Dick. The more he ran after her the more she despised him. Also the more she flouted Dick the wilder he drank and gambled. Now here comes the pitiful part of it. Jim Blake went utterly to the bad, so your father says, though Lucy hopes and believes she can save him. I do too. Jim was only weak. Jard Hardman ruined him. Finally Dick enlisted his father in his cause and they forced Jim to try to make Lucy marry Dick. She refused. She left her father's place and went to live with her Uncle Bill, who was an honest fine man. But he was shot in the Yellow Mine. By accident, they gave out, but your father scouts that idea . . . Oh, those dreadful gambling hells! Life is cheap here. . . . Lucy came to live with us. She taught the school. But she had to give that up. Dick Hardman and other wild young fellows made her life wretched. Besides she was never safe. We persuaded her to give it up. And then the—the worst happened."

Mrs. Smith paused, wiping her wet eyes, and appeared to dread further disclosure. She lifted an appealing hand to Pan.

"What—what was it, Mother?" he asked, fearfully.

"Didn't—she—Lucy tell you anything?" faltered his mother.

"Yes—the greatest thing in the world—that she loved me," burst out Pan with exultant passion.

"Oh, how terrible!"

"No, Mother, not that, but beautiful, wonderful, glorious. . . . Go on."

"Then—then they put Jim Blake in jail," began Mrs. Smith.

"What for?" flashed Pan.

"To hold him there, pending action back in Texas. Jim Blake was a cattle thief. There's little doubt of that, your father says. You know there's law back east, at least now in some districts. Well, Jard Hardman is holding Jim in jail. It seems Hardman will waive trial, provided—provided. . . . Oh, how can I tell you!"

"My God! I see!" cried Pan, leaping in fierce passion. "They will try to force Lucy to marry Dick to save her father."

"Yes. That's it . . . and Pan, my son . . . she has consented!"

"So that was what made her act so strange! . . . Poor Lucy! Dick Hardman was a skunk when he was a kid. Now he's a skunk-bitten coyote. Oh, but this is a mess!"

"Pan, what *can* you do?" implored his mother.

"Lucy *hasn't* married him yet? Tell me quick," cried Pan suddenly.

"Oh, no. She has only promised. She doesn't trust those men. She wants papers signed to clear her father. They laugh at her. But Lucy is no fool. When she sacrifices herself it'll not be for nothing."

Pan slowly sank down into the chair, and his brooding

gaze fastened on the big blue gun with which Bobby was playing. It fascinated Pan. Sight of it brought the strange cold sensation that seemed like a wind through his being.

"Mother, how old is Lucy?" he asked, forcing himself to be calm.

"She's nearly seventeen, but looks older."

"Not of age yet. Yes, she looks twenty. She's a woman, Mother."

"What did Lucy do and say when she saw you?" asked his mother, with a woman's intense curiosity.

"Ha! She did and said enough," replied Pan radiantly. "I didn't recognize her. Think of that, Mother."

"Tell me, son," implored Mrs. Smith.

"Mother, she ran right into my arms. . . . We just met, Mother, and the old love leaped."

"Mercy, what a terrible situation for you both, especially for Lucy. . . . Pan, what *can* you do?"

"Mother, I don't know, I can't think. It's too sudden. But I'll never let her marry Dick Hardman. Why, only last night I saw a painted little hussy hanging over him. Bad as that poor girl must be, she's too good for him. . . . *He* doesn't worry me, nor his schemes to get Lucy. But how to save Jim Blake."

"Pan, you think it can be done?"

"My dear Mother, I know it. Only I can't think now. I'm new here. And handicapped by concern for you, for Lucy, for Dad. . . . Lord, if I was back in the Cimarron—it'd be easy!"

"My boy, don't be too concerned about Lucy, or me or your dad," replied his mother with surprising coolness. "I mean don't let concern for us balk you. Thank God you have come home to us. I feel a different woman. I am frightened, yes. For—for I've heard of you. What a name for my boy!"

"Well, you're game, Mother," said Pan, with a laugh, as he embraced her. "That'll help a lot. If only Lucy will be like you."

"She has a heart of fire. Only save her father, Pan, and you will be blessed with such woman's love as you never dreamed of. It may be hard, though, for you to change her mind."

"I won't try, Mother."

"Go to her, then, and fill her with the hope you've given me."

7

◈

FROM a thick clump of trees Pan had watched Lucy, spied upon her with only love, tenderness, pity in his heart. But he did not know her. It seemed incredible that he could confess to himself he loved her. Had the love he had cherished for a child suddenly, as if by magic, leaped into love for a woman? What then was this storm within him, this outward bodily trembling from the tumult within?

Lucy stood like a statue, gazing into nothingness. Then she paced to and fro, her hands clenched on her breast. This was a secluded nook, where a bench had been built between two low-branching trees, on the bank of the stream. Pan stealthily slipped closer, so he could get clearer sight of her face. Was her love for him the cause of her emotion?

Presently he halted, at a point close to one end of her walk, and crouched down. It did not occur to him that he was trespassing upon her privacy. She was a stranger whom he loved because she was Lucy Blake, grown from child to woman. He was concerned with finding himself, so that when he faced her again he would know what to do, to say.

Pan had not encountered a great many girls in the years he had ridden the ranges. But he had seen enough to recognize beauty when it was thrust upon him. And Lucy had that. As she paced away from him the small gold head, the heavy braid of hair, the fine build of her, not robust, yet strong and full, answered then and there the wondering query of his admiration. Then she turned to pace back. This would be an ordeal for him. She was in trouble, and he could not hide there much longer. Yet he wanted to watch her, to grasp from this agitation fuel for his kindling passion. She had been weeping, yet her face was white. Indeed she did look older than her seventeen years. Closer she came. Then Pan's gaze got as far as her eyes and fixed there. Unmasked now, true to the strife of her soul, they betrayed to Pan the thing he yearned so to know. Not only her love but her revolt!

That was enough for him. In a few seconds his feelings underwent a tremendous gamut of change, at last to set with the certainty of a man's love for his one woman. This conviction seemed consciously backed by the stern fact of his cool reckless spirit. He was what the cowboy's range of that period had made him. Perhaps only such a man could cope with the lawless circumstances in which Lucy had become enmeshed. By the time she had paced her beat again and was once more approaching his covert, he knew what the situation would demand and how he would meet it. But he would listen to Lucy, to his mother, to his father, in the hope that they might extricate her from her dilemma. He believed, however, that only extreme measures would ever free her and her father. Pan knew men of the Hardman and Matthews stripe.

He stepped out to confront Lucy, smiling and cool.

"Howdy, Lucy," he drawled, with the cowboy sang-froid she must know well.

"Oh!" she cried, startled, and drawing back. Then she recovered. But there was a single instant when Pan saw her unguarded self expressed in her face.

"I was hiding behind there," he said, indicating the trees and bushes.

"What for?"

"I wanted to *see* you really, without you knowing."

"Well?" she queried, gravely.

"As I remember little Lucy Blake she never had any promise of growing so—so lovely as you are now."

"Pan, don't tease—don't flatter me now," she implored.

"Reckon I was just stating a fact. Let's sit down on the seat there, and get acquainted."

He put her in the corner of the bench so she would have to face him, and he began to talk as if there were no black trouble between them. He wanted her to know the story of his life from the time she had seen him last; and he had two reasons for this, first to bridge that gap in their acquaintance, and secondly to let her know what the range had made him. It took him two hours in the telling, surely the sweetest hours he had ever spent, for he watched her warm to intense interest, forget herself, live over with him the lonely days and nights on the range, and glow radiant at his adventures, and pale and trembling over those bloody encounters that were as much a part of his experience as any others.

"That's my story, Lucy," he said, in conclusion. "I'd have come back to you and home long ago, if I'd known. But I was always broke. Then there was the talk about me. Panhandle Smith! So the years sped by. It's over now, and I've found you and my people all well, thank God. Nothing else mattered to me. And your trouble and Dad's bad luck do not scare me. . . . Now tell me your story."

He had reached her. It had been wise for him to go back to the school days, and spare nothing of his experience. She began at the time she saw him last—she remembered the day, the date, the clothes he wore, the horse he rode—and she told the story of those lonely years when his few letters were epochs, and the effect it had when they ceased. So, with simple directness, she went on to relate the downfall of her father and how the disgrace and heartbreak had killed her mother. When she finished her story she was crying.

"Lucy, don't cry. Just think—here we are!" he exclaimed, as she ended.

"That's what—makes me cry," she replied brokenly.

"Very well. Here. Cry on my shoulder," he said forcefully, and despite her resistance he drew her into his arms and her head to his breast. There he held her, feeling the strain of her muscles slowly relax. She did not weep violently, but in a heartbroken way that yet seemed relief.

"Pan, this is—is foolish," she said, presently stirring. "I mean my crying here in your arms, as if it were a refuge. But, oh! I—I have needed someone—something so terribly."

"I don't see where it's foolish. Reckon it's very sweet and wonderful for me. . . . Lucy, let's not rush right into arguments. We're bound to disagree. But let's put that off. . . .

70

I'm so darned glad to see you, *know* you, that I'm the foolish one."

"You're a boy, for all your size. How can we help but talk of my troubles? . . . Of this horrible fix I'm in! . . . How can I lay my head on your shoulder? . . . I didn't. You forced me to."

"Well, if you want to deny me such happiness, you can," replied Pan.

"Is it happiness for you—knowing it's wrong—and can never be again?" she whispered.

"Pure heaven!" he said. "Lucy, don't say this is wrong. You belong to *me*. My mother told me once you'd never have lived but for me."

"Yes, my mother told me the same thing. . . . Oh, how sad it is!"

"Sad, nothing! It was beautiful. And I tell you that you do belong to me."

"My soul does, yes," she returned, dreamily. And then as if reminded of her bodily weakness she moved away from him to the corner of the bench.

"All right, Lucy. Have it your way now. But you'll only have all the more to make up to me later," said Pan, with resigned good nature.

"Pan, you don't seem to recognize anything but your own will," she returned, pondering. "I've *got* to save my father. . . . There's only one way."

"Don't talk such rot to me," he flashed, sharply. "I'd hoped you would let us get acquainted first. But if you won't, all right. . . . You've been frightened into a deal that is terrible for you. No wonder. But you're only a kid yet. What do you know of men? These Hardmans are crooked. They pulled out of Texas because they were crooked. Matthews, magistrate or marshal, whatever he calls himself, he's crooked too. I *know* such men. I've met a hundred of them. Slowly they've been forced farther west, beyond the Rockies. And here they work their will. But it can't last. Why, Lucy, I'm amazed that some miner or cowboy or gunfighter hasn't stopped them long ago."

"Pan, you must be wrong," she declared, earnestly. "Hardman cheated Dad, yes. But that was only Dad's fault.

71

His blindness in business. Hardman is a power here. And Matthews, too. You talk like a—a wild cowboy."

"Sure," replied Pan, with a grim laugh. "And it'll take just a wild cowboy to clean up this mess. . . . Now, Lucy, don't go white and sick. I promise you I'll listen to Dad and you before I make a move. I'll go to see your father. And I'll call on Hardman. I'll talk sense and reason, and business to these men. I know it'll not amount to beans, but I'll do it just to show you I can be deliberate and sane."

"Thank you—you frightened me so," she murmured. "Pan, there was something terrible about you—then."

"Listen, Lucy," he began, more seriously. "I've been here in Marco only a few hours. But this country is no place for us to settle down to live. It's mostly a mining country. I've heard a lot about Arizona. I'm going to take you all down there. Dad and Mother will love the idea. I'll get your father out of jail—"

"Pan, are you dreaming?" she interrupted, in distress. "Dad is a rustler. He admits it. Back in Texas he can be jailed for years. All Hardman has to do is to send for officers to come take Dad. And I've got to marry Dick Hardman to save him."

"You poor little girl! . . . Now, Lucy, let me tell you something funny. This will stagger you. Because it's gospel truth, I swear. . . . Rustler you call your dad. What's that? It means a cowman who has appropriated cattle not his own. He has driven off unbranded stock and branded it. There's no difference. Lucy, my dad rustled cattle. So have all the ranchers I ever rode for."

"Pan!" she gasped, with dilating eyes. "What are you saying?"

"I'm trying to tell you one of the queer facts about the ranges," replied Pan. "I've known cowmen to shoot rustlers. Cowmen who had themselves branded cattle not their own. This was a practice. They didn't think it crooked. They all did it. But it *was* crooked, when you come down to truth. And though that may not be legally as criminal as the stealing of branded cattle, to my mind it is just as bad. Your father began that way, Hardman caught him, and perhaps forced him into worse practice."

"Pan, are you trying to give me some hope?"

72

"Reckon I am. Things are not so bad. My Lord, suppose I'd been a month later!"

Lucy shook her head despondently. "It's worse *now* for me than if you had come—"

"Why?" interrupted Pan. She would say the things that hurt.

"Because to see you—be with you like this—before I'm—if I have to be married—is perfectly terrible. . . . Afterward, when it would be too late and I had lost something—self-respect or more—then I might not care."

That not only made Pan lose patience but it also angered him. The hot blood rushed to his face. He bit his tongue and struggled to control himself.

"Lucy! Haven't I told you that you're not going to marry Dick Hardman," he burst out.

"Oh, but I'll have to," she replied stubbornly, with a sad little shake of her head.

"No!"

"I must save Dad. You might indeed get him out of jail some way. But that would not save him."

"Certainly it would," rejoined Pan, curtly. "In another state he would be perfectly safe."

"They'll trail him anywhere. No, that won't do. We haven't time. Dick is pressing me hard to marry him at once, or his father will prosecute Dad. I promised. . . . And today—this morning—Dick is coming here to get me to set the day."

"What?" cried Pan, passionately.

His word, swift as a bullet, made her jump, but she repeated what she had said almost word for word.

"And your answer?" queried Pan, in hot scorn.

"Sooner the—better," she replied, mournfully. "I can't stand—this—you—oh, anything would be—easier than your hope . . . your—your love making!"

"Lucy Blake, have *you* gone down hill like your father?" asked Pan, hoarsely. "What kind of a woman are you? If you love me, it's a crime to marry him. Women do these things, I know—sell themselves. But they kill their souls. If you could save your father from being hanged, it would still be wrong. Suppose he *did* go to jail for a few years. What's that compared to hell for you all your life? You're out of

73

your head. You've lost your sense of proportion. . . . You must *care* for this damned skunk Dick Hardman."

"Care for him!" she cried, shamefaced and furious. "I hate him."

"Then if you marry him you'll be crooked. To yourself! To me! . . . Why, in my eyes you'd be worse than that little hussy down at the Yellow Mine."

"Pan!" she whispered. "How can you? How dare you?"

"Hard facts deserve hard names. You make me say such things. Why, you'd drive me mad if I listened—if I believed you. Don't you dare say you'll marry Dick."

"I will—I must—"

"Lucy!" he thundered. It was no use to reason with this girl. She had been trapped like a wild thing and could not see any way out. He shot out a strong hand and clutched her shoulder and with one heave he drew her to him, so her face was under his. It went pale. The telltale eyes dilated in sudden fear. She beat at him with weak fluttering hands.

"Say you love me!"

He shook her roughly, then held her tight. "I don't maul any other man's woman," he went on, fiercely. "But if you love me—that's different. You said it a little while ago. Was it true? Are you a liar?"

"No—no—Pan," she whispered, in distress. "I—I do."

"Do what?"

"I—I love you," she said, the scarlet blood mounting to her pale face. She was weakening—sinking toward him. Her eyes held a sort of dark spell.

"How do you love me?" he queried relentlessly, with his heart mounting high.

"Always I've love you—since I was a baby."

"As a brother?"

"Yes."

"But we're man and woman now. This is my one chance for happiness. I don't want you—I wouldn't have you unless you love me as I do you. Be honest with me. Be square. Do you love me now as I do you?"

"God help me—yes," she replied, almost inaudibly, with eyes of remorse and love and agony on his.

Pan could not withstand this. He crushed her to him, and lifted her arms around his neck, and fell to kissing her with all the starved hunger of his lonely loveless years on the ranges. She was not proof against this. It lifted her out of her weakness, of her abasement to a response that swept away all fears, doubts, troubles. For the moment, at least, love conquered her.

Pan was wrenched out of the ecstasy of that moment by the pound of hoofs and the crashing of brush. He could not disengage himself before a horse and rider were upon them. Nevertheless Pan recognized the intruder and leaped away from the bench with the instinctive swiftness for defense that had been ingrained in him.

Dick Hardman showed the most abject astonishment. His eyes stuck out, his jaw dropped. No other emotion seemed yet to have dawned in him. He stared from Lucy to Pan and back again. A slow dull red began to creep into his cheeks. He ejaculated something incoherent. His amaze swiftly grew into horror. He had caught his fiancée in the arms of another man. Black fury suddenly possessed him.

"You—you—" he yelled stridently, moving to dismount.

"Stay on your horse," commanded Pan.

"Who the hell are you?" bellowed Hardman, sliding back in the saddle.

"Howdy, Skunk Hardman," rejoined Pan, with cool impudence. "Reckon you ought to know me."

"Pan Smith!" gasped the other, hoarsely, and he turned lividly white. "By God, I knew you last night. But I couldn't place you."

"Well, Mr. Dick Hardman, I knew you the instant I set eyes on you—sitting there gambling—with the pretty barearmed girl on your chair," returned Pan, with slow deliberate sarcasm.

"Yes, and you got that little —— over to you about as quick," shouted Hardman.

"Be careful of your language. There's a lady present," replied Pan, menacingly.

"Of all the nerve! You—you damned cowpuncher," raved Hardman in a fury. "It didn't take you long to get to *her*, either, did it? Now you make tracks out of here or I'll—I'll—it'll be the worse for you, Pan Smith. . . . Lucy Blake is as good as married to me."

"Nope, you're wrong, Dick," snapped Pan insolently. "I got here just in time to save her from that doubtful honor."

"You'd break her engagement to me?" rasped Hardman huskily, and he actually shook in his saddle.

"I have broken it."

"Lucy, tell me he lies!" begged Hardman, turning to her in poignant distress. If he had any good in him it showed then.

Lucy came out from the shade of the tree into the sunlight. She was pale, but composed.

"Dick, it's true," she said, steadily. "I've broken my word. I can't marry you. . . . I love Pan. I've loved him always. It would be a sin to marry you now."

"*Hell's fire!*" shrieked Hardman. His face grew frightful to see—beastly with rage. "You're as bad as that hussy who threw me down for him. I'll fix you, Lucy Blake. And I'll put your cow-thief father behind the bars for life."

Pan leaped at Hardman and struck him a body blow that sent him tumbling out of his saddle to thud on the ground. The frightened horse ran down the path toward the gate.

"You dirty-mouthed cur," said Pan. "Get up, and if you've got a gun—throw it."

Hardman laboriously got to his feet. The breath had been partly knocked out of him. Baleful eyes rolled at Pan. Instinctive wrath, however, had been given a setback. Hardman had been forced to think of something beside the frustration of his imperious will.

"I'm—not—packing—my gun," he panted, heavily. "You saw—that—Pan Smith."

"Well, you'd better pack it after this," replied Pan with contempt. "Because I'm liable to throw on you at sight."

"I'll have—you—run—out of this country," replied Dick huskily.

"Bah! don't waste your breath. Run me out of this country? Me! Reckon you never heard of Panhandle Smith. You're so thickheaded you couldn't take a hunch. Well, I'll give you one, anyway. *You* and your crooked father, and your two bit of a sheriff pardner would do well to leave this country. Savvy that! Now get out of here pronto."

Hardman gave Pan a ghastly stare and wheeled away to stride down the path. Once he turned to flash his convulsed face at Lucy. Then he passed out of sight among the trees in search of his horse.

Pan stood gazing down the green aisle. He had acted true to himself. How impossible to meet this situation in any other way! It meant the spilling of blood. He knew it—accepted it—and made no attempt to change the cold passion deep within him. Lucy—his mother and father would suffer. But wouldn't they suffer more if he did not confront this conflict as his hard training dictated? He was almost afraid to turn and look at Lucy. Just a little while before he had promised her forbearance. So his amaze was great when she faced him, violet eyes ablaze, to clasp him, and creep close to him, with lingering traces of fear giving way to woman's admiration and love.

"Panhandle Smith!" she whispered, gazing up into his face. "I heard your story. It thrilled me. . . . But I never understood—till you faced Dick Hardman. . . . Oh, what have you done for me? . . . Oh, Pan, you have saved me from ruin."

8

◇

PAN and Lucy did not realize the passing of time until they were called to dinner. As they stepped upon the little porch Lucy tried to withdraw her hand from Pan's, but did not succeed.

"See here," said he, very seriously, yielding to an urge he could not resist. "Wouldn't it be wise for us to—to get married at once?"

Lucy blushed furiously. "Pan Smith! Are you crazy?"

"Reckon I am," he replied, ruefully. "But I got to thinking how I'll be out after wild horses. . . . And I'm afraid something might happen. Please marry me this afternoon?"

"Pan! You're—you're terrible," cried Lucy, and snatching away her hand, scarlet of face she rushed into the house ahead of him.

He followed, to find Lucy gone. His father was smiling, and his mother had wide-open hopeful eyes. A slim young girl with freckles, grave sweet eyes and curly hair was standing by a window. She turned and devoured him with those shy eyes. From that look he knew who she was.

"Alice! Little sister!" he exclaimed, meeting her. "Well, by golly, this is great."

It did not take long for Pan to grasp that a subtle change had come over his mother and father. Not the excitement of his presence nor the wonder about Lucy accounted for it, but a difference, a lessening of strain, a relief. Pan sensed a reliance upon him that they were not yet conscious of.

"Son, what was the matter with Lucy?" inquired his father, shrewdly.

"Why nothing to speak of," replied Pan, nonchalantly. "Reckon she was a little flustered because I wanted her to marry me this afternoon."

"Good gracious!" cried his mother. "You *are* a cowboy. Lucy marry you when she's engaged to another man!"

"Mother, dear, that's broken off. Don't remind me of it. I want to look pleasant, so you'll all be glad I'm home."

"Glad!" his mother laughed, with a catch in her voice. "My prayers have been answered. . . . Come now to dinner. Remember, Pan, when you used to yell, 'Come an' get it before I throw it out'?"

Bobby left Pan's knee and made a beeline for the kitchen. Alice raced after him.

"Pan, I met Dick Hardman on the road. He looked like hell, and was sure punishin' his horse. I said when I seen him, I'd bet he's run into Pan. How about it?"

"Reckon he did," laughed Pan. "It was pretty tough on him, I'm bound to admit. He rode down the path and caught me—well, the truth is, Dad, I was kissing the young lady he imagined belonged to him."

"You range-ridin' son-of-a-gun!" ejaculated his father, in unmitigated admiration and gladness. "What come off?"

"I'll tell you after dinner. Gee, I smell applesauce! . . . Dad, I never forgot Mother's cooking."

They went into the little whitewashed kitchen, where Pan had to stoop to avoid the ceiling, and took seats at the table. Pan feasted his eyes. His mother had not been idle during the hours that he was out in the orchard with Lucy, nor had she forgotten the things that he had always liked. Alice acted as waitress, and Bobby sat in a high chair beaming upon Pan. At that juncture Lucy came in. She had changed her gray blouse to one of white, with wide collar that was cut a little low and showed the golden contour of her superb neck. She had put her hair up. Pan could not take his eyes off her. In hers he saw a dancing subdued light, and a beautiful rose color in her cheeks.

"Well, I've got to eat," said Pan, as if by way of explanation and excuse for removing his gaze from this radiant picture.

Thus his homecoming proved to be a happier event than he had ever dared to hope for. Lucy was quiet and ate but little. At times Pan caught her stealing a glimpse at him, and each time she blushed. She could not meet his eyes again. Alice too stole shy glances at him, wondering, loving. Bobby was hungry, but he did not forget that Pan sat across from him. Mrs. Smith watched Pan with an expression that would have pained him had he allowed remorse to come back then. And his father was funny. He tried to be natural, to meet Pan on a plane of the old western insouciance, but it was impossible. No doubt such happiness had not reigned in that household for years.

"Dad, let's go out and have a talk," proposed Pan, after dinner.

As they walked down toward the corrals Pan's father was silent, yet it was clear he labored with suppressed feeling.

"All right, fire away," he burst out at last, "but first tell me, for Gawd's sake, how'd you do it?"

"What?" queried Pan, looking round from his survey of the farm land.

"Mother! She's *well*. She wasn't well at all," exclaimed the older man, breathing hard. "An' that girl! Did you ever see such eyes?"

"Reckon I never did," replied Pan, with joyous bluntness.

"This mornin' I left Lucy crushed. Her eyes were like lead. An' now! . . . Pan, I'm thankin' God for them. But tell me how'd you do it?"

"Dad, I don't know women very well, but I reckon they live by their hearts. You can bet that happiness for them means a lot to me. I felt pretty low down. That's gone. I could crow like Bobby . . . but, Dad, I've a big job on my hands, and I think I'm equal to it. Are you going to oppose me?"

"Hell, no!" spat out his father, losing his pipe in his vehemence. "Son, I lost my cattle, my ranch. An' then my nerve. I'm not makin' excuses. I just fell down . . . but I'm not too old to make another start with you to steer me."

"Good!" replied Pan with strong feeling, and he laid a hand on his father's shoulder. They halted by the open corral. "Then let's get right down to straight poker."

"Play your game, Pan. I'm sure curious."

"First off then—we don't want to settle in this country."

"Pan, you've called me right on the first hand," declared his father, cracking his fist on the corral gate. "I know this's no country for the Smiths. But I followed Jard Hardman here, I hoped to—"

"Never mind explanations, Dad," interrupted Pan. "We're looking to the future. We won't settle here. We'll go to Arizona. I had a pard who came from Arizona. All day long and half the night that broncho buster would rave about Arizona. Well, he won me over. Arizona must be wonderful."

"But, Pan, isn't it desert country?"

"Arizona is every kind of country," replied Pan earnestly. "It's a big territory, Dad. Pretty wild yet, too, but not like these mining claim countries, with their Yellow Mines. Arizona is getting settlers in the valleys where there's water and grass. Lots of fine pine timber that will be valuable some day. I know just where we'll strike for. But we needn't waste time talking about that now. If it suits you the thing is settled. We go to Arizona."

"Fine, Pan," said his father rubbing his hands. Pan had struck fire from him. "*When* will we go?"

"That's to decide," answered Pan, thoughtfully. "I've got some money. Not much. But we could get there and start on it. I believe, though, that we'd do better to stay here—this fall anyway—and round up a bunch of these wild horses. Five hundred horses, a thousand at twelve dollars a head—why, Dad, it would start us in a big way."

"Son, I should smile it would," returned Smith, with fiery enthusiasm. "But can you do it?"

"Dad, if these broomies are as thick as I hear they are I sure can make a stake. Last night I fell in with two cowboys—Blinky Moran and Gus Hans. They're chasing wild horses, and want me to throw in with them. Now with you and maybe a couple of more riders we can make a big drive. You've got to know the tricks. I learned a heap from a Mormon wild-horse wrangler. If these broomtails are thick here—well, I don't want to set your hopes too high. But wait till I show you."

"Pan, there's ten thousand wild horses in that one valley across the mountain there. Hot Springs Valley they call it."

"Then, by George, we've got to take the risk," declared Pan decisively.

"Risk of what?"

"Trouble with that Hardman outfit. It can't be avoided. I'd have to bluff them out or fight them down, right off. Dick is a yellow skunk. Jard Hardman is a bad man in any pinch. But not on an even break. I don't mean that. If *that* were all. But he's treacherous. And his henchman, this two bit of a sheriff, he's no man to face you on the square. I'll swear he can be bluffed. Has he any reputation as a gun thrower?"

"Matthews? I never heard of it, if he had. But he brags a lot. He's been in several fracases here, with drunken miners an' Mexicans. He's killed a couple of men since I've been here."

"Ah-huh, just what I thought," declared Pan, in cool contempt. "I'll bet a hundred he elected himself town marshal, as he calls it. I'll bet he hasn't any law papers from the territory, or government, either. . . . Jard Hardman will be the hard nut to crack. Now, Dad, back in Littleton I learned what he did to you. And Lucy's story gave me another angle on that. It's pretty hard to overlook. I'm not swearing I can do so. But I'd like to know how you feel about it."

"Son, I'd be scared to tell you," replied Smith in a husky voice, dropping his head.

"You needn't, Dad. We'll stay here till we catch and sell a bunch of horses," said Pan curtly. "Can you quit your job at the wagon shop?"

"Any time—an' Lord, won't I be glad to do it," returned Smith fervently.

"Well, you quit just then," remarked Pan dryly. "So much is settled. . . . Dad, I've got to get Jim Blake out of that jail."

"I reckon so. It might be a job an' then again it mightn't. Depends on Jim. An' between you an' me, Pan, I've no confidence in Jim."

"That doesn't make any difference. I've got to get him out and send him away. Head him for Arizona where we're going. . . . Is it a real jail?"

"Dobe mud an' stones," replied his father. "An Indian or a real man could break out of there any night. There are three guards, who change off every eight hours. One of them is a tough customer. Name's Hill. He used to be an outlaw. The other two are lazy loafers round town."

"Anybody but Jim in just now?"

"I don't know. Matthews jailed a woman not long ago. He arrests somebody every day or so."

"Where is this calaboose belonging to Mr. Matthews?"

"You passed it on the way out, Pan. Off the road. Gray flat buildin'. Let's see. It's the third place from the wagon shop, same side."

"All right, Dad," said Pan with cheerful finality. "Let's go back to the house and talk Arizona to Lucy and Mother for a little. Then I'll rustle along toward town. Tomorrow you come over to the boys' camp. It's on the other side of town, in a cedar flat, up that slope. We've got horses to try out and saddles to buy."

9

◈

As Pan strode back along the road toward Marco the whole world seemed to have changed.

For a few moments he indulged his old joy in range and mountain, stretching, rising on his right, away into the purple distance. Something had heightened its beauty. How softly gray the rolling range land—how black the timbered slopes! The town before him sat like a hideous blotch on a fair landscape. It forced his gaze over and beyond toward the west, where the late afternoon sun had begun to mellow and redden, edging the clouds with exquisite light. To the southward lay Arizona, land of painted mesas and storied canyon walls, of thundering streams and wild pine forests, of purple-saged valleys and grassy parks, set like mosaics between the stark desert mountains.

But his mind soon reverted to the business at hand. It was much to his liking. Many a time he had gone to extremes, reckless and fun loving, in the interest of some cowboy who had gotten into durance vile. It was the way of his class. A few were strong and many were weak, but all of them held a constancy of purpose as to their calling. As they hated wire fences so they hated notoriety-seeking sheriffs and unlicensed jails. No doubt Jard Hardman, who backed the Yellow Mine, was also behind the jail. At least Matthews pocketed the ill-gotten gains from offenders of the peace as constituted by himself.

Pan felt that now for the first time in his life he had a mighty incentive, something tremendous and calling, to bring out that spirit of fire common to the daredevils of the range. He had touched only the last fringe of the cowboy re-gime. Dodge and Abilene, the old Chisholm Trail, the hard-drinking hard-shooting days of an earlier Cimarron had gone. Life then had been but the chance of a card, the wink of an eye, the flip of a quirt. But Pan had ridden and slept with men who had seen those days. He had absorbed from them, and to him had come a later period, not comparable in any sense, yet rough, free, untamed and still bloody. He knew how to play his cards against such men as these. The more boldly he faced them, the more menacingly he went out of his way to meet them, the greater would be his ad-vantage. If Matthews were another Hickok the situation would have been vastly different. If there were any real fighting men on Hardman's side Pan would recognize them in a single glance. He was an unknown quantity to them, that most irritating of newcomers to a wild place, the man with a name preceding him.

Pan came abreast of the building that he was seeking. It was part stone and part adobe, heavily and crudely built, with no windows on the side facing him. Approaching it, and turning the corner, he saw a wide-arched door leading into a small stone-floored room. He heard voices. In a cou-ple of long strides Pan crossed the flat threshold. Two men were playing cards with a greasy deck, a bottle of liquor and small glasses on the table between them. The one whose back was turned to Pan did not see him, but the other man jerked up from his bench, then sagged back with strangely altering expression. He was young, dark, coarse, and he had a bullet hole in his chin.

Pan's recognition did not lag behind the other's. This was Handy Mac New, late of Montana, a cowboy who had drifted beyond the pale. He was one of that innumerable band whom Pan had helped in some way or other. Handy had become a horse thief and a suspected murderer in the year following Pan's acquaintance with him.

"Howdy, men," Pan greeted them, giving no sign that he had recognized Mac New. "Which one of you is on guard here?"

"Me," replied Mac New, choking over the word. Slowly he got to his feet.

"You've got a prisoner in there named Blake," went on

84

Pan. "I once lived near him. He used to play horse with me and ride me on his back. Will you let me talk to him?"

"Why, shore, stranger," replied Mac New, with nervous haste, and producing a key, he inserted it in the lock of a heavy whitewashed door.

Pan found himself ushered into a large room with small iron-barred windows on the west side. His experience of frontier jails had been limited, but those he had seen had been bare, empty, squalid cells. This, however, was evidently a luxurious kind of a prison house. There were Indian blankets and rugs on the floor, an open fireplace with cheerful blaze, a table littered with books and papers, a washstand, a comfortable bed upon which reclined a man smoking and reading.

"Somebody to see you, Blake," called the guard, and he went out, shutting the door behind him.

Blake sat up. As he did so, moving his bootless feet, Pan's keen eye espied a bottle on the floor.

Pan approached leisurely, his swift thoughts revolving around a situation that looked peculiar to him. Blake was very much better cared for there then could have been expected. Why?

"Howdy, Blake. Do you remember me?" asked Pan halting beside the table.

He did not in the least remember Lucy's father in this heavy blond man, lax of body and sodden of face.

"Somethin' familiar aboot you," replied Blake, studying Pan intently. "But I reckon you've got the best of me."

"Pan Smith," said Pan shortly.

"Wal!" he ejaculated, as if shocked into memory, and slowly he rose to hold out a shaking hand. "Bill's kid—the little boy who stuck by my wife—when Lucy was born."

"Same boy, and he's damn sorry to find you in this fix," responded Pan, forcefully. "And he's here to get you out."

Blake sagged back as slowly as he had risen. His face changed like that of a man suddenly stabbed. And he dropped his head. In that moment Pan saw enough to make him glad. Manifestly the good in him had not been wholly killed by evil. Jim Blake might yet be reclaimed or at least led away from evil life.

"Mr. Blake, I've been to see Lucy," went on Pan, and

85

swiftly he talked of the girl, her unhappiness, and the faith she still held in her father. "I've come to get you out of here, for Lucy's sake. We're all going to Arizona. You and Dad can make a new start in life."

"My God, if I only could," groaned the man.

Pan reached out with quick hand and shook him. "Listen," he said, low and eagerly. "How long is this guard Mac New on duty?"

"Mac New? The fellow outside is called Hurd. He's on till midnight."

"All right, my mistake," went on Pan, swiftly. "I'll be here tonight about eleven. I'll have a horse for you, blanket, grub, gun, and money. I'll hold up this guard Hurd—get you out some way or other. You're to ride away. Take the road south. There are other mining camps. You'll not be followed. Make for Siccane, Arizona."

"Siccane, Arizona," echoed Blake, as a man in a dream of freedom.

"Yes, Siccane. Don't forget it. Stay there till we all come."

Pan straightened up, with deep expulsion of breath, and tingling nerves. He had reached Blake. Whatever his doubts of the man, and they had been many, Pan divined that he could stir him, rouse him out of the lethargy of sordid indifference and forgetfulness. He would free him from this jail, and the shackles of Hardman in any case, but to find that it was possible to influence him gladdened Pan's heart. What would this not mean to Lucy!

The door opened behind Pan.

"Wal, stranger, reckon yore time's up," called the jailer.

Pan gave the stunned Blake a meaning look, and then without a word, he left the room. The guard closed and locked the door. Then he looked up, with cunning, yet not wholly without pleasure. His companion at the card game had gone.

"Panhandle Smith!" whispered the guard, half stretching out his hand, then withdrawing it.

"Shake, Mac," said Pan in a low voice. "It's a small world."

"By Gord, it shore is," replied Mac New, wringing Pan's hand. "I'm known here as Hurd."

"Ah-huh. . . . Well, Hurd, I'm not a talking man. But I want to remind you that you owe me a good turn."

"You shore don't have to remind me of thet," returned the other.

"It pays to do good turns. . . . I'm lucky, old-timer."

"I savvy, Panhandle Smith," said Hurd, with gleaming eyes, and he crooked a stubby thumb toward the door of Blake's jail.

"All right, cowboy," returned Pan, with a meaning smile. "I'll drop around tonight about eleven."

Pan slowed up in his stride when he reached the business section of the town, and strolled along as if he were looking for someone. He was. He meant to have eyes in the back of his head henceforth. But he did not meet anyone he knew or see anyone who glanced twice at him.

He went into Black's general merchandise store to look at the saddle Moran had recommended. It was a bargain and Pan purchased it on sight. Proof indeed was this that there were not many cowboys in and around Marco. While he was there, Pan bought a Winchester carbine and a saddle sheath for it. Thus burdened, he walked out to the camp.

Lying Juan had supper about ready and the boys were noisy up at the corral. Some of their language was indicative of trouble and mean horses. Pan found a seat by the fire very welcome. Emotion had power to exhaust him far beyond physical exertion. Darkness had just about merged from dusk when the boys dragged themselves in, smelling of dust and horses. They went into the water basins like ducks. Pan lighted the lantern and put it on the table. Then the boys came straddling the bench like cowboys mounting horses. Their faces were red and shiny, their wet hair was pasted down.

"Wal, if heah ain't ole Pan Smith," announced Blinky, vociferously. "Gus, take a peep at him. I'll bet he's got hold of a grand hoss. Nothin' else could make him look like thet."

"No. I just got back my girl," replied Pan gaily.

"Gurl! Say, cowboy," began Blinky, in consternation. "You didn't run foul of thet little Yellow Mine kid?"

"Eat your supper, you hungry-looking galoot," replied

Pan. "And you too, Gus . . . Because if I begin to shoot off my chin now you'll forget the grub."

Thus admonished, and with curious glances at Pan, the cowboys took his advice and attacked the generous meal Juan had set before them. Their appetites further attested to a strenuous day. Pan did not seem to be hungry, which fact caused Juan much concern.

"Ahuh! It's the way a fellar gets when he's in love with a gurl," observed the keen Blinky. "I been there."

After supper they got together before the stove and rolled their cigarettes. The cold night wind, with its tang of mountain heights, made the fire most agreeable. Pan spread his palms to the heat.

"Wal, pard, throw it off your chest before you bust," advised Blinky shrewdly.

"What kind of a day did you boys have?" countered Pan with a laugh.

"Good an' bad," replied Gus, while Blinky shook his head. "Some hoss thieves have been runnin' off our stock. We had some fine hosses, not broke yet. Some we wanted to keep."

"What's the good news?" queried Pan, as Hans hesitated.

"Pan, I'll be doggoned if we didn't see a million broomies today," burst out Blinky.

"No. Now, Blink, talk sense," remonstrated Pan. "You mean you saw a thousand?"

"Wal, shore a million is stretchin' it some," acknowledged the cowboy. "But ten thousand wouldn't be nothin'. We tracked some of our hosses twenty miles an' more over heah, farther'n we'd been yet. An' climbed a high ridge we looked down into the purtiest valley I ever seen. Twice as big as Hot Springs Valley. Gee, it lay there gray an' green with hosses as thick as greasewood bushes on the desert. Thet valley hasn't been drove yet. It's purty rough gettin' up to where you can see. An' there's lots of hosses closer to town. Thet accounts."

"Blinky, is this talk of yours a leaf out of Lying Juan's book?" asked Pan incredulously. "It's too good to be true."

"Pan, I'll swear it on a stack of Bibles," protested Blinky. "Ask Gus. He seen them."

"For onct Blinky ain't out of his haid," corroborated Hans. "Never saw so many wild hosses. An' if we can find a way to ketch some of them we'll be rich."

"Boys, you told me you'd been trapping horses at the water holes," said Pan.

"Shore, we've been moonshinin' them," replied Blinky. "We build a corral round a water hole. Make a wide gate we can shut quick. Then we lay out on moonlight nights waitin' for 'em to come in to drink. We've done purty darn good at it, too."

"That's fun, but it's a two-bit way to catch wild horses," rejoined Pan.

"Wal, they're all doin' it thet way. Hardman's outfit, an' a couple more besides us. I figgured myself it was purty slow, but no better way come to me. Do you know one?"

"Do I? Well, I should smile. I know more than one that'll beat your moonshining. Back on the prairie where it's all wide and bare there's no chance for a small outfit. But this is high country, valleys, canyons, cedars. Boys, we can make one big stake before the other outfits get on to us."

"By gosh, one's enough for us," declared Blinky. "Then we can shake this gold-claim country where they steal your empty tin cans an' broken shovels."

"One haul will do me, too," agreed Pan. "Then Arizona for me."

"Ah-uh! . . . Pan, how aboot this gurl?"

Briefly then Pan told his story, and the situation as it looked to him at the moment. The response of these cowboys was what he had expected. He knew them. Warm-hearted, simple, elemental, they responded in different ways, but with the same fire. Gus Hans looked his championship while Blinky raved and swore.

"Then you're both with me?" asked Pan, tersely. "Mind, it's no fair deal, my getting your support here for helping you with a wild horse drive."

"Fair, hell!" returned Blinky, forcibly. "It ain't like you to insult cowboys."

"I'm begging your pardon," replied Pan, hastily. "But we'd never been pardners and I hesitated to draw you into a scrap that'll almost sure go to gun throwing."

"Wal, we're your pardners now, an' damn proud of it, Panhandle Smith."

Silently and grimly they all shook hands on it. Not half a dozen times in his range life had Pan been party to a compact like that.

"This Blake fellar, now," began Blinky, as he lighted another cigarette. "What's your idea of gettin' him out?"

"I want a horse, a blanket, some grub and a gun. I'm to take them down to the jail at eleven o'clock."

"Huh! Goin' to hold up the guard?" queried Blinky.

"That was my intention," replied Pan, "but I know that fellow Hurd, who'll be on guard then. I'll not have to hold him up."

"Hurd? I know him. Hard nut, but I think he's square."

"Reckon Hurd will lose his job," said Pan reflectively. "If he does, let's take him with us on the wild horse deal."

"Suits me. An' he'll shore love thet job. Hurd hasn't any use for Matthews."

"Blinky, do you know another man we can hire or get to throw in with us? We've got five now counting my dad, and we'll need at least six."

"Why so many? It'll cut our profits."

"No, it'll increase them. One good rider means a great deal to us."

"Then let's get thet miner. Charley Brown."

"But he's working a gold claim."

"Wal, if I know anythin' he'll not be workin' it any longer than findin' blue dirt. Gus an' me seen Jard Hardman with two men ridin' out thet way this mawnin'."

"Ah! . . . So Hardman is here now. We'll hunt up Brown and see what he says. Suppose we walk downtown now."

"All right, but let me get a hoss up for Blake," replied Blinky. "Gus, you find thet old saddle of mine, an' a blanket. There's an old canvas saddlebag an' water bottle heah somewheres. Ask Juan. An' get him to pack the grub."

The night of the sabbath was no barrier to the habitués of the Yellow Mine. But early in the evening it was not yet in full swing. The dance was on with a few heavy-footed miners and their gaudy partners, and several of the gambling tables were surrounded.

Pan stalked about alone. His new-found cowboy friends had been instructed to follow him unobtrusively. Pan did not wish to give an impression that he had taken up with allies. He was looking for Charley Brown, but he had a keen roving eye for every man in sight. It was doubtful if Hardman or Matthews could have espied Pan first, unless they were hidden somewhere. He took up a position, presently, behind one of the poker games, with his back to the wall, so that he had command of the room. A stiff game was in progress, which Pan watched casually. Blinky and Gus lounged around, with apparently no more aim than other idle drinking visitors of the place.

Gradually more men came in, the gaming tables filled up, and the white-armed girls appeared to mingle with the guests.

Pan espied the girl Louise before she had become aware of his presence. She appeared to be more decently clad, a circumstance that greatly added to her charm, in his opinion. Curiously he studied her. Women represented more to Pan than to most men he had had opportunity to meet or observe. He never forgot that they belonged to the same sex as his mother. So it was natural he had compassion for this unsexed dance-hall, gambling-lure girl. She was pretty in a wild sort of way, dissolute, abandoned, yet not in any sense weak. A terrible havoc showed in her face for anyone with eyes to see beneath the surface. Pan noted a strange restlessness in her that at first he imagined was the seeking instinct of women of her class. But it was only that she could not sit or stand still. Her hawklike eyes did not miss anyone there, and finally they located him. She came around the tables up to Pan, and took hold of his arm.

"Howdy, Handsome," she said, smiling up at him.

Pan doffed his sombrero and bade her good evening.

"Don't do that," she said. "It irritates me."

"But, Louise, I can't break a habit just to please you," he replied, smiling.

"You could stay out of here. Didn't I warn you not to come back?"

"Yes, but I thought you were only fooling. Besides I *had* to come."

"Why? You don't fit here. You've got too clean a look."

Pan gazed down at her, feeling in her words and presence something that prompted him to more than kindliness and good nature.

"Louise, I can return the compliment. You don't fit here."

"Damn you!" she flashed. "I'll fall in love with you."

"Well, if you did, I'd sure drag you out of this hell," replied Pan, bluntly.

"Come away from these gamblers," she demanded, and drew him from behind the circle to seats at an empty table. "I won't ask you to drink or dance. But I'm curious. I've been hearing about you."

"That so? Who told you?"

"I overheard Dick Hardman tonight, just before supper. He has a room next to mine in the hotel here, when he stays in town. He was telling his father about you. Such cussing I never heard. I'm giving you a hunch. They'll do away with you."

"Thanks. Reckon it's pretty fine of you to put me on my guard."

"I only meant behind your back. What has Dick against you?"

"We were kids together back in Texas. Just natural rivals and enemies. But I hadn't seen him for years till last night. Then he didn't know me."

"He knows you now all right. He ran into you today?"

"I reckon he did," replied Pan, with a grim laugh.

"Panhandle, this is getting sort of warm," she said, leaning across the table to him. "I'm not prying into your affairs. But I could be your friend. God knows I like a *man.*"

"That's the second compliment you've paid me tonight. What're you up to, Louise?"

"See here, cowboy, when I pay any two-legged hombre compliments you can gamble they are sincere."

"All right, no offense meant."

"Do you resent my curiosity?"

"No."

"I've got you figured right when I say you're in trouble. You're *looking* for someone?"

"Yes."

"I knew it," she retorted, snapping her fingers. "And

that's Hardman and his outfit . . . I didn't hear all Dick said. When he talked loud he cussed. But I heard enough to tie up Panhandle Smith with this girl Lucy and the Hardman outfit."

Pan eyed her steadily. She was encroaching upon sacred ground. But her feeling was genuine, and undoubtedly she had some connection with a situation which began to look complex. The same instinct that operated so often with Pan in his relation to men of the open now subtly prompted him. Regardless of circumstances he knew when to grasp an opportunity.

"Louise, you show that you'd risk taking a chance on me—a stranger," he replied, with quick decision. "I return that compliment."

The smile she gave him was really a reward. It gave him a glimpse of the depths of her.

"Who's this girl Lucy?" she queried.

"She's my sweetheart, ever since we were kids," returned Pan with emotion. "I went to riding the ranges, and well, like so many cowboys, I didn't go back home. When I did go Lucy was gone, my family was gone. I trailed them here—to find that Dick Hardman was about to force Lucy to marry him."

"The —— —— ——!" she burst out. Then after her excitement cooled: "How'd he aim to force her?"

Quickly Pan explained the situation as related to Jim Blake.

"Aha! Easy to savvy. That's where Jard Hardman and Matthews come in. . . . Panhandle, they're a dirty outfit and the dirtiest of them is Dick Hardman!"

"What's he to you, Louise?" inquired Pan gravely. "You'll excuse me if I say I can't see you in love with him."

"In love with Dick Hardman?" she whispered, hotly. "My God! I wouldn't soil even my hands on him—if I didn't have to. . . . He met me in Frisco. He brought me to this damned stinking rough hole. He made me promises he never kept. Not to marry me. Don't get the wrong hunch. He has doublecrossed me. And I *had* to sink to this! . . . Drunk? Yes, sure I was drunk. Don't you understand I have to be drunk to stand this life? I'm not drunk now because you got here early. . . . Something deep must be behind my meeting you, Panhandle Smith."

"I hope to heaven it will be to your good—as I know meeting you will be to mine," replied Pan fervently.

"We're off the track," she broke in, and Pan imagined he saw a deeper red under her artificial color. "I despise Dick Hardman. He's stingy, conceited, selfish. He's low down, and he's sinking to worse."

"His father ruined mine," Pan told her. "That's what brought Dad out here—to try to get something back from Jard Hardman. No use. He only got another hard deal."

"That cowboy who was in here with you last night—Blinky Moran. His claim was jumped by Hardman."

"Louise, how'd you know that?" asked Pan in surprise.

"Don't give me away. Blinky told me. He's one of my friends and he's a white man if I ever saw one. . . . He has been in love with me. Wanted me to marry him! Poor crazy boy! I sure had to fight—and get drunker—to keep from more than liking him. He spent all his money on me and I had to make him quit."

"Well, that little bow-legged cowboy liar! He's as deep as the sea."

"Keep it secret, Panhandle," she responded seriously. "I don't want to hurt his feelings. . . . To get back to the Hardmans. They've taken strong hold here. The old man owns half of Marco. He's in everything. But it's my hunch I'm giving you—that he's in the straight deals only to cover the crooked ones. That's where the money is."

"Yet Jard Hardman will not square up with Dad!" exclaimed Pan.

"Now tell me why you come into the Yellow Mine. Is it to court trouble? You're taking an awful chance. Every night or so some tipsy miner gets robbed or knifed, or shot."

"Louise, in dealing with men of really dangerous quality your only chance is to face them with precisely the same thing. As for the fourflushers like Matthews and men of the Hardman stamp, the one thing they can't stand is nerve. They haven't got it. They don't understand it. They fear it. It works on their consciousness. They begin to figure on what the nervy man means to do before they do anything. . . . If I did not show myself in the street, and here, the

94

Hardman outfit would soon run true to their deals. So by appearing to invite and seek a fight I really avoid one."

"So that's why they call you Panhandle Smith?" queried the girl, meditatively. "I mean with the tone old man Hardman used. They call me Angel. But that doesn't mean what it sounds, does it?"

"I can't figure you, Louise," replied Pan dubiously.

"I'm glad you can't. . . . Hello, there's Blinky and his pard Gus. What're they up to?"

"They are looking pretty hard, but it can't be for you and me. They saw us long ago."

"There! Hardman and Matthews, coming from behind the bar. There's a private office in behind. You can see the door. . . . Panhandle, let me tell you Hardman seldom shows up here."

Pan leisurely got to his feet. His eye quickly caught Matthews' black sombrero, then the big ham of a face, with its drooping mustache. Pan could not see anyone with him until they got out from behind the crowded bar. Then Pan perceived that Matthews' companion was a stout man, bearded, dressed like a prosperous rancher.

"Louise, is that man with Matthews the gentleman we have been discussing?" asked Pan.

"That's the rich fat bloated —— —— ——," replied the girl, with eyes like a hawk. "You don't talk straight, Panhandle."

"I'm not quite so free as you are with bad language," replied Pan, smiling down on her. Then with deft movement he hitched his belt round farther forward on his hip. It was carelesss, it might have been accidental, but it was neither. And the girl grasped its meaning. She turned white under her paint, and the eyes that searched Pan were just then like any other woman's.

"Cowboy, what're you going to do?" she whispered, reaching for him.

"I don't know exactly. You can never tell how actions are going to be taken. But I mean well."

"Stop!" she called low after him. "You smiling devil!"

Pan moved leisurely in among the tables toward the bar and the two men standing rather apart from the crowd. He maneuvered so that Matthews' roving glance fell upon him.

Then Pan advanced straight. He saw the sheriff start, then speak hurriedly to Hardman.

Pan halted within six feet of both men. He might never have seen Jard Hardman so far as any recognition was concerned. He faced a man of about fifty years of age, rather florid of complexion, well fed and used to strong drink.

"Excuse me," spoke Pan, with most consummate coolness, addressing the shorter man. Apparently he did not see Matthews. "Are you Jard Hardman?"

"Reckon I am, if that's any of your business," came a gruff reply. Light, hard, speculative eyes took Pan in from head to feet.

"Do you recognize me?" asked Pan, in the same tone.

"No, sir, I never saw you in my life," retorted Hardman, his bearded chin working up and down with the vehemence of his speech. And he turned away.

Pan made a step. His long arm shot out, and his hand, striking hard on Hardman's shoulder, whirled him round.

"My name's Smith," called Pan, in vibrant loud voice that stilled the room. "Panhandle Smith!"

"I don't know you, sir," replied Hardman, aghast and amazed. He began to redden. He turned to Matthews, as if in wonder that this individual permitted him to be thus affronted.

"Well, you knew my dad—to his loss," declared Pan. "And that's my business with you."

"You've no business with me," fumed Hardman.

"Reckon you're mistaken," went on Pan, slowly and easily. "I'm Bill Smith's boy. And I mean to have an accounting with you on that Texas cattle deal."

These deliberate words, heard by all within earshot, caused little less than a deadlock throughout the room. The bartenders quit, the drinkers poised glasses in the air, the voices suddenly hushed. Pan had an open space behind him, a fact he was responsible for. He faced Matthews, Hardman, and then the length of the bar. He left the gamblers behind to Blinky and Gus, who stood to one side. Pan had invited an argument with the owner of the Yellow Mine and his sheriff ally. Every westerner in the room understood its meaning.

"You upstart cowpuncher!" presently shouted Hardman. "Get out of here or I'll have you arrested."

"Arrest me! What for? I'm only asking you for an honest deal. I can prove you cheated my father out of cattle. You can't arrest me for that."

Hardman guffawed boisterously. "Get out of here with your insolent talk about cattle deals."

"I won't get out. You can't put me out, even if you do own the place."

"I'll—I'll—" choked Hardman, his body leaping with rage, his face growing purple under his beard. Then he turned to Matthews. "Throw this drunken cowboy out."

That focused attention upon the sheriff. Pan read in Matthews' eyes the very things he had suspected. And as he relaxed the mental and muscular strain under which he had waited, he laughed in Matthews' face.

"Bah! Hardman, you're backed by the wrong man. And at last you've run into the wrong man. Haven't you sense enough to see that? . . . You cheated my father. Now you're going to make it good."

Hardman, furious and imperious, never grasped the significance that had frozen Matthews. He was thick, arrogant. He had long been a power wherever he went. Yielding to rage he yelled at Pan.

"Bill Smith sicked his cowpuncher on me, hey? Like father, like son! You're a rustler breed. I'll drive you—"

Pan leaped like a tiger and struck Hardman a terrible blow in the face. Like something thrown from a catapult he went into the crowd next the bar, and despite this barrier and the hands grasping at his flying arms he crashed to the floor. But before he fell Pan had leaped back in the same position he had held in front of Matthews.

"He lied," cried Pan. "My dad, Bill Smith, was as honest a cattleman as ever lived. . . . Mr. Sheriff, do you share that slur cast on him?"

"I don't know Bill Smith," replied Matthews hastily. "Reckon I'm not talkin' agin men I don't know. . . . An' as I'm not armed I can't argue with a gun-packin' cowboy."

Thus he saved his face with the majority of those present. But he did have a gun. Pan knew that as well as if he had seen it. Matthews was not the "even break" stripe of sheriff.

97

"Ah-huh!" ejaculated Pan sardonically. "All right. Then I'll be looking for you to arrest me next time we meet."

"I'll arrest you, Panhandle Smith, you can gamble on thet," declared Matthews harshly.

"Arrest nothing," replied Pan with ringing scorn. "You're a four-flush sheriff. I'll gamble you elected yourself. I know your kind, Matthews. And I'll gamble some more that you don't last long in Màrco."

This was, as Pan deliberately intended, raw talk that any man not a coward could not swallow. But Matthews was a coward. That appeared patent to all onlookers, in their whispers and nodding heads. Whatever prestige he had held there in that rough mining community was gone, until he came out to face this fiery cowboy with a gun. White and shaking he turned to the group of men who had gotten Hardman to his feet. They led him out the open door and Matthews followed.

Pan strode back to the table where Louise sat tense and wide eyed. The hum of voices began again, the clatter of glasses, the clink of coin. The incident had passed.

"Well, little girl, I had them figured, didn't I?" asked Pan, calling a smile to break his tight cold face.

"I don't—know what—ails me," she said, breathlessly. "I see fights every night. And I've seen men killed—dragged out. But this got my nerve."

"It wasn't much to be excited about. I didn't expect any fight."

"Your idea was to show up Hardman and Matthews before the crowd You sure did. The crowd was with you. And so am I, Panhandle Smith." She held out a slim hand. "I've got to dance. Good night."

10

◆

PAN's exit from the Yellow Mine was remarkable for the generous space accorded him by its occupants.

Outside he laughed a little, as he stood under the flare of the yellow light and rolled a cigarette. Knots of men stood on the corners of the street. But the area in front of the saloon was significantly vacant.

"Now if Dad had only been there," soliloquized Pan. "That might have put some life in him."

He sauntered down into the street, and as he went he heard the jangle of spurs behind him. Blinky and Gus covering his rear! Presently, beyond the circle of yellow light, they joined him, one on each side.

"Wal, Pan I was shore in on thet," said Blink, gripping Pan's arm.

"Say, you called 'em flat. Made 'em swaller a hell of a lot," added Gus, with a hard note in his voice. "When it come down to hard pan they wasn't there."

"Pan, you remember me tellin' you aboot Purcell, who jumped my claim with young Hardman?" queried Blinky. "Wal, Purcell was there, settin' some tables back of where you made your stand. I seen him when we first went in. Course everybody quit playin' cards when you called old Hardman. An' I made it my particular biz to get close to Purcell. He was pullin' his gun under the table when I kicked him. An' when he looked up he seen somethin', you can bet on thet. . . . Wal, Purcell is one man in Hardman's outfit we'll have to kill. . . . Gus will back me up on thet."

"I shore will. Purcell's a Nevada claim jumper, accordin' to talk. Somebody hinted he belong to thet Plummer gang

99

thet was cleaned out at Bannock years ago. He's no spring chicken, thet's shore."

"Point Purcell out to me the first chance you get," replied Pan. "Don't figure I expect to bluff everybody. It can't be done. Somebody will try me out—if only to see what I can do. That's the game, you know."

"Hell, yes. An' all you got to do, Pan, is to be there first."

"Reckon tomorrow will be shore interestin'," remarked Gus.

"That girl Louise gave me a hunch," said Pan thoughtfully. "Struck me she was square. Blink, you've talked to her, of course?"

"Me? . . . Aw!—Couple of times. I reckon. Bought her drinks. . . . She won't look at me unless she's drunk," replied Blink, both confused and gloomy.

"You've got Louise figured wrong, cowboy," returned Pan. "I'll prove it to you sometime. . . . Now let's get down to business, and plan Blake's release from jail. I want to lead the horse round about, so I won't be seen by anybody."

"Shore, thet'll be easy," replied Blinky. "I'll go with you. We can keep to the slope a ways an' then go down an' come up on the other side of town. No roads an' no houses."

They returned to camp, and replenishing the fire sat around it talking of the wild-horse drive.

About ten o'clock Blinky went to the corral, saddled a horse, and led him back to the tent. There they put on the blanket and saddlebags. Blinky produced a gun he could spare, and then thoughtfully added a small bag of grain for the horse.

"It's darker'n the milltail of Hades," announced Blinky, "an' thet's good fer this kind of work. I'll go ahaid, pickin' out the way, an' you lead the hoss."

So they set out into the black night, working along the base of the slope. No stars showed, and the raw wind hinted of rain or snow. The lights of the town shone dimly. Keen on the breeze floated the discordant music and revelry, from the Yellow Mine and other like dives, in full blast.

Descending the slope required careful slow work. The incline was steep, of soft earth and loose shale. But Blinky knew where to feel his way, and eventually they reached the flat, to find easier progress. Blinky made a detour, and finally, as they gradually approached several lamp-lights, far apart, he whispered: "You wait heah. I ain't so darn shore which one of them lights comes from the jail."

Pan waited what seemed a long while. At last he heard steps, then made out an object blacker than the black background.

"Found the jail easy, but got off comin' back. Pronto now. Must be near eleven."

Pan kept the dark silent moving form in sight. The dim light grew larger. Then the low flat building loomed up faintly in the dense gloom.

"Go ahead," whispered Blinky. "I'll hold the hoss."

Pan went swiftly up to the wall, and thence along it to the corner. The light came from an open door. He listened. There was no sound. Luckily Hurd was alone. Pan slipped round the corner and entered. Hurd sat at the table in the flare of a lamp, turned down low.

"Ha! Was waitin' fer you, an' beginnin' to worry," he said, in hoarse whisper.

"Plenty of time, if Blake's all ready," replied Pan.

"I'm givin' you a hunch. He's damn queer fer a fellar who expects to break jail."

"No matter. Let's get at it, pronto."

Hurd got up, and laid his gun on the table. Then he turned over the bench, threw papers on the floor. "Thar's the key, an' heah's a rope. Hawg-tie me."

With that he turned his back. Swiftly Pan bound him securely, and let him down upon the floor. Then he unlocked the door, opened it. Pitch darkness inside and no sound! He called in low voice. Blake did not reply. Muttering in surprise, Pan took the lamp and went into the room. He found Blake asleep, though fully dressed. Pan jerked him roughly out of that indifferent slumber.

"It's Smith," he said bluntly. "You sure must *want* to get out. . . . Damn you, Blake, this whole deal looks fishy to me! . . . Come on."

Leaving the lamp there, Pan dragged the man out, through the dark entrance room, into the night. In another moment they had reached the horse and Blinky.

"Here's money and a gun," whispered Pan, swiftly. "You'll find grub, blanket, grain on your saddle. Get on!"

Pan had to half lift Blake on his horse. He felt of the stirrups. "They're all right. . . . The road is that way, about fifty yards. Turn to the left and ride. Remember, Siccane."

Blake rode away into the darkness without a word. Pan watched and listened. Presently he heard the hard clip-clop of hoofs on the road, making to the left.

"Good! He'll ride past where Lucy's sleeping. I wish she could know," muttered Pan.

"Was he drunk?" queried Blinky, in a hoarse whisper. "Shore acted funny fer a sober man."

"He didn't breathe like he was drunk," replied Pan. "But he flabbergasted me. Found him asleep! And he never said a darned word . . . Blink, it sticks in my craw. Reckon he didn't want to leave that nice warm bed."

"Ahuh! Wal, let's rustle back to our warm beds," said the cowboy gruffly.

Pan awakened during the latter part of the night. Rain was pattering on the tent. The wind moaned. He thought of Blake, not clad for bad weather and in unfit condition for a long ride, facing the storm. Even then a vague doubt penetrated his drowsy mind.

Morning dawned bright and sparkling after the rain. The air was keen and crisp. The cedars glistened as if decked with diamonds. Pan felt the sweet scent of the damp dust, and it gave him a thrill and a longing for the saddle and the open country.

"Wal, reckon this heah'll be our busy day," drawled Blinky, after making a hearty breakfast of bacon and flapjacks. "Pan, what's first on the ticket?"

"Show me a horse, you bow-legged grub destroyer," replied Pan eagerly.

"Come out to the corral. We got a sorrel as is a real shore enough hoss if you can ride him."

There were a dozen or more horses in the corral. Pan, glancing over them with appraising eye, decided the cowboys had not spoken of them with the degree of satisfaction that they really merited.

"Fine string, Blinky," said Pan, with glistening eyes. "Is that sorrel the one I can't ride?"

"Yep, thet's him. Ain't he a real hoss?"

"Best of the bunch, at first sight. Blinky, are you sure you're not giving me your own horse?"

"Me? I don't care nothin' aboot him," declared Blinky, lying glibly. "Shore he's the orfullest pitchin son-of-a-gun I ever forked. But mebbe you can ride him."

It developed presently that Pan could ride the sorrel, and that Blinky had done the horse a great injustice. How good to be back in the saddle. Pan wanted to ride down at once to show Lucy his first mount west of the Rockies. Indeed he was possessed of a strong yearning desire to hurry to see Lucy, a feeling that he had to dispel. If all went well he could go to his mother's for dinner. Meanwhile he must meet the exigencies here in Marco.

"Wal, what's next on the ticket?" queried Blinky, who appeared to be rather jerky this morning.

"I'm going downtown," replied Pan.

"Ahuh. I want to trail along with you."

"No, I'll go alone. I'll make my bluff strong, Blinky, or draw Matthews out. Honest, I don't think he'll show."

"Thet yellow dawg? He won't face you, Pan. But he's in thet Hardman outfit, an' one of them—mebbe Purcell—might take a shot at you from a winder. It's been done heah. Let me go with you."

"Well, if they're that low down your being with me wouldn't help much," replied Pan, pondering the matter. "I'll tell you, Blink. Here's how I figure. Marco is a pretty big place. It's full of men. And western men are much alike anywhere. Matthews is no fool. He couldn't risk murdering me in broad daylight, from ambush."

"I'm not trustin' him," said Blinky, somberly. "But I admit the chances are he won't do thet."

"You and Gus pack up for the wild-horse drive," went on Pan briskly. "We ought to get off in the morning. One of you ride out to see if Charley Brown will throw in with us. I'll see Dad at dinner. He'll need horse and outfit. It may turn out we can get our jailer friend, Hurd. Wonder if he lost his job. . . . Ha! Ha! Well, boys, I'll know more when I see you again."

Pan strolled down toward the town. A familiar unpleasant mental strain dominated his consciousness. His slow, cool, easy nonchalance was all outward. He had done this thing before, but that seemed long ago. His father, Lucy, his mother, somehow made an immense difference between the cowboy reactions of long ago and this stern duty he had set himself today. He hated what his actions meant, what might well ensue from them, yet he was glad it was in him to meet the issue in this way of the West.

By the time he had reached a point opposite the stage office all reflections had passed out of his mind to give place to something sinister.

His alert faculties of observation belied the leisurely manner of his approach to the main street. He was a keen-strung, watching, listening machine. The lighting and smoking of a cigarette was mechanical pretense—he did not want to smoke.

Two men stood in front of the stage office. One was Smith, the agent. Pan approached them, leaned on the hitching rail. But he favored his right side and he faced the street.

"Mornin', cowboy," Smith greeted him, not without nervousness. "See you're down early to git arrested."

"Howdy, Smith. Can you give me a drink?" returned Pan.

"Sorry, but I haven't a drop."

The other man was an old fellow, though evidently he was still active, for his boots and clothes showed the stain and wear of mining.

"Tell you, cowboy," he spoke up dryly, "you might buy a bottle at the Yellow Mine."

Pan made no reply, and presently the old man shambled away while Smith entered his office. Pan kept his vigil there, watching, waiting. He was seen by dozens of passing men, but none of them crossed toward the stage office. Down the street straggling pedestrians halted to form little groups. In an hour the business of Marco had apparently halted.

Its citizens, the miners who had started to work, the teamsters, Mexicans, cowboys who happened upon the street, suddenly struck attitudes of curious attention, with faces turned toward Pan. They too were waiting, watching.

The porch of the Yellow Mine was in plain sight, standing out on a corner, scarcely more than a hundred yards down the street. Pan saw Hardman and Matthews come out of the hotel. They could not fail to observe the quiet, the absence of movement, the waiting knots of men.

This was the climax of strain for Pan. Leisurely he strolled away from the hitching rail, out into the middle of the street, and down. The closer groups of watchers vanished.

Hardman could be seen gesticulating, stamping as if in rage; and then he went into the hotel, leaving Matthews standing alone. Other men, in the background, disappeared. The sheriff stood a moment irresolute, sagging, with his pale hamlike face gleaming. Then he wheeled to enter the hotel.

He had damned himself. He had refused the even break, the man-to-man, the unwritten edict of westerners.

Pan saw this evasion with grim relief. The next move was one easier to perform, though fraught with great peril. Every man in Marco now knew that Pan had come out to meet the men he had denounced. They had been aware of his intention. They had seen him sauntering down the middle of the street. And they had showed what the West called yellow. But they had not showed their claws, if they had any. Pan could well have ended his quest then and there. But to follow it up, to beard the jackals in their den—that was the last word.

As Pan proceeded slowly down the middle of the street the little groups of spectators disintegrated, and slipped out of sight into the stores and saloons. Those farthest from him moved on to halt again. And when any neared the Yellow Mine, they scurried completely out of sight. Pan had the main street to himself. For a few moments not a single man showed himself. Then they began to reappear behind him out of range, slowly following him.

At the entrance to the Yellow Mine, Pan threw away his cigarette, and mounted the steps. He was gambling his life on the code of westerners. The big hall-like saloon was vacant except for the two bartenders behind the bar, and a Mexican sweeping out the sawdust. Pan had heard subdued voices, the shuffle of feet, the closing of doors. Every muscle in his body was cramped with tension, ready to leap like lightning into action. Advancing to the bar he called for a drink.

"On the house this mawnin'," replied the nearest bartender, smiling. He showed a little nervousness with his hands, otherwise he was composed, and his offer to treat expressed his sentiment. Pan took the bottle with his left hand, poured out some liquor, set the bottle down, and lifted the glass. He had his drink. His tension relaxed.

"Sort of quiet this morning," he said.

"Reckon it is, just now," replied the bartender, significantly.

"Is this Sunday?" went on Pan casually.

"No. Yestiddy was Sunday, so this must be Monday."

"Reckon I might as well move along," remarked Pan, but he did not stir. The bartender went on cleaning glasses. Sounds of footsteps came from outside. Presently Pan walked back through the open door, then halted a moment, to light another cigarette. His back was turned to the bar and the doors. That seemed the climax of his effrontery. It was deliberate, the utter recklessness of the cowboy who had been trained in a hard school. But all that happened was the silence breaking to a gay wild sweet voice: "Call again, cowboy, when there's somebody home!"

Louise had been watching him through some secret peephole. That had been her tribute to him and her scorn of his opponents. It about closed the incident, Pan concluded. Men were now coming along the street in both directions, though not yet close. Some wag yelled from a distance: "Thar ain't no sheriff, Panhandle."

Pan retraced his steps up the street, finding, as before, a clear passage. Men hailed him from doorways, from windows, from behind obstructions. He did not need to be told that they were with him. Marco had been treated to precisely what it wanted. Pan was quick to grasp the mood of these residents who had been so keen about his endeavor to draw out Hardman and Matthews. That hour saw the beginning of the end for these dominant factors in the evil doings of Marco. What deep gratification it afforded Pan! They might thrive for a time, but their heyday had passed. Matthews would be the laughing stock of the town. He could never retrieve. He had been proclaimed only another in the long list of self-appointed officers of the law.

By the time Pan got back to camp his mood actually harmonized with his leisurely, free and careless movements. Still he was hiding something, for he wanted to yell. Blinky saw him coming and yelled for him. The cowboy was beside himself with a frenzy of delight. It had been hard for him to stay there in camp. He cursed radiantly.

"How's the pack job? All done?" queried Pan, when he could get a word in.

"Pack hell! We plumb forgot," replied Blinky. "What you think—you—you—"

Blinky failed to find adequate words to express his sentiments. Gus was quiet as usual, but he too showed relaxation from a severe ordeal.

"Well, let's get at it now," suggested Pan. "I'll start you boys on it, then ride down to Mother's."

In the succeeding hour, leading to noon, what with sundry trips down to the store, the trio learned some news that afforded much satisfaction. Jim Blake had assaulted a guard and broken jail. No doubt he must have had outside assistance. According to rumor Matthews accused Hurd, the guard, of being party to the escape, and had discharged him. Sentiment in town was not equally divided. Most everybody, according to the informers, was glad Blake had escaped. It developed that the jail was not a civic institution. Already there had been talk of the permanent citizens getting together.

All this was exceedingly welcome to Pan. He could hardly wait till noon to saddle the sorrel, to ride over to his mother's.

"Aw, cowboy, hug thet gurl fer me!" sang Blinky, with ecstatic upward gaze. "Shore she's put the devil in you. An' this heah outfit is steppin' high!"

On the way out to the farm, halfway beyond the outskirts of town, Pan met his father rushing up the road. At sight of Pan he almost collapsed.

"Just—heard—the news," he panted, as Pan reined in the sorrel.

"What news, Dad?" queried Pan, gazing down with both thrill and anxiety at that haggard face, slowly warming out of its havoc.

"Bill Dolan an' his—boys—stopped at the ranch to—tell

me," replied Smith, wiping his clammy face. "They just left town. . . . Bill saw you take that walk down main street."

"Well, what's that to be all set up about?"

"Reckon I was scared wild . . . Bill says to me, 'Bill, you oughtn't show yellow like thet. You shore don't savvy thet boy of yours.' . . . I thought I did, son, but when it come to a showdown I was chickenhearted. Your comin' home was a Godsend to Mother an' Lucy. An' more to me! Then to think you might get shot right off. . . . Wal, it was too much for my stomach."

"Dad, I bluffed them—that's all. I braced them quick and hard, before they could figure. It worked and I believe I got most of the town with me."

"Pan, is it true that you accused Jard Hardman of robbin' me—an' you knocked him flat?"

"Sure it's true."

"Lord, but I'd like to have seen that," declared Smith vehemently. "An' son, you got Jim Blake out of jail. Bill didn't hint you had anythin' to do with that. But I knew. It was sure great. If only Jim does his part!"

"You doubt that, Dad?"

"Shore do. But I'll tell you, Pan. If we could be with Jim all the time we could pull him up."

"Let's hope he's far on the way to Siccane by now. . . . Does Lucy know? I hope you didn't tell her about my meeting with Hardman and Matthews?"

"I didn't. But Bill shore did," replied his father. "Reckon I would have squealed, though. Mother an' Lucy have a lot more nerve than me. Fact is, though, Bill didn't give 'em time to go to pieces. He just busted out with news of Blake's escape. Say, boy, you should have seen Lucy."

"I will see her pronto," replied Pan eagerly. "Come on. What're you holding me up for, anyhow?"

Pan walked the horse while his father kept pace alongside.

"Some more news I most forgot," Smith went on. "Bill told about a shootin' scrape out in Cedar Gulch. Them claim jumpers drove a miner named Brown off his claim. They had to fight for it. Brown said he wounded one of 'em. They chased him clean to Satlee's ranch. Shore wanted to kill him or scare him off for good."

"I know Brown," replied Pan. "And from what he told me I've a hunch I know the claim jumpers."

"Wal, that'd be hard to prove. In the early days of a minin' boom there's a lot of trouble. A miner is a crazy fellar often. He'll dig a hole, then move on to dig another. Then if some other prospector comes along to find gold on his last diggin's he yells claim jumpin'. As a matter of fact most of them haven't a real claim till they find gold. An' all that makes the trouble."

"I'll hunt Brown up and persuade him to make the wild-horse drive with us. He's—"

"By George, I forgot some more," interrupted Smith, slapping his leg. "Bill said Wiggate broke with Jard Hardman. Wiggate started this wild-hoss buyin' an' shippin' east. Hardman had to get his finger in the pie. Now Wiggate is a big man an' he has plenty of money. I always heard him well spoken of. Now I'll gamble your callin' Jard Hardman the way you did had a lot to do with Wiggate's break with him."

"Shouldn't wonder," rejoined Pan. "And it's darned good luck for us. The boys ran across a valley full of wild horses over here about twenty miles. Dad, I believe I can trap several thousand wild horses."

"No!" ejaculated his father, incredulously.

"If the boys aren't loco, I sure can," declared Pan positively.

"I can vouch for numbers myself," replied Smith. "An' I've not a doubt in the world but that there valley's not yet hunted. But to ketch the darned scooters, that's the hell of it! Pan, even a thousand head would give me a new start somewhere."

"It's as good as done. Before the snow flies we will be on the way to Siccane."

"Lord! I'm a younger man than I was a few days ago. Before the snow flies? That's hardly another month. Pan, how'll we travel?"

"Wagons and horseback. We can buy wagon outfits for next to nothing. There's a corral full of them at Black's. Second hand, but good enough."

"Mother an' Lucy will be glad. They hate this country. I don't mind wind if it's not too cold."

"There! Isn't that Lucy at the gate now?" suddenly queried Pan, with piercing gaze ahead.

"Reckon it is," replied his father. "Ride ahead, son. I'll take my time."

Pan urged the sorrel into a lope, then a gallop, and from that to a run. In just a few rods Pan took the measure of this splendid horse. Swift, strong, sure footed and easy gaited, and betraying no sign of a mean spirit, the sorrel won Pan. What a liar Blinky was! He had lied to be generous.

Lucy waved to Pan as he came clattering down the road. Then she disappeared in the green foliage. Arriving at the gate he dismounted and went in. He expected to see her. But she had disappeared. Leading his horse he hurried in toward the house, looking everywhere. The girl, however, was not to be seen.

Bobby was occupied with little wooden playthings on the porch. Pan's gay shout to him brought forth his mother, but no Lucy.

He dropped his bridle, and mounted the porch to embrace his mother, who met him with suppressed emotions. Her hands were more expressive than her words.

"Oh, I'm all here, Mother," he laughed. "Where's Lucy? She was at the gate. Waved to me."

"Lucy ran through the house like a whirlwind," replied his mother, with smile. "The truth is, my son, she has been quite beside herself since she heard of her father's release from jail. She *knew* you got him out. She stared at me with her eyes black and wide. 'Mother, he laughed at me—at my fears. He said it'd be easy to free Dad.'. . . So she knows, Pan, and I rather think she didn't want us to see her when she meets you. You'll find her in the orchard or down by the brook."

"All right, Mother, I'll find her," replied Pan happily. "We'll be in to dinner pronto. There's a lot to talk about. Dad will tell you."

Pan did not seek Lucy in the orchard. Leaping upon the sorrel he loped down the sandy hard-packed path toward the brook and the shady tree with its bench. Pan knew she would be there. Dodging the overhanging branches he kept peering through the aisles of green for a glimpse of white or a golden head. Suddenly he was rewarded. Lucy stood in the middle of the sunny glade.

Pan rode to her side and leaped from the saddle. Her face was pale, and wet with tears. But her eyes were now dry, wide and purple, radiant with unutterable gladness. She rushed into his arms.

Dinner that day appeared to be something only Bobby and Pan had thought or need of. Mrs. Smith and Lucy, learning they might have to leave in two weeks, surely in four, became so deeply involved in discussion of practical details of preparation, of food supplies for a long wagon trip, of sewing and packing, that they did not indulge in the expression of their joy.

"Dad is hopeless," said Pan, with a grin. "He's worse than a kid. I'll have to pack his outfit, if he has anything. What he hasn't got, we'll buy. So, Mother, you trot out his clothes, boots, some bedding, a gun, chaps, spurs, everything there is, and let me pick what's worth taking."

It was indeed a scant and sad array of articles that Pan had to choose from.

"No saddle, no tarp, no chaps, no spurs, no gun!" ejaculated Pan, scratching his head. "Poor Dad! I begin to have a hunch how he felt."

It developed that all his father possessed made a small bundle that Pan could easily carry into town on his saddle.

"We'll buy Dad's outfit," said Pan briskly. "Mother, here's some money. Use it for what you need. Work now, you and Lucy. You see we want to get out of Marco pronto. The very day Dad and I get back with the horses. Maybe we can sell the horses out there. I'd take less money. It'll be a big job driving a bunch of wild horses into Marco. Anyway, we'll leave here pronto."

To Lucy he bade a fond but not anxious good-by. "We won't be away long. And you'll be busy. Don't go into town! Not on any account. Send Alice. Or Mother can go when necessary. But *you* stay home."

"Very well, boss, I promise," replied Lucy roguishly.

11

◆

BEFORE dark that night Pan had most of his preparations made, so that next morning there would be nothing to do but eat, pack the horses, saddle up and ride.

At suppertime Charley Brown and Mac New, alias Hurd, called at the camp. The latter was a little the worse for the bottle. Charley was sober, hard, gloomy.

"Howdy, boys. Help yourself to chuck. Then we'll talk," said Pan.

The outcome of that visit was the hiring of both men to go on the wild-horse drive. Brown's claim had been jumped by strangers. It could not be gotten back without a fight. Brown had two horses and a complete outfit; Mac New had only the clothes on his back.

"Fired me 'thout payin' my wages," he said, sullenly.

"Who fired you, Mac?" inquired Pan.

"Hardman, the —— —— ——!" replied Mac New.

"Well! That's strange. Does he own the jail?"

"Huh! Hardman owns this heah whole damn burg."

"Nix," spoke up Blinky. "Don't fool yourself there, pardner. Jard Hardman has a long string on Marco, I'll admit, but somebody's goin' to cut it."

Brown had an interesting account to give of his meeting with Dick Hardman down at Yellow Mine. The young scion of the would-be dictator of Marco fortunes had been drunk enough to rave about what he would do to Panhandle Smith. Some of his maudlin threats, as related by Brown, caused a good deal of merriment in camp, except to Blinky, who grew perfectly furious.

"Hey, cowboy, are you goin' to stand fer thet?" he queried, belligerently.

Pan tried to laugh it off, but Blinky manifestly had seen red at the mention of Dick Hardman's name. He was going over to the Yellow Mine and pick a fight. Pan, finding Blinky stubborn and strange, adopted other tactics. Drawing the irate cowboy aside he inquired kindly and firmly: "It's because of Louise?"

"What's because?" returned Blinky, blusteringly.

"That you want to pick a fight with Dick?"

"Naw," replied Blinky, averting his face.

"Don't you lie to me, Blinky," went on Pan earnestly, shaking the cowboy. "I've guessed your trouble and I'm your friend."

"Wal, Pan, I'm darn glad an' lucky if you're my friend," said Blinky, won out of his sullenness. "But what trouble are you hintin' aboot?"

Pan whispered: "You're in love with Louise."

"What if I am?" hissed Blinky in fierce shame. "Are you holdin' thet agin me?"

"No, I'm damned if I don't like you better for it."

That was too much for Blinky. He gazed mutely up at Pan, as a dog at his master. Pan never saw such eyes of misery.

"Blinky, that girl is wicked," went on Pan. "She's full of hellfire. But that's only the drink. She couldn't carry on that life without being drunk. She told me so. There's something great about that little girl. I felt it, Blink. I liked her. I told her she didn't belong there. I believe she could be made a good woman. Why don't you try it? I'll help you. She likes you. She told me that, too."

"But Louise won't ever see me unless she's drunk," protested Blinky sorrowfully.

"That's proof. She doesn't want you wasting your time and money at the Yellow Mine. She thinks you're too good for that—when she's sober. . . . Talk straight now, Blink. You do love her, bad as she is?"

"So help me I do!" burst out the cowboy abjectly. "It's purty near killed me. The more I see of her the more I care. I'm so sorry fer her I cain't stand it. . . . Dick Hardman fetched her out heah from Frisco. Aw! She must have been

113

bad before thet, I know. But she wasn't low down. Thet dive has done it. Wal, he never cared nothin' fer her an' she hates him. She swears she'll cut his heart out. An' I'm afraid she'll do it. Thet's why I'd like to stick a gun into his belly."

"Marry Louise. Take her away. Come south with us to Arizona," replied Pan persuasively.

"My Gawd, pardner, you're too swift fer me," whispered Blinky huskily, and he clutched Pan. "Would you let us go with you?"

"Sure. Why not? Lucy and my mother know nothing about Louise. Even if they did they wouldn't despise a poor girl you and I believe is good at heart and has been unfortunate. I'd rather not tell them, but I wouldn't be afraid to."

"But Louise won't marry me."

"If we can't talk her into it when she's sober, by heaven we'll get her drunk. . . . Now Blink, it's settled. Let's stay away from there tonight. Forget it. We'll go out and do the hard riding stunt of our lives. We'll sell horses. With some money we can figure on homes far from this bitter country—*homes*, cowboy, do you savvy that? With cattle and horses—some fine open grassy rolling country—where nobody ever heard of Blinky Moran and Panhandle Smith."

"Pard, it ain't—my—right name, either," mumbled Blinky leaning against Pan. He was crying.

"No difference," replied Pan, holding the boy tight a moment. "Brace up, now, Blink. It's all settled. Go to bed now, I'll help Gus with the horses."

Pan left the cowboy there in the darkness, and returned to camp. His conscience questioned him, but he had only satisfaction, even gladness in reply. Blinky had been one of the wild cowboys, and had been going from bad to worse. If an overpowering love gripped him, a yielding to it in a right way might make a better man of him. Pan could not see anything else. He had known more than one good-for-nothing cowboy, drinking and gambling himself straight to hell, who had fooled his detractors and had taken the narrow trail for a woman others deemed worthless. There was something about this kind of fight that appealed to Pan As for the girl, Louise Melliss, and her reaction to such a desperate climax,

114

Pan had only his strange faith that it might create a revolution in her soul. At least he was absolutely sure she would never return to such a life, and she was young.

Pan sought his blankets very late, and it seemed he scarcely had closed his eyes when Juan called him. It was pitch dark outside. The boys were stirring, the horses pounding, the campfire crackling. He pulled on his boots with a will. Glad he was to return to the life of camps, horses, cold dawns, hard fare and hard riding. He smelled the frying ham, the steaming coffee.

"Mawnin', pardner," drawled Blinky. "Shore thought you was daid. Grab a pan of grub heah.... An' say, cowboy, from now on you can call me Somers—Frank Somers. I'm proud of the name, but I reckon it was ashamed of me."

"Ah-huh! All right, Blink Somers, replied Pan cheerfully. "You'll always be Blink to me."

They ate standing and sitting before the campfire, in the chill blackness just beginning to turn gray. Then swift hands and lean strong arms went at beds and packs, horses and saddles. When dawn broke the hunters were on their way, far up on the cedar slope.

Pan gazed back and down upon Marco, a ragged one-street town of motley appearance, its white tents, its adobe huts, its stone buildings, and high board fronts, mute and still in the morning grayness. What greed, what raw wild life slept there!

Far beyond the town he saw the green-patched farm, the little gray cabin where his mother and Lucy slept, no doubt dreaming of the hopes he had fostered in them. Some doubt, some fear, intangible and inexplicable, passed over him as he looked. Would all be well with Lucy? There was indeed much to be feared, and he could never give happiness full rein until he had her safe away from Marco.

Once out of sight of the town Pan forced himself to the job ahead. And as always, to ride a good-gaited horse with open country ahead lulled his mind into content.

Blinky was first, leading a pack horse. Pan followed next, and the other four men strung out behind, with bobbing pack horses between. This ridge was the high ground between Marco Valley and Hot Springs Valley Soon the trail led down, and it was dusty. The rising sun killed the chill in the air, and by the time the hunters had reached level ground again it was hot. There was alkali dust to breathe, always an abomination. From above, Pan had espied a green spot fifteen miles or more down the valley. A number of dust devils were whirling around it.

"What's that, Blink?" Pan had asked, pointing.

"Thet's Hot Springs, an' the dust comes from wild hosses comin' in to drink."

They rode across the valley, which appeared to be five or six miles wide, to begin ascending another slope. The pack horses lagged and had to be driven. Up and up the hunters climbed, once more into the cedars. Pan had another view of Hot Springs and the droves of wild horses. He was surprised at their numbers.

"Blink, there must be lots of horses water there."

"Yep. Three thousand or more at this time of the year. Many more later, when the droves get run out of the high country by man. An' you see Hardman's outfit has been chasin' them hosses fer two months. They're shore purty well boggered."

"Are many of them branded?"

"Darn few," replied Blinky. "Not more'n five or six in a hundred. The Mexicans call them Arenajos. These wild hosses haven't been worth ketchin' until lately. Most all broomtails. But now an' then you shore see a bunch of dandy mustangs, with a high-steppin' stallion."

"Ah, now, cowboy, you're talking," declared Pan. "You're singing to me. It'll be darn hard for me to sell horses like that."

"Pard, I reckon we won't sell 'em," replied Blinky. "Cain't we use a few strings of real hosses down there in Arizonie?"

"I should smile," replied Pan.

They climbed and crossed that ridge, which could have been called a foothill if there had been any mountains near. Another valley, narrow and rough, not so low as the last, lay between this ridge and the next one, a cedared rise of rock and yellow earth that promised hard going. Beyond it rose the range of mountains, black and purple, and higher still, white peaked into the blue. They called to Pan. This was

116

wild country, and even to see it in the distance was all satisfying.

This narrow valley also showed some wild-horse bands, but not many, for there appeared to be scant grass and water. These horses were going or coming, all on a trot, but when they sighted the hunters they would halt stockstill. Soon a stallion trotted out a hundred paces or more, snorted and whistled, then taking to his heels he led his band away in a cloud of dust. Some of these bands would run a long way; others would halt soon to look back.

The water which they had come to drink was not very good, according to Pan's taste. His sorrel did not like it. This was Pan's first experience with hot alkali water. It came out almost boiling, too hot to drink, but a few rods from the spring it cooled off.

The spring was surrounded by low trees still green, though many of the leaves had turned yellow. While the hunters watered there, Pan espied another herd of wild horses that trooped in below, and drank from the stream. He counted ten horses, mostly blacks and bays. The leader was a buckskin, and Pan would not have minded owning him. The others were not bad looking, of fair size, weighing around a thousand pounds, but they showed inbreeding. After they had drunk their fill they pawed the mud and rolled in the water, to come up most unsightly beasts. Pan let out a loud yell. Swift as antelopes the horses swept away.

"Shore they left there!" drawled Blinky. Then talking to his own horse, which he slapped with his sombrero, he said: "Now you smelled them broomies, didn't you? Want to run right off an' turn wild, huh? Wal, I'll shore keep a durn sharp eye on you, an' hobble you too."

All the saddle horses, and even some of the pack animals, were affected by the scent of the wild herd. Freedom still lived deep down in their hearts. That was why a broken horse, no matter how gentle, became the wildest of the wild when he got free.

Pan had been right in his judgment of the lay of the land on the next ridge. Climbing it was difficult.

"When we ketch the wild hosses we can drive them down the valley an' round to the road," said Blinky, evi-

117

dently by way of excuse. "It'll be longer, but easy travelin'. Shore we couldn't drive any broomtails heah."

The summit of this ridge was covered with piñons and cedars, growing in heavy clumps around outcropping of ledges. Pan espied the blue flash of deer, through the gray and green. Deer sign was plentiful, a fact he observed with pleasure, for he liked venison better than beef.

It was rather a wide-topped ridge, and not until Pan had reached an open break on the far side could he see what kind of country lay beyond.

"Wal, there she is, my wild hoss valley," said Blinky, who sat his horse alongside of Pan. "An' by golly, thet's the name for her—Wild Hoss Valley. Hey, pard?"

Pan nodded his acquiescence. In truth he had been rendered quite speechless by the wildness and beauty of the scene below and beyond him. A valley that had some of the characteristics of a canyon yawned beneath, so deep and wide that it appeared like a blue lake, so long that he could only see the north end, which notched under a rugged mountain slope, green and black and golden and white according to the successive steps toward the heights.

The height upon which he stood was the last of the ridges, for the elevation that lay directly across was a noble range of foothills, timbered, canyoned, apparently insurmountable for horses. Gray cliffs stood out of the green, crags of yellow rock mounted like castles.

But it was the blue floor of the valley that longest held Pan's enraptured gaze. It looked level, though to an experienced eye that was deceitful. Grass and sage! What were the innumerable colored rock or bushes or dots that covered the whole floor of the valley? Pan wondered. Then he did not need to ask. They were wild horses!

"Aw, Blink! This'll be hard to leave!" he expostulated, as if his friend were to blame for this unexpected and bewildering spectacle.

"You bet your sweet life it will," agreed Blinky. "But we cain't hang up heah, moon eyed an' ravin'. We're holdin' up the outfit an' it's a long way down to water."

"Have you picked out a place where we'll be away—out of sight?" queried Pan quickly.

"Wal, pard, I'm no wild hoss wrangler like you say you

are, but I've got hoss sense," drawled Blinky, as he urged his animal back into the yellow trail.

Pan dismounted to walk, a habit he had always conformed to on steep trails, when his horse needed freeing of a burden, and his own legs were the better for action. At time he got a glimpse of the valley through a hole in the trees, but for the most part he could not see downward at all. Then he gazed across the open gulf to the mountains. These were not like the Rockies he knew so well by sight, the great white-crowned sky-piercing peaks of Montana. These belonged more to the desert, were wilder, with more color, not so lofty, and as ragged as jagged rock and fringed timber could make them. Gradually, as he descended the trail, this range dropped back out of his sight.

At near the sunset hour, when the journey was ended, Pan had to compliment Blinky on the beautiful place to which he had guided them. It was isolated, and singularly fitted to their requirements. The slope they had descended ran out into an immense buttress jutting far into the valley. A low brushy arm of the incline extended out a half mile to turn toward the main slope and to break off short, leaving a narrow opening out into the valley. The place was not only ideal for a hidden camp site, with plenty of water, grass, wood, but also for such a wild-horse trap as Pan had in mind. What astonished Pan was that manifestly Blinky had not seen the possibilities of this peculiar formation of slope as a trap into which wild horses could be chased.

"How wide is that gap?" asked Pan.

"Reckon it cain't be more'n the length of two lassoes," replied Blinky.

"Rope it off high, boys, and turn the stock loose. This corral was made for us," said Pan, enthusiastically.

They set to work, each with self-assumed tasks that soon accomplished the whole business of pitching camp. Suppertime found them a cheerful, hungry, hopeful little band. Pan's optimism dominated them. He believed in his luck, and they believed in him.

Dusk settled down into this neck of the great valley. Coyotes barked out in the open. From the heights pealed down the mournful bloodcurdling, yet beautiful, bay of a wolf. The rosy afterglow of sunset lingered a long time. The

119

place was shut in, closed about by brushy steeps, redolent of sage. A tiny stream of swift water sang faintly down over rocks. And before darkness had time to enfold hollow and slope and horizon, the moon slid up to defeat the encroaching night and blanch the hills with silvery light.

Interrogation by Pan brought out the fact that Blinky had never been down this trail at all. It was only a wild horse trail anyway. Blinky had viewed the country from the heights above, and this marvelously secluded arm of the valley had been as unknown to him as to Pan.

"Luck!" burst out Pan when the circumstance became clear. "Say, Blink, if your horse would jump you off a cliff you'd come up with Queen Victoria on your arm!"

Lying Juan sometimes broke into the conversation, very often by reason of his defective hearing and his appalling habit of falsehood, bringing his companions to the verge of hysterics.

"Yes, yes, I was over to her place two, tree times," began Juan, brightening with each word. "I drive en to many horse to her ranch. You bet I sell some damn good horse to Queen Victorie. I can tell you myself Queen Victorie is a fine little woman I ever seen on my life. She make big a dance for me when I never seen so much supper on my life. I dance with her myself an' she ata me an' say, 'Juanie, I never dance lika this en my life till I dance with you,' yes, that's sure what she tell me to my own face an' eyes."

Pan was the only one of Juan's listeners who had power of speech left, and he asked: "Juan, did you play any monte or poker with the queen?"

"You bet. She playa best game of poker I ever seen on my life an' she won tree hundred dollars from me."

Whereupon Pan succumbed to the riotous mirth. This laughter tickled Lying Juan's supreme vanity. He was a veritable child in mentality, though he spoke English better than most Mexican laborers. Blinky was the only one who ever tried to match wits with Lying Juan.

"Juan, thet shore reminds me of somethin'," began Blinky impressively. "Yea, hit shore does. Onct I almost got hitched up with Victorie. I was sort of figgerin' on marryin' her, but she got leery o' my little desert farm back in

Missourie. She got sorter skeered o' coyotes an' Injins. Now, I ain't got no use fer a woman like her an' thet's why me an' Queen Victorie ain't no longer friends."

"Most of the talk, however, invariably switched back to the burning question of the hour—wild horses. Pan had to attempt to answer a hundred queries, many of which were not explicit to his companions or satisfactory to himself. Finally he lost patience.

"Say, you long-eared jackasses," he exploded. "I tell you it all depends on the lay of the land. I mean the success of a big drive. If round the corner here there's good running ground—well, it'll be great for us. We'll look the ground over and size up the valley for horses. Find where they water and graze. If we decide to use this place as a trap to drive into we'll throw up two blind corrals just inside that gateway out there. Then we'll throw a fence of cedars as far across the valley as we can drag cedars. The farther the better. It'll have to be a fence too thick and high for horses to break through or jump over. That means work, my buckaroos, *work!* When that's done we'll go up the valley, get behind the wild horses and drive them down."

Loud indeed were the commendations showered upon Pan's plan.

Blinky, who alone had not voiced his approval, cast an admiring eye upon Pan.

"Shore I've got dobe mud in my haid fer brains," he said with disgust. "Simple as apple pie, an' I never onct thought of ketchin' wild hosses thet a way."

"Blink, that's because you never figured on a wholesale catch," replied Pan. "Moonshining wild horses, as you called it, and roping, and creasing with a rifle bullet, never answered for numbers. It wouldn't pay us to try those methods. We want at least a thousand head in one drive."

"Aw! Aw! Pan, don't work my hopes to believin' thet," implored Blinky, throwing up his hands.

"Son, I'm cryin' for mercy too," added Pan's father. "An' I'm goin' to turn in on that one."

Lying Juan, either from design or accident, found this an admirable opening.

"My father was a big don in Mexico. He hada tree tousand *vacqueros* on our rancho. We chase wild horse many days, more horse than I ever see on my life. I helpa lass more horse than I ever see in my life. I make tree tousand peso by my father's rancho."

"Juan, I pass," declared Pan. "You've got my hand beat. Boys, let's unroll the tarps. It has been a sure enough riding day."

12

◆

PAN's father was an early riser, and next morning he routed everybody out before the clear white morning star had gone down in the velvet blue sky.

Before breakfast, while the others were wrangling horses, packing wood and water, he climbed the steep end of the bluff between camp and valley. Upon his return he was so excited over the number of wild horses which he claimed to have seen that Pan feared he had fallen victim to Lying Juan's malady.

"I hope Dad's not loco," said Pan. "But our luck is running heavy. Let's play it for all we're worth. I'll climb that bluff, too, and see for myself. Then we'll ride out into the valley, get the lay of the land, and find the best place for our trap."

Blinky accompanied Pan to the ridge which they climbed at a point opposite camp. Probably it was four or five hundred feet high, and provided a splendid prospect of the valley. Pan could scarcely believe his eyes. He saw wild horses—so many that for the time being he forgot the other important details. He counted thirty bands in a section of the valley no more than fifteen miles long and less than half as wide. These were individual bands, keeping to themselves, each undoubtedly having a leader.

Blinky swore lustily in his enthusiasm, evidently thinking

of the money thus represented. "—— —— —— who'd
ever think of these heah broomies turnin' into a gold mine?"
he ended his tribute to the scene.

But to Pan it meant much more than fortune; indeed
at first he had no mercenary thought whatsoever. Horses
had been the passion of his life. Cattle had been only beef,
hoofs, horns to him. Horses he loved. Naturally then wild
horses would appeal to him with more thrill and transport
than those that acknowledged the mastery of man.

Cowboys were of an infinite variety of types, yet they all
fell under two classes: Those who were brutal with horses
and those who were gentle. The bronco, the outlaw, the wild
horse had to be broken to be ridden. Many of them hated
the saddle, the bit, the rider, and would not tolerate them
except when mastered. These horses had to be hurt to be
subdued. Then there were cowboys, great horsemen, who
never wanted any kind of a horse save one that would kick,
bite, pitch. It was a kind of cowboy vanity. Panhandle
Smith did not have it. He had broken bad horses and he
had ridden outlaws, but because of his humanity he was
not so great a horseman as he might have been. In almost
every outfit where Pan had worked there had always been
one cowboy, sometimes more, who could beat him riding.

Because of this genuine love for horses, the beautiful
wild-horse panorama beneath Pan swelled his heart. He
gazed and gazed. From near to far the bands dotted the
green-gray valley. Far away this valley floor shaded into
blue. Near at hand the colors were easily distinguishable.
Blacks and bays, whites and chestnuts, pintos that resembled zebras dotted this wild pasture land. The closest band
to where Pan and Blinky stood could not have been more
than a mile distant, in a straight line. A shiny black stallion
was the leader of this herd. He was acting strangely, too,
trotting forward and halting, tossing his head and long
black mane.

"Stallion!" exclaimed Pan, pointing. "What a jim-dandy
horse! Blink, he has spotted us, sure as you're born. Talk
about eyesight!"

"Wal, the broomtailed son-of-a-bronc!" drawled Blinky,
tapping a cigarette against his palm. "Reckon, by gosh,
you're correct."

"Blink, that's a wild stallion—a wonderful horse. I'll bet he's game and fast," protested Pan.

"Wal, you're safe to gamble on his bein' fast, anyways."

"Didn't you ever really *care* for a horse?" queried Pan.

"Me? Hell no! I've been kicked in the stummick—bit on the ear—piled onto the mud—drug in the dust too darn often."

"You'll admit, though, that there are some fine horses among these?" asked Pan earnestly.

"Wal, Pan, to stop kiddin' you, now an' then a fellar sees a real hoss among them broomies. But shore them boys are the hard ones to ketch."

The last of Blinky's remark forced Pan's observation upon the cardinally important point—the lay of the land. A million wild horses in sight would be of no marketable value if they could not be trapped. So he bent his keen gaze here and there, up and down the valley, across to the far side, and upon the steep wall near by.

"Blink, see that deep wash running down the valley? It looks a good deal closer to the far side. That's a break in the valley floor all right. It may be a wonderful help to us, and it may ruin our chances."

"Reckon we cain't tell much from heah. Thet's where the water runs, when there is any. Bet it's plumb dry now."

"We'll ride out presently and see. But I'm almost sure it's a deep wide wash, with steep walls. Impassable! And by golly, if that's so—you're a rich cowboy."

"Haw! Haw! Gosh, the way you sling words around."

"Now let's work along this ridge, down to the point where Dad went. Wasn't he funny?"

"He's shore full of ginger. Wal, I reckon he's perked up since you come."

Brush and cactus, jumbles of sharp rocks, thickets of scrub oak and clumps of dwarf cedars, all matted along the narrow hog-back, as Blinky called it, made progress slow and tedious. No cowboy ever climbed and walked so well as he rode. At length, however, Pan and Blinky arrived at the extreme end of the capelike bluff. It stood higher than their first lookout.

Pan, who arrived at a vantage point ahead of Blinky, let

out a stentorian yell. Whereupon his companion came running.

"Hey, what's eatin' you?" he panted. "Rattlesnakes or wild hosses?"

"Look!" exclaimed Pan, waving his hand impressively.

The steep yellow slope opposite them, very close at the point where the bluff curved in, stretched away almost to the other side of the valley. Indeed it constituted the southern wall of the valley, and was broken only by the narrow pass below where the cowboys stood, and another wider break at the far end. From this point the wash that had puzzled Pan proved to be almost a canyon in dimensions. It kept to the lowest part of the valley floor and turned to run parallel with the slope.

"Blink, suppose we run a fence of cedars from the slope straight out to the wash. Reckon that's two miles and more. Then close up any gaps along this side of the valley. What would happen?" suggested Pan, with bright eyes on his comrade.

Blinky spat out his cigarette, a sign of unusual emotion for him.

"You doggone wild-hoss wrangler!" he ejaculated, with starting eyes and healthy grin. "Shore I begin to get your hunch. Honest, I never till this heah minnit thought so damn much of your idee. You shore gotta excuse me. A blind man could figger this deal heah. . . . Big corrals hid behind the gate under us—long fence out there to the wash—close up any holes on this side of valley—then make a humdinger of a drive. . . . Cowboy, shore's you're born I'm seein' my Arizona ranch right this minnit!"

"Reckon I'm seeing things too," agreed Pan in suppressed excitement. "I said once before it's too good to be true. Dad wasn't loco. No wonder he raved. . . . Blink, is there *any* mistake?"

"What about?"

"The market for wild horses."

"Absolutely, no," declared Blinky vehemently. "It's new. Only started last summer. Wiggate made money. He said so. Thet's what fetched the Hardmans nosin' into the game. Mebbe this summer will kill the bizness, but right now we're safe. We can sell all the hosses we can ketch, right

125

heah on the hoof, without breakin' or drivin'. It's only a day's ride from Marco, less than thet over the hills the way we come. We can sell at Marco or we can drive to the railroad. I'd say sell at ten dollars a haid right heah an' whoop."

"I should smile," replied Pan. "It'll take us ten days or more working like beavers to cut and drag the cedars to build that fence. More time if there are gaps to close along this side. Then all we've got to do is drive the valley. One day will do it. Why, I never saw or heard of such a trap. You can bet it will be driven only once. The wild horses we don't catch will steer clear of this valley. But breaking a big drove, or driving them to Marco—that'd be a job I'd rather dodge. It'd take a month, even with a small herd."

"Hardman an' Wiggate have several outfits working, mebbe fifty riders all told. They've been handlin' hosses. Reckon Wiggate would jump at buyin' up a thousand haid, all he could get. He's from St. Louis an' what he knows aboot wild hosses ain't a hell of a lot. I've talked with him."

"Blinky, old-timer, we've got the broomies sold. Now let's figure on catching them," replied Pan joyfully. "And we'll cut out a few of the best for ourselves."

"An' a couple fer our lady friends, hey, pard!" added Blinky, with violence of gesture and speech.

Down the steep slope, through brush and thickets, they slid like a couple of youngsters on a lark. Pan found the gateway between bluff and slope even more adaptable to his purposes than it had appeared from a distance. The whole lay of the land was miraculously advantageous to the drive and the proposed trap.

"Oh, it's too darn good," cried Pan, incredulously. "It'll be too easy. It makes me afraid."

"Thet somethin' unforseen will happen, huh?" queried Blinky, shrewdly. "I had the same idee."

"But what could happen?" asked Pan, darkly speculative.

"Wal, to figger the way things run fer me an' Gus out heah I'd say this," replied Blinky, with profound seriousness. "We'll do all the cuttin' an' draggin' an' buildin'. We close up any gaps. We'll work ourselves till we're daid in our boots. Then we'll drive—drive them wild hosses as hosses was never drove before."

126

"Well, what then?" queried Pan sharply.

"Drive 'em right in heah where Hardman's outfit will be waitin'!"

"My God, man," flashed Pan hotly. "Such a thing couldn't happen."

"Wal, it just could," drawled Blinky, "an' we couldn't do a damn thing but fight."

"Fight?" repeated Pan passionately. The very thought of a contingency such as Blinky had suggested made the hot red blood film his eyes.

"Thet's what I said, pard," replied his comrade coolly. "An' it would be one hell of a fight, with all the best of numbers an' guns on Hardman's side. We've got only three rifles besides our guns, an' not much ammunition. I fetched all we had an' sent Gus for more. But Black didn't send thet over an' I forgot to go after it."

"We can send somebody back to Marco," said Pan broodingly. "Say, you've given me a shock. I never thought of such a possibility. I see now it *could* happen, but the chances are a thousand to one against it."

"Shore. It's hardly worth guessin' aboot. But there's thet one chance. An' we're both afeared of something strange. All we can do, Pan, is gamble."

On the way back to camp, Pan, pondering very gravely over the question, at last decided that such a bold raid was a remote possibility, and that his and Blinky's subtle reaction to the thought came from their highly excited imaginations. The days of rustling cattle and stealing horses on a grand scale were gone into the past. Hardman's machinations back there in Marco were those of a crooked man who played safe. There was nothing big or bold about him, none of the earmarks of the old frontier rustler. Matthews was still less of a character to fear. Dick Hardman was a dissolute and depraved youth, scarcely to be considered. Purcell, perhaps, or others of like ilk, might have to be drawn upon sooner or later, but that being a personal encounter caused Pan no anxiety. Thus he allayed the doubts and misgivings that had been roused over Blinky's supposition.

"Let's see," he asked when he reached camp. "How many horses have we, all told?"

127

"Thirty-one, countin' the pack hosses, an' thet outlaw sorrel of yours," replied Blinky.

"Reckon we'll have to ride them all. Dragging cedars pulls a horse down."

"Some of 'em we cain't ride, leastways I cain't."

"Grab some ropes and nose bags, everybody, and we'll fetch the string into camp," ordered Pan.

In due time all the horses were ridden and driven back to camp, where a temporary corral had been roped off in a niche of the slope.

"Wal, fellars, it's find a hoss you haven't rid before," sang out Blinky, "an' everyone fer himself."

There was a stout, round-barreled buckskin that Pan's father had his eye on.

"Don't like his looks, Dad," warned Pan. "Say, Blink, how about this wormy-looking buck?"

"Wal, he's hell to get on, but there never was a better hoss wrapped up in thet much hide."

Pan caught him and led him out of the corral. Just as the horse stepped over the rope fence which Pan held down, he plunged and made a break to get loose, dragging Pan at the end of a thirty-foot lasso. There was a lively tussle, which Pan finally won.

"Whoa, you bean-headed jasper," he yelled. "I'll ride you myself."

His father caught a brown bald-faced horse, nothing much to look at, that acted gentle enough until he was mounted. Then! He arched his back, jumped up stiff legged, and began to pitch. Evidently Smith had been a horseman in his day. He stayed on.

"Hang on, Dad," yelled Pan in delight.

"Ride him, cowboy," shrieked Blinky.

Fortunately for Smith, the horse was not one of the fiery devilish species that would not be ridden. He straightened out presently and calmed down.

"He was goin' to pile me—shore," declared Smith.

Charley Brown caught a blue-gray, fine looking horse, whose appearance, no doubt had attracted the miner; but he turned out to be a counterfeit, and Charley "bit the dust," as Blinky called it. Whereupon Charley had recourse to the animal he had ridden from Marco. Hurd showed he was a judge of horses and could ride. Blinky evidently was laboring under the urge that caused so much disaster among riders—he wanted to try a new horse. So he caught a jugheaded bay that did not look as if he could move out of his own way.

"Blink, you must be figuring on sleeping some?" inquired Pan.

"Humph! he'll walk back," snorted Gus. "I tried thet pack animal. He's hell for breakfast."

"Gus, if I was goin' to walk I'd leave my saddle heah in the camp," drawled Blinky.

"Blink, I'll let you ride in behind me," added Pan.

As a matter of fact, Pan was not having much luck propitiating the horse he had selected. Every time Pan would reach under for the cinch the horse would kick at him and throw off the saddle.

"Hey, Blink, come here," called Pan impatiently. "Hold this nice kind horse. What'd you call him?"

"Dunny," replied Blink. "An' he's a right shore enough good hoss. . . . I'll hold him."

Blinky grasped the ears of the horse but that did not work, so Pan roped his front feet. Blinky held the beast while Pan put the saddle on, but when he gave the cinch a pull Dunny stood up with a wild shriek and fell over backwards. He would have struck square on the saddle if Blinky had not pulled him sideways. Fortunately for Pan the horse rolled over to the right.

"Pan, turn that thing loose an' catch a horse you can get on," called his father.

"Don't worry, Dad. I'm ararin' to ride this bird."

"Pard, Dunny will be nice after you buckle down thet saddle an' get forked on him good," drawled Blinky, with his deceitful grin. "He's shore a broomie-chasin' devil."

Pan said: "Blink, I'll fool you in a minute . . . Hold him down now. Step on his nose." Pulling the right stirrup out from under the horse Pan drew the cinch a couple of holes tighter, and then straddled him.

"Let him up, Blink."

"All right, pard. Tell us where you want to be buried," replied Blinky, loosing the lasso and jumping free.

With a blast of rage Dunny got up. But he cunningly got

up with his back first, head down between his legs, and stiff as a poker. He scattered the horses and whooping men, bucked over the campfire and the beds; then with long high leaps, he tore for the open.

"High, wide an' handsome," yelled Blinky, in a spasm of glee. "Ride him, you Texas cowpunchin' galoot! You'll shore be the first one who ever forked him fer keeps."

"Blink—if he—piles me—I'll lick you!" yelled back Pan.

"Lick nothin," bawled Blinky, "you'll need a doctor."

But Pan stayed on that horse, which turned out to be the meanest and most violent bucker he had ever bestrode. Less powerful horses had thrown him. Eventually the plunging animal stopped, and Pan turned him back to camp.

"Wal, you son-of-a-gun!" ejaculated Blinky, in genuine admiration. "How'd you ever keep company with him?"

"Grin, you idiot," panted Pan, good humoredly. "Now, men—we're ready to look the valley over. I'll take Dad with me. Blink, you and Gus turn the corner here and keep close under the slope all the way up the valley. Look out for places where the wild horses might climb out. Charley, you and Mac New cross to the other side of the valley, if you can. Look the ground over along that western wall. And everybody keep eyes peeled for wild horses, so we can get a line on numbers."

They rode out through the gateway into the valley, where they separated into pairs. Pan, with his father, headed south along the slope. He found distances somewhat greater than he had estimated from the bluff, and obstacles that he had not noted at all. But by traveling farther down he discovered a low ledge of rock, quite a wall in places, that zigzagged out from the slope for a goodly distance. It had breaks here and there which could easily be closed up with brush. This wall would serve very well for part of the fence, and from the end of it out to the wash there was comparatively level ground. Half a mile up the slope the cedars grew thickly, so that the material for the fence was easily accessible.

The wash proved to be a perpendicularly walled gorge fifty or more feet deep with a sandy dry floor. It wound somewhat west by north up the valley, and as far as he could see did not greatly differ in proportion from the point where the fence was to touch.

"Dad, there are likely to be side washes or cuts up toward the head, where horses could get down," said Pan. "We'll fence right across here. So if we do chase any horses into the wash we'll stop them here. Sure, this long hole would make a great trap."

From that point they rode up the wash and gradually out into the middle of the valley. Bands of wild horses trooped away in the distance. Clouds of moving dust beyond the rolling ridges of the valley told of others in motion. They were pretty wild, considering that they had never been chased. At length Pan decided that many of these herds had come into this valley from other points nearer to Marco. Some bands stood on ridge tops, with heads erect, manes flying, wild and ragged, watching the two riders move along the wash.

Pan did not observe any evidence of water, but he hardly expected to find any in that wash. A very perceptible ascent in that direction explained the greater number of horses. The sage was stubby and rather scant near at hand, yet it lent the beautiful color that was so appreciable from a distance.

Intersecting washes were few and so deep and steep-walled that there need be no fear of horses going down them into the main wash. Outcroppings of rock were rare; the zone of cactus failed as the valley floor lost its desert properties; jack rabbits bounded away before the approach of the horses; a few lean gray coyotes trotted up to rises of ground, there to watch the intruders.

Pan had been deceived in his estimate of the size of the valley. They rode ten miles west before they began to get into rougher ground, scaly with broken rock, and gradually failing in vegetation. The notch of the west end loomed up, ragged and brushy, evidently a wild jumble of cliffs, ledges, timber and brush. The green patch at the foot meant water and willows. Pan left his father to watch from a high point while he rode on five miles farther. The ascent of the valley was like a bowl. The time came when he gazed back and down over the whole valley. Before him lines and dots of green, widely scattered, told of more places where water ran. Strings of horses moved to and fro, so far away that they were scarcely distinguishable. Beyond these points no horses could be seen. The wash wound like a black ribbon out of sight. The vast sloping lines of valley swept majestically down from the wooded bluff—like sides. It was an austere, gray hollow of the earth, with all depressions and ridges blending beautifully into the soft gray-green dotted surface.

Pan rode back to join his father.

"It's a big place, and we've got a big job on our hands," he remarked.

"While you was gone a band of two hundred or more run right under me, comin' from this side," replied Smith with beaming face. "Broomtails and willowtails they may be, as those boys call them, but I'll tell you, son, some of them are mighty fine stock. The leader of this bunch had a brand on his flank. He was white an' I saw it plain. I'd shore like to own him.

"Dad, I'll bet we catch some good ones to take with us to Arizona. If we only had more time!"

"Pan, it'd pay us to work here all winter."

"You bet. But, Dad, I—I want to take Lucy away from Marco," replied Pan hesitatingly. "When I let myself think, I'm worried. She's only a kid, and she might be scared or driven."

"Right, son," said Smith soberly. "Those Hardmans would try anythin'."

"We'll stick to the original plan, and that's to make a quick hard drive—then rustle out of New Mexico."

When they rode into the gateway the day was far spent, and the west was darkly ablaze with subdued fire.

Pan's father showed his unfamiliarity with long horseback rides and he made sundry remarks, mirth provoking to his son.

"I'll make a cowboy and horse wrangler of you again," threatened Pan.

By the time Lying Juan had supper ready Blinky and Gus rode into camp.

"Hungrier'n a wolf," said Blinky.

132

"Well, what's the verdict?" asked Pan with a smile.

"Wuss an' more of it," drawled Blinky. "We seen most five thousand hosses, an' I'll be doggoned if I don't believe we'll ketch them all."

"You found this side of the valley a regular hole-proof wing for our trap, I'll bet," asserted Pan.

"Wal, there's places where hosses could climb out easy, but they won't try it," replied Blinky. "The valley slopes up long an' easy to the wall. But when we drive them hosses they'll keep down in the center, between the risin' ground an' thet wash. They'll run far past them places where they could climb out. I shore lose my breath whenever I think of what's comin' off. I reckon the valley is a made-to-order corral."

"Blink, you have some intelligence after all," replied Pan, chaffingly. "Did you see any sign of Brown and Mac New?"

"Not after we separated this mawnin'," returned Blinky. "An' that reminds me, pard, I've got somethin' to tell you. This fellar Hurd—or Mac New as you call him—has a pocketful of gold coin."

"How do you know?" queried Pan bluntly.

"Gus kicked his coat this mawnin', over there where Mac New had his bed, an' a pile of gold eagles rolled out. Just by accident. Gus wanted somethin' or other. He was plumb surprised, an' he said Mac New was plumb flustered. Now what you make of thet?"

"By golly, Blink, I don't know. There's no reason why he shouldn't have some money, yet it strikes me queer. How much gold?"

"Aw, two or three hundred easy," rejoined Blinky. "It struck me sort of queer, too. I recollected thet he told us he'd only been doin' guard duty at the jail fer a couple of months. An' Gus recollected how not long before Mac New went to work he'd been a regular grub-line runner. We fed him heah, or Juan did. Now, pard, it may be all right an' then again it mayn't. Are you shore aboot him?"

"Blink, you make me see how I answer to some feeling that's not practical," returned Pan, much perturbed. "Mac was an outlaw in Montana. Maybe worse. Anyway I saved him one day from being strung up. That was on the

Powder River, when I was riding for Hurley's X Y Z outfit. They were a hard lot. And Mac's guilt wasn't clear to me. Anyway, I got him out of a bad mess, on condition he'd leave the country."

"Ahuh! Wal, I see. But it's a shore gamble he's one of Hardman's outfit now, same as Purcell."

"Reckon he was. But he got fired."

"Thet's what *he* says."

"Blink, you advise me not to trust Mac New?" queried Pan dubiously.

"I ain't advisin' nobody. If you want my opinion, I'd say, now I know what you done fer Mac New, thet he wouldn't double-cross you. When it comes down under the skin there ain't much difference between outlaws an' other range men in a deal like thet."

"Well, I'll trust him just because of that feeling I can't explain," returned Pan.

He did not, however, forget the possible implication, and it hovered in his mind. It was after dark when Mac New and Brown rode into camp. Pan and the others were eating their supper.

"We had to ride clean to the end of the valley to cross that wash," said Brown. "It's rough country. Horses all down low. Didn't see so many, at that, until we rimmed around way up on this side."

"Fine. You couldn't have pleased me more," declared Pan. "Now Mac, what do you say?"

"About this heah hoss huntin'?" queried Mac New.

"Yes. Our prospects, I mean. You've chased wild horses."

"It'll be most as bad as stealin' hosses," replied the outlaw, laconically. "Easy work an' easy money."

"Say, you won't think it's easy work when you get to dragging cedars down that hill in the hot sun all day. I don't know anything harder."

Early next morning the labor began and proceeded with the utmost dispatch. The slope resounded with the ring of axes. Pan's father was a capital hand at chopping down trees, and he kept two horsemen dragging cedars at a lively rate. The work progressed rapidly, but the fence did not seem to grow in proportion.

As Pan dragged trees out to the sloping valley floor, raising a cloud of dust, he espied a stallion standing on the nearest ridge, half a mile away. How wild and curious!

"You better look sharp, you raw-boned sage eater!" called Pan.

Twice more this same horse evinced intelligent curiosity. Pan could not see any signs of a band with him. But other wild horses showed at different points, none however so close as this gray black-spotted stallion. Blinky was sure this horse had not always been wild. Manifestly he knew the ways of his archenemy, man.

With three cutters and three riders dragging cedars, allowing for a rest of an hour at noon the fence grew to a length of a quarter of a mile from the slope.

"Not so good," declared Pan, when they left off work for the day. "But that fence is high and thick. It will take an old stallion like that gray to break through it."

"Wal, my idee is thet we did grand," replied Blinky, wiping his sweaty face. "Besides all the choppin' and haulin' Gus found time to kill a deer."

It was a tired, sweaty and dust-begrimed party of hunters that descended upon Lying Juan for supper. After their hearty meal they gathered round the campfire to smoke and talk. This night Mac New joined the group, and though he had nothing to say he listened attentively and appeared to fit in more. Pan was aware of how the former outlaw watched him. The conversation, of course, centered round the plan and execution of work, and especially the wonderful drive they expected to make. If they could have at once started the drive, it would have been over and done with before their interest had time to grow intense. But the tremendous task of preparation ahead augmented the anticipation and thrill of that one day when they must ride like the wind.

Next day they did not go back to the fence, but worked at the gateway on the blind corrals. Pan constructed the opening to resemble a narrow aisle of scrub oak. Material for this they cut from the bluff and slid it down to the level. By sunset one corral had been almost completed. It was large enough to hold a thousand horses. One third of it was fenced by the bluff.

Two more days were required to build the second blind corral, which was larger, and though it opened from the first it did not run along the bluff. As this one was intended for chasing and roping horses, as well as simply holding them, the fence was made an almost impenetrable mass of thick foliaged cedars reinforced, where necessary, with stuffings of scrub-oak brush. Pan was so particular that he tried to construct a barrier which did not have sharp projecting spikes of dread branches sticking out to cut a horse.

"By gum, I shore don't believe you ever was a regular cowpuncher," declared Blinky testily, after having been ordered to do additional labor on a portion of the fence.

"Blink, we're dealing with horses, not cows," answered Pan.

"But, good Lord, man, a cow is as feelin' as a hoss any day," protested Blinky.

"You'll be swearing you love cows next," laughed Pan. "Nope. We'll do our work well. Then the chances are we won't spike any of those thoroughbreds we want to break for Arizona."

"Say, I'll bet two bits you won't let us sell a single goshdarned broomie," added Blinky.

"Go to bed, Blink," rejoined Pan, in pretended compassion. "You're all in. This isn't moonshining wild horses."

In the succeeding days Pan paced up the work, from dawn until dark. A week more saw the fence completed. It was an obstacle few horses could leap. Pan thought he would love to se the stallion that could do it.

Following the completion of the fence, they built a barrier across the wash. And then to make doubly sure Pan divided his party into three couples, each with instructions to close all possible exits along the branches of the wash, and the sides of the slope.

During the latter part of this work, the bands of wild horses moved farther westward. But as far as Pan could tell, none left the valley. They had appeared curious and wary, then had moved out of sight over the ridges in the center of the great oval.

The night that they finished, with two weeks of unremitting toil in dust and heat behind them, was one for explosive satisfaction.

"Fellars, my pard Panhandle is one to tie to," declared Blinky, "but excoose me from ridin' any range where he was foreman."

"Blink, you'll soon be cowboy, foreman, boss—the whole outfit on your own Arizona ranch."

"Pard, I'll shore drink to thet, if anybody's got any licker."

If there were any other bottles in the camp, Mac New's was the only one that came to light. It was passed around.

"Now, men, listen," began Pan when they had found comfortable seats around the campfire. "It's all over but the shouting—and the riding. You listen too, Juan, for you've got to fork a horse and drive with us. As soon as it's light enough to see, we'll take the fresh horses we've been saving and ride across the valley. It's pretty long around, but I want to come up behind all these bands of wild horses. Pack your guns and all the shells you've got. We'll take stands at the best place, which we'll decide from the location of the horses. Reckon that'll be about ten miles west. You'll all see when we get there how the neck of the valley narrows down till it's not very wide. Maybe a matter of two miles of level ground, with breaks running toward each slope. We'll string across this, equal distances apart and begin our drive. If we start well and don't let any horses break our line, we'll soon get them going and then each band will drive with us. Ride like hell, shoot and yell your head off to turn back any horses that charge to get between us. Soon as we get a few hundred moving, whistling trampling and raising the dust, that'll frighten the bands ahead. They'll begin to move before they see us. Naturally as the valley widens we've got to spread. But if we once get a wide scattering string of horses running ahead of us we needn't worry about being separated. When we get them going strong, there'll be a stampede. Sure a lot of horses will fool us one way or another, but we ought to chase half the number on this side of the valley clear to our fence. That'll turn them toward the gate to the blind corrals. We'll close in there, and that'll take riding, my buckaroos!"

Blinky was the most obstreperously responsive to Pan's

137

long harangue. Pan thought he understood the secret of the cowboy's strange elation. After all, what did Blinky care for horses or money? He had been a homeless wandering range rider, a hard-drinking reckless fellow with few friends, and those only for the hour or the length of a job. The success of this venture, if it turned out so, meant that Blinky would do the one big act of his life. He would take the girl Louise from her surroundings, give her a name that was honest and a love that was great, and rise or fall with her. Pan had belief in human nature. In endless ways his little acts of faith had borne fruit.

The hunters stayed up later than usual, and had to be reminded twice by Pan of the strenuous morrow.

When Pan made for his own bed Mac New followed him in the darkness.

"Smith, I'd like a word with you," said the outlaw, under his breath. His eyes gleamed out of his dark face.

"Sure, Mac, glad to hear you," replied Pan, not without a little shock.

"I've stuck on heah, haven't I?" queried Mac New.

"You sure have. I wouldn't ask a better worker. And if the drive is all I hope for, I'll double your money."

"Wal, I didn't come with you on my own hook," rejoined the other hurriedly. "Leastways it wasn't my idee. Hardman got wind of your hoss-trappin' scheme. Thet was after he'd fired me without my wages. Then he sent fer me, an' he offered me gold to get a job with you an' keep him posted if you ketched any big bunch of hosses."

Here the outlaw clinked the gold coin in his coat pocket.

"I took the gold, an' said I'd do it," went on Mac New deliberately. "But I never meant to double-cross you, an' I haven't. Reckon I might have told you before. It jest didn't come, though, till tonight."

"Thanks, Mac," returned Pan, extending his hand to the outlaw. "I wasn't afraid to trust you . . . Hardman's playing a high hand, then?"

"Reckon he is, an' thet's a hunch."

"All right, Mac. I'm thinking you're square with me," replied Pan.

After the outlaw left, Pan sat on his bed pondering this latest aspect of the situation. Mac New's revelation was what Pan would have expected of such a character. Bad as he was, he seemed a white man compared with this underhanded, greedy Hardman. Even granting Hardman's gradual degeneration, Pan could not bring himself to believe the man would attempt any open crooked deal. Still this attempt to bribe Mac New had a dubious look. Pan did not like it. If his wild horse expedition had not reached the last day he would have sent Blinky back to Marco or have gone himself to see if Hardman's riders could be located. But it was too late. Pan would not postpone the drive, come what might.

13

◆

At last the cold night wind reminded Pan that he had not yet rolled in his blankets, which he had intended to do until Mac New's significant statement had roused somber misgiving. He went to bed, yet despite the exertions of the long day, slumber was a contrary thing that he could not woo.
- He lay under the transparent roof of a makeshift shelter of boughs through which the stars showed white and brilliant. For ten years and more he had lain out on most nights under the open sky, with wind and rain and snow working their will on him, and the bright stars, like strange eyes, watching him. Duing the early years of his range life he used to watch the stars in return and wonder what was their message. And now, since his return home, he seemed so much closer to his beloved boyhood. Tonight the stars haunted him. Over the ridge tops a few miles, they were shining in the window of Lucy's tiny room, perhaps lighting her fair face. It seemed that these stars were telling him all was not well in Lucy's mind and heart. He could not shake the insidious vague haunting thought, and longed for

dawn, so that in the sunlight he could dispel all morbid doubts and the shadows that came in the night.

So for hours he lay there, absorbed in mind. It was not so silent a night as usual. The horses were restless, as if some animal were prowling about. He could hear the sudden trampling of hoofs as a number of horses swiftly changed their location. The coyotes were in full chorus out in the valley. A cold wind fitfully stirred the branches, whipped across his face. One of his comrades, Blinky he thought, was snoring heavily.

Pan grew unaccountably full of dread of unknown things. His sensitive mind had magnified the menace hinted at by Mac New. It was a matter of feeling which no intelligent reasoning could dispel. Midnight came before he finally dropped into restless slumber.

At four o'clock Lying Juan called the men to get up. He had breakfast almost ready. With groans and grunts and curses the hunters rolled out, heavy with sleep, stiff of joints, vacant of mind. Blinky required two calls.

They ate in the cold gray dawn, silent and glum. A hot breakfast acted favorably upon their mental and physical make-ups, and some brisk action in catching and saddling horses brought them back to normal. Still there was not much time for talk.

The morning star was going down in an intense dark blue sky when the seven men rode out upon their long-planned drive. The valley was a great obscure void, gray, silent, betraying nothing of its treasure to the hunters. They crossed the wash below the fence, where they had dug entrance and exit, and turned west at a brisk trot. Daylight came lingeringly. The valley cleared of opaque light. Like a gentle rolling sea it swept away to west and north, divided by its thin dark line, and faintly dotted by bands of wild horses.

In the eastern sky, over the far low gap where the valley failed, the pink light deepened to rose, and then to red. A disk of golden fire tipped the bleak horizon. The whole country became transformed as if with life. The sun had risen on this memorable day for Pan Smith and his father, and for Blinky Somers. Nothing of the black shadows and doubts and fears of night! Pan could have laughed at himself in scorn. Here was the sunrise. How beautiful the valley! There were the wild horses grazing near and far, innumerable hundreds and thousands of them. The thought of the wonderful drive gripped Pan in thrilling fascination. Horses! Horses! Horses! The time, the scene, the impending ride called to him as nothing ever had. The thrilling capture of wild horses would alone have raised him to the heights. How much more tremendous, then, an issue that meant a chance of happiness for all his loved ones.

It was seven o'clock when Pan and his men reached the western elevation of the valley, something over a dozen miles from their fence and trap. From this vantage point Pan could sweep the whole country with far-sighted eyes. What he saw made them glisten.

Wild horses everywhere, like dots of brush on a bare green rolling prairie!

"Boys, we'll ride down the valley now and pick a place where we split to begin the drive," said Pan.

"Hosses way down there look to me like they was movin' this way," observed Blinky, who had eyes like a hawk.

Pan had keen eyes, too, but he did not believe his could compare with Blinky's. That worthy had the finest of all instruments of human vision—clear light-gray eyes, like those of an eagle. Dark eyes were not as far-seeing on range and desert as the gray or blue. And it was a fact that Pan had to ride down the valley a mile or more before he could detect a movement of wild horses toward him.

"Wal, reckon mebbe thet don't mean nothin'," said Blinky. "An' then agin mebbe it does. Horses run around a lot of their own accord. An' agin they get scared of somethin'. If we run into some bunches haidin' this way we'll turn them back an' thet's work for us."

Pan called a halt there, and after sweeping his gaze over all the valley ahead, he said: "We split here. . . . Mac, you and Brown ride straight toward the slope. Mac take a stand a half mile or so out. Brown, you go clear to the slope and build a fire so we can see your smoke. Give us five minutes, say, to see your smoke, and then start the drive. Reckon we'll hold our line all right till they get to charging us. And when we close in down there by the gate it'll be every man for himself. I'll bet it'll be a stampede."

Pan sent Lying Juan to take up a stand a mile or more outside of Mac New. Gus and Blinky were instructed to place equal distances between themselves and Juan. Pan's father left with them and rode to a ridge top in plain sight a mile away. Pan remained where he had reined his horse.

"Sort of work for them, even to Dad," soliloquized Pan, half amused at his own tremendous boyish eagerness. All his life he had dreamed of some such great experience with horses.

He could see about half of the valley floor which was to be driven. The other half lay over the rolling ridges and obscured by the haze and yellow clouds of dust rising here and there. Those dust clouds had not appeared until the last quarter of an hour or so, and they caused Pan curiosity that almost amounted to anxiety. Surely bands of horses were running.

Suddenly a shot rang out over to Pan's left. His father was waving hat and gun. Far over against the green background of slope curled up a thin column of blue smoke. Brown's signal! In a few moments the drive would be on.

Pan got off to tighten cinches.

"Well, Sorrel, old boy, you look fit for the drive," said Pan, patting the glossy neck. "But I'll bet you'll not be so slick and fat tonight."

When he got astride again he saw his father and the next driver heading their horses south. So he started Sorrel and the drive had begun. He waved his sombrero at his father. And he waved it in the direction of home, with a message to Lucy.

Pan rode at a trot. It was not easy to hold in Sorrel. He wanted to go. He scented the wild horses. He knew there was something afoot, and he had been given a long rest. Soon Pan was riding down into one of the shallow depressions, the hollows that gave the valley its resemblance to a ridged sea. Thus he lost sight of the foreground. When, half a mile below, he reached a wave crest of ground he saw bands of wild horses, enough to make a broken line half across the valley, traveling toward him. They had their heads north, and were moving prettily, probably a couple of miles distant. Beyond them other bands scattered and in-

142

distinct, but all in motion, convinced Pan that something had startled the horses, or they had sensed the drive.

"No difference now," shouted Pan aloud. "We're going to run your legs off, and catch a lot of you."

The long black line of horses did not keep intact. It broke into sections, and then into bands, most of which sheered to the left. But one herd of about twenty kept on toward Pan. He halted Sorrel. They came within a hundred yards before they stopped as if frozen. How plump and shiny they were! The lean wild heads and ears all stood up.

A mouse-colored mare was leading this bunch. She whistled shrilly, and then a big roan stallion trotted out from behind. He jumped as if he had been struck, and taking the lead swung to Pan's left, manifestly to get by him. But they had to run up hill while Pan had only to keep to a level. He turned them before they got halfway to a point even with the next driver. Away they swept, running wild, a beautiful sight, the roan and mare leading, with the others massed behind, manes and tails flying, dust rolling from under their clattering hoofs.

Then Pan turned ahead again, working back toward his place in the driving line. He had a better view here. He saw his father and Gus and Blinky ride toward each other to head off a scattered string of horses. The leaders were too swift for the drivers and got through the line, but most of the several herds were headed and turned. Gun shots helped to send them scurring down the valley.

Two small bands of horses appeared coming west along the wash. Pan loped Sorrel across to intercept them. They were ragged and motley, altogether a score or more of the broomtails that had earned that unflattering epithet. They had no leader and showed it in their indecision. They were as wild as jack rabbits, and upon sighting Pan they wheeled in their tracks and fled like the wind, down the valley. Pan saw them turn a larger darker-colored herd. This feature was what he had mainly relied upon. Wonderful luck of this kind might attend the drive: even a broken line running the right way would sweep the valley from wash to slope. But that was too much for even Pan's most extravagant hopes.

Again he lost sight of the horses and his comrades, as he

rode down a long swell of the valley sea. The slope ahead was long and gradual, and it mounted fairly high. Pan was keen to see the field from that vantage point. Still he did not hurry. Any moment a band of horses might appear, and he wanted always to have plenty of spare room to ride across to left or right. Once they got the lead of him or even with him it would be almost impossible to turn them.

Not, however, until he had surmounted the next ridge did he catch sight of any more wild horses. Then he faced several miles of almost level valley, with the only perceptible slope toward the left. For the first time he saw all the drivers. They were holding a fairly straight line. As Pan had anticipated, the drive was slowly leading away from the wash, diagonally toward the great basin that constituted the bottom of the valley floor. Bands of horses were running south, bobbing under the dust clouds. There were none within a mile of Pan. The other men, beyond the position of Pan's father, would soon be called upon to do some riding.

As Pan kept on at a fast trot, he watched in all directions, expecting to see horses come up out of a hollow or over a ridge; also he took a quick glance every now and then in the direction of his comrades. They were working ahead of him more and more to the left. Therefore a wide gap soon separated Pan from his father.

This occasioned him uneasiness because they would soon be down on a level, where palls of dust threatened to close over the whole valley, and it would be impossible to see any considerable distance. If the wild horses then took a notion to wheel and run back up the valley the drive would not yield great results.

Suddenly, way over close to the wash Pan espied a string of horses emerging from the thin haze of dust. He galloped down and across to intercept them. As he drew closer he was surprised to see they were in a dead run. These horses were unusually wild, as if they had been frightened. They appeared bent on running Pan down, and he had to resort to firing his gun to turn them. It was a heavy forty-five caliber, the report of which was loud. Then after they had veered, he had to race back across a good deal more than his territory to keep them from going round him.

At last they headed back into the dusty-curtained, blackstreaked zone which constituted the bowl of the valley. This little race had warmed Sorrel. He had entered into the spirit of the drive. Pan found that the horse sighted wild horses more quickly than he, and wanted to chase them all.

Pan rode a mile to the left, somewhat up hill and also forward. He caught sight of his father, and two other riders, rather far ahead, riding, shooting either behind or in front of a waving pall of dust. The ground down there was dry, and though covered with grass and sage, it had equally as much bare surface, from which the plunging hoofs kicked up the yellow smoke.

Pan had a front of two miles and more to guard, and the distance was increasing every moment. The drive swept down to the left, massing toward the apex where the fence and slope met. This was still miles away. Pan could see landmarks he recognized, high up on the horizon. Many bands of horses were now in motion. They streaked to and fro across lighter places in the dust cloud. Pan wanted to stay out in the clear, so that he could see distinctly, but he was already behind his comrades. No horses were running up the wash. So he worked over toward where he had last observed his father, and gave up any attempt at further orderly driving.

It was plain that his comrades had soon broken the line. Probably in such a case, where so many horses were running, it was not possible to keep a uniform front. But Pan thought they could have done better. He saw strings of horses passing him to the left. They had broken through. This was to be expected. No doubt the main solid mass was now on a stampede toward the south.

Pan let stragglers and small bunches go by him. There were, however, no large bands of horses running back, at least that he could see. He rode to and fro, at a fast clip, across this dust-clouded basin, heading what horses happened to come near him. The melee of dust and animals thickened. He now heard the clip-clop of hoofs, here, there, everywhere, with the mass of sound to the fore. Presently he appeared surrounded by circles of dust and stringing horses. It was like a huge corral full of frightened animals running wild through dust so thick that they could not be seen a hundred feet distant. Pan turned horses back, but he could not tell how quickly they would wheel again and elude him.

Once he thought he saw a rider on a white mount, yet could not be sure. Then he decided he was mistaken, for none of Blinky's horses were white.

This melee down in the dusty basin was bad. Driving was hampered by the obscurity. Pan could only hope the main line of wild horses was sweeping on as it had started.

After a long patrol in the dust and heat of that valley flat, Pan emerged, it seemed, into clearer atmosphere. He was working up. Horses were everywhere, and it was ridiculous to try to drive all those he encountered. At length there were none running back. All were heading across, to and fro, or down the valley. And when Pan reached the long ascent of that bowl he saw a magnificent spectacle.

A long black mass of horses was sweeping onward toward the gateway to the corrals, and to the fence. Dust columns, like smoke, curled up from behind them and swung low on the breeze. Pan saw riders behind them, and to the left. He had perhaps been the only one to go through that valley bowl. The many bands of horses, now converged into one great herd, had no doubt crossed it. They were fully four miles distant. Pan saw his opportunity to cut across and down to the right toward where the fence met the wash. If the horses swerved, as surely some or all of them would do, he could head them off. To that end he gave Sorrel free rein and had a splendid run of several miles to the point halfway between the fence and the wash.

Here from a high point of ground he observed the moving pace of dust and saw the black wheel-shaped mass of horses sweep down the valley like a storm. The spectacle was worth all the toil and time he had given, even if not one beast was captured. But Pan, with swelling heart and beaming eye, felt assured of greater success than he had hoped for. There were five thousand horses in that band, more by ten times than he had ever before seen driven. They could not all get through that narrow gateway to the corrals. Pan wondered how his few riders could have done so well. Luck! The topography of the valley! The wild horses took the lanes of least resistance; and the level or downhill ground favored a broad direct line toward the fence trap Pan and his men had contrived.

"Looks like Dad and all the rest of them have swung round on this side," soliloquized Pan, straining his eyes.

That was good, but Pan could not understand how they had ever accomplished it. Perhaps they had been keen enough to see that the wild horses would now have to go through the gateway or turn south along the fence.

Pan watched eagerly. Whatever was going to happen must come very soon, as swiftly as those fast wild horses could run another mile. He saw them sweep down on the bluff and round it, and then begin to spread, to disintegrate. Again dust clouds settled over one place. It was in the apex. What a vortex of furious horses must be there! Pan lost sight of them for some moments. Then out of the yellow curtain streaked black strings, traveling down the fence toward Pan, across the valley, back up the way they had come. Pan let out a stentorian yell of victory. He knew the action indicated that the horses had poured in a mass into the apex between bluff and fence.

"Whoopee!" yelled Pan, to relieve his surcharged emotions. "It's a sure bet we've got a bunch!"

Then he spurred Sorrel to meet the horses fleeing down along the fence. They came in bunches, in lines, stringing for a mile or more along the barrier of cedars.

Pan met them with yells and shouts. Frantic now, the animals wheeled back. But few of them ran up out of the winding shallow ground along which the fence had been cunningly built. He drove them back, up over the slow ascent, toward the great dusty swarm of horses that ran helter-skelter under the dust haze.

Suddenly Pan espied a black stallion racing toward him. He remembered the horse. And the desire to capture this individual took strong hold upon him. The advantage lay all with Pan. So he held back to stop this stallion.

At the most favorable moment Pan spurred Sorrel to intercept the stallion. But the black, maddened with terror and instinct to rage, would not swerve out of Pan's way. On he came, swift as the wind, lean black head out, mane flying, a wild creature at once beautiful and fearful. Pan had to jerk

147

Sorrel out of his way. Then Pan, having the black between himself and the fence, turned Sorrel loose. The race began—with Pan still holding the advantage. It did not, however, last long that way. The black ran away from Pan. He wanted to shoot but thought it best not to use his last shells. What a stride! He was a big horse, too, ragged, rangy, with action and power that delighted Pan. Knowing he could not catch the black, Pan cut across toward the wash. Then the stallion, seeing the yawning gulf ahead, turned toward the fence, and quickening that marvelous stride he made a magnificent leap right at the top of the obstruction. He cleared the heavy wood and crashed through the branches to freedom.

"You black son-of-a-gun!" yelled Pan in sheer admiration, and halting the sorrel he watched the stallion disappear.

Dust-begrimed and wet, Pan once more headed toward the goal. His horse was tired and so was he. Far as he could view in a fan-shaped spread, wild horses were running back up the valley. Pan estimated he saw thousands, but there were no heavy black masses, no sweeping stormlike clouds of horses, such as had borne down on that corner of the valley.

He was weary, but he could have sung for very joy. Happily his thoughts reverted to Lucy and the future. He would pick out a couple of beautiful ponies for her, and break them gently. He would find some swift sturdy horses for himself. Then, as many thousands of times, he thought of his first horse Curly. None could ever take his place. But how he would have loved to own the black stallion!

"I'm just as glad, though, he got away," mused Pan.

The afternoon was half gone and hazy, owing to the drifting clouds of dust that had risen from the valley. As Pan neared the end of the fence, which was still a goodly distance from the gateway, he was surprised that he did not see any horses or men. The wide brush gates had been closed. Beyond them and over the bluff he saw clouds of dust, like smoke, rising lazily, as if just stirred.

"Horses in the corrals!" he exclaimed. "I'll bet they're full. . . . Gee! now comes the problem. But we could hold a thousand head there for a week—maybe ten days. There's water and grass. Reckon, though, I'll sell tomorrow."

He would have hurried on but for the fact that Sorrel had begun to limp. Pan remembered going over a steep soft bank where the horse had stumbled. Dismounting, Pan walked the rest of the way to the bluff, beginning to think it strange he did not see or hear any of his comrades. No doubt they were back reveling in the corrals full of wild horses.

"It's been a great day. If only I could get word to Lucy!"

Pan opened the small gate, and led Sorrel into the lane. Still he did not see anything of the men. He did hear, however, a snorting, trampling of many horses, over in the direction of the farther corral.

At the end of the bluff, where the line of slope curved in deep, Pan suddenly saw a number of saddled horses, without riders.

With a violent start he halted.

There were men, strange men, standing in groups, lounging on the rocks, sitting down, all as if waiting.

A little to the left of these Pan's lightning swift gaze took in another group His men! Not lounging, not conversing, but aloof from each other, lax and abject, or strung motionless!

Bewildered, shocked, Pan swept his eyes back upon the strangers.

"Hardman! Purcell!" he gasped, starting back as if struck.

Then his mind leaped to conclusions. He did not need to see Blinky approach him with hard sullen face. Hardman and outfit had timed the wild-horse drive. No doubt they had participated in it, and meant to profit by that, or worse, they meant to claim the drive, and by superior numbers force that issue.

Such a terrible fury possessed Pan that he burned and shook all over. He dropped his bridle and made a dragging step to meet Blinky. But so great was his emotion that he had no physical control. He waited. After that bursting of his heart, he slowly changed. This then was the strange untoward thing that had haunted him. All the time fate had held this horrible crisis in abeyance, waiting to crush at the last moment his marvelous good fortune. That had been the doubt, the misgiving, the inscrutable something which had opposed all Pan's optimism, his hope, his love. An icy sickening misery convulsed him for a moment. But that could not exist in the white heat of his wrath.

Blinky did not stride up to Pan. He hated this necessity. His will was forcing his steps, and they were slow.

"Blink—Blink," whispered Pan, hoarsely. "It's come! That damned hunch we feared, but wouldn't believe!"

"By Gawd, I—I couldn't hev told you," replied Blinky, just as hoarsely. "An' it couldn't be worse."

"Blink—then we made a good haul?"

"Cowboy, nobody ever heerd of such a haul. We could moonshine wild hosses fer a hundred years an' never ketch as many."

"How—many?" queried Pan, sharply, his voice breaking clear.

"Reckon we don't agree on figgerin' thet. I say fifteen hundred haid. Your dad, who's aboot crazy, reckons two thousand. An' the other fellars come in between."

"Fifteen hundred horses!" ejaculated Pan intensely. "Heavens, but it's great!"

"Pan, I wish to Gawd we hadn't ketched any," declared Blinky, in hard fierce voice.

That brought Pan back to earth.

"What's their game?" he asked swiftly, indicating the watching whispering group.

"I had only a few words with Hardman. Your dad went out of his haid. Reckon he'd have done fer Hardman with his bare hands, if Purcell hadn't knocked him down with the butt of a gun."

Again there was a violent leap of Pan's blood. It jerked his whole frame.

"Blink, did that big brute—" asked Pan hoarsely, suddenly breaking off.

"He shore did. Your dad's got a nasty knock over the eye.   No, I hadn't any chance to talk to Hardman. But his game's as plain as that big nose of his."

"Well, what is it?" snapped Pan.

"Shore he'll grab our hosses, or most of them," returned Blinky.

"You mean straight horse stealing?"

"Shore, thet's what it'll be. But the hell of it is, Hardman's outfit helped make the drive."

"No!"

"You bet they did. Thet's what galls me. Either they was layin' fer the day or just happened to ride up on us, an' figgered it out. Mebbe thet's where Mac New comes in."

"Blink, I don't believe he's double-crossed us," declared Pan stoutly.

"Wal, he's an outlaw."

"No difference. I just don't believe it. But we'll find out. . . . So you think Hardman will claim most of our horses or take them all?"

"I shore do."

"Blink, if he gets *one* of our horses it'll be over my dead body. You fellows sure showed yellow clear through—to let them ride in here without a fight."

"Hell's fire!" cried Blinky, as if stung. "What you think? . . . There wasn't a one of us thet had a single lead left fer our guns. Thet's where the rub comes in. We played their game. Wasted a lot of shells on them damn broomies! So how could we fight?"

"Ah-huh!" groaned Pan, appalled at the fatality of the whole incident.

"Pan, I reckon you'd better swaller the dose, bitter as it is, an' bluff Hardman into leavin' us a share of the hosses."

"Say, man, are you drunk or loco?" flashed Pan scornfully.

With that he whirled on his heel and strode toward where Hardman, Purcell, and another man stood somewhat apart from the lounging riders.

Slowly Blinky followed in Pan's footsteps, and then Mac New left the group in the shade of the wall, and shuffled out into the sunlight. His action was that of a forceful man, dangerous to encounter.

In the dozen rods or more that Pan traversed to get to Hardman he had reverted to the old wild spirit of the Cimarron. That cold dark wind which had at times swept his soul returned with his realization of the only recourse here. When he had walked the streets of Marco waiting for Matthews to prove his mettle or show his cowardice, he had gambled on the latter. He had an uncanny certainty that he

151

had only to bluff the sheriff. Here was a different proposition. It would take bloodshed to halt this gang.

As Pan approached, Purcell swung around square with his hands low, a significant posture. Hardman evinced signs of extreme nervous tension. The third man walked apart from them. All the others suddenly abandoned their lounging attitude.

"Hardman, what's your game?" queried Pan bluntly, as he halted.

The words, the pause manifestly relieved Hardman, for he swallowed hard and braced himself.

"Game?" he parried gruffly. "There's no game about drivin' a million wild hosses through the dust. It was work."

"Don't try to twist words with me," replied Pan fiercely. "What's your game? Do you mean a straight out and out horse-thief deal? Or a share and share divvy on the strength of your riding in where you weren't asked?"

"Young man, I'm warnin' you not to call me a hoss thief," shouted Hardman, growing red under his beard.

"I'll call you one, damn quick, if you don't tell your game."

"We made the drive, Smith," returned Hardman. "You'd never made it without us. An' that gives us the biggest share. Say two-thirds, an' I'll buy your third at ten dollars a head."

"Hardman, that's a rotten deal," burst out Pan. "Haven't you any sense? If you could make it, you'd be outlawed in this country. Men won't stand for such things. You may be strong in Marco but I tell you even there you can't go too far. We planned this trap. We worked like dogs. And we made the drive. You might account for more horses trapped, but no difference. You had no business here. We can *prove* it."

"Wal, if I've got the hosses I don't care what *you* say," retorted Hardman, finding bravado as the interview progressed.

It was no use to try to appeal to any sense of fairness in this man. Pan saw that and his passionate eloquence died in his throat. Coldly he eyed Hardman and then the greasy dust-caked face of Purcell. He could catch only the steely speculation in Purcell's evil eyes. He read there that, if the man had possessed the nerve, he would have drawn on him at the first.

Meanwhile Blinky had come up beside Pan and a moment later Mac New. Neither had anything to say but their actions, especially Mac New's, were not to be misunderstood. The situation became intense. Hardman suddenly showed the strain.

Pan's demeanor, however, might have been deceiving, except to the keenest of men, long versed in such encounters.

"Jard Hardman, you're a low-down horse thief," said Pan deliberately.

The taunt, thrown in Hardman's face, added to the tension of the moment. He had lost the ruddy color under his beard. His eyes stood out. He recognized at last something beyond his power to change or stop.

"Smith, reckon you've cause for temper," he said, huskily. "I'll take half the hosses—an' buy your half."

"No! Not one damn broomtail do you get," returned Pan in a voice that cut. "Look out, Hardman! I can prove you hatched up this deal to rob me."

"How, I'd like to know?" blustered the rancher, relaxing again.

"Mac New can prove it."

"Who's he?"

"Hurd here. His real name is Mac New. You hired him to get in with me—to keep you posted on my movements."

Again Hardman showed his kind of fiber under extreme provocation: "Yes, I hired him—an' he's double-crossed you as well as me."

"Did he? Well, now *you* prove that," flashed Pan who had read the furious falseness of the man.

"Purcell here," replied Hardman hoarsely, "he's been camped below. Hurd met him at night—kept him posted on your work. Then, when all was ready for the drive Purcell sent for me. Ask him yourself."

Pan did not answer to the suggestion. "Mac, what do you say to that?" he queried, sharply, but he never took his eyes off Purcell.

"Hardman, you're a liar!" roared Mac New sonorously. If ever Pan heard menace in a voice, it was then.

"Take it back!" went on the outlaw, now with a hiss. "Square me with Panhandle Smith!"

"Mac, he doesn't have to square you. Anyone could see he's a liar," called Pan derisively.

"Hurd, I—I'll have you shot—I'll shoot you myself," burst out Hardman, wrestling his arm toward his hip.

A thundering report close beside Pan almost deafened him. Hardman uttered a loud gasp. His eyes rolled—fixed in an awful stony stare. Then like a flung sack he fell heavily.

"Thar, Jard Hardman," declared the outlaw, "I had one bullet left." And he threw his empty gun with violence at the prostrate body.

Purcell's long taut body jerked into swift action. His gun spurted red as it leaped out. Pan, quick as he drew and shot, was too late to save Mac New. Both men fell without a cry, their heads almost meeting.

"Blink, grab their guns!" yelled Pan piercingly, and leaping over the bodies he confronted the stricken group of men with leveled weapon.

"Hands up! *Quick,* damn you!" he ordered, fiercely.

His swiftness, his tremendous passion, following instantly upon the tragedy, had shocked Hardman's men. Up went their hands.

Then Blinky ran in with a gun in each hand, and his wild aspect most powerfully supplemented Pan's furious energy and menace.

"Fork them hosses, you — — —!" yelled Blinky. Death for more of them quivered in the balance. As one man, Hardman's riders rushed with thudding boots and tinkling spurs to mount their horses. Several did not wait for further orders, but plunged away down the lane toward the outlet.

"Rustle, hoss thieves," added Blinky, with something of the old drawl in his voice, that yet seemed the more deadly for it. With quick strides he had gotten behind most of the riders. "Get out of heah!"

With shuffling, creaking of leather, and suddenly cracking hoofs the order was obeyed. The riders soon disappeared around the corner of the bluff.

14

◈

THE TWO horses left, belonging to Hardman and Purcell, neighed loudly at being left behind, and pulled on their halters.

Pan's quick eye caught sight of a rifle in a sheath on one of the saddles. He ran to get it, but had to halt and approach the horse warily. But he secured the rifle—a Winchester —fully loaded.

Blinky, observing Pan's act, repeated it with the other horse.

"Pard, I ain't figgerin' they'll fight, even from cover," said Blinky. "By gosh, this hoss must have been Purcell's. Shore. Stirrups too long for Hardman. An' the saddle bag is full of shells."

"Slip along the fence and see where they went," replied Pan.

"Aw, I can lick the whole outfit now," declared Blinky recklessly.

"You keep out of sight," ordered Pan.

Whereupon Blinky, growling something, crashed away through the cedar fence and disappeared.

Pan hurriedly sheathed his gun, and with the rifle in hand, ran back to the overhanging bluff, where he began to climb through the brush. Fierce action was necessary to him then. He did not spare himself. Moreover he half-expected some kind of attack from the men who had been driven away. Soon he had reached a point where he could work round to the side of the bluff. When he looked out upon the valley he espied Hardman's outfit two miles down the slope, beyond the cedar fence. They had set fire to the cedars. A column of yellow smoke rolled away across the valley.

"Ah-huh! They're rustling—all right," panted Pan. "Wonder what—kind of a -story—they'll tell. Looks to me—like they'd better keep clear of Marco."

Then a reaction set in upon Pan. He crawled into the shade of some brush and stretched out, letting his tight muscles relax. The terrible something released its hold on mind and heart. He was sick. He fought with himself until the spasm passed.

When he got back to his men, Blinky had just returned.

"Did you see them shakin' up the dust?" queried Blinky.

"Yes, they're gone. Reckon we've no more to fear from them."

"Huh! We never had nothin'. Shore was a yellow outfit. They set fire to our fence, the —— —— ——!"

It took some effort for Pan to approach his father. The feeling deep within him was inexplicable. But, then, he had never before been compelled to face his father after a fight. Pan's relation to him seemed of long ago.

"How are you, Dad?" he asked with constraint.

"Little shaky—I guess—son," came the husky reply. But Smith got up and removed his hand from the bloody wound on his forehead. It was more of a bruise than a cut, but the flesh was broken and swollen.

"Nasty bump, Dad. I'll bet you'll have a headache. Go to camp and bathe it in cold water. Then get Juan to bandage it."

"All right," replied his father. He forced himself to look up at Pan. His eyes were warming out of deep strange shadows of pain, of horror. "Son, I—I was kind of dazed when—when you—the fight come off. . . . I heard the shots, but I didn't see . . . Was it you who—who killed Jard Hardman?"

"No, Dad," replied Pan, placing a steady hand on his father's shoulder. Indeed he seemed more than physically shaken. "But I meant to."

"Then how—who?" choked Smith.

"Mac New shot him," replied Pan, hurriedly. "Hardman accused Mac of double-crossing me. Mac called him.

I think Hardman tried to draw. But Mac killed him. . . . I got Purcell too late to save Mac."

"Awful!" replied Smith, hoarsely.

"Pan, I seen Purcell's eyes," spoke up Blinky. "Shore he meant to drop Mac an' you in two shots. But he wasn't quite previous enough."

"I was—too slow myself," rejoined Pan haltingly. "Mac New was an outlaw, but he was white compared to Hardman."

"Wal, it's all over. Let's kinda get set back in our saddles," drawled Blinky. "What'll we do with them stiffs?"

"By George, that's a stumper," replied Pan, sitting down in the shade.

"Huh! Reckon you figger we ought to pack them back to Marco an' give them church services," said Blinky, in disgust. "Jest a couple of two-bit rustlers!"

"Somebody will come out here after their bodies, surely. Dick Hardman would want to—"

"Mebbe someone will, but not thet hombre," declared Blinky. "But I'm gamblin' Hardman's outfit won't break their necks tellin' aboot this. Now you jest see."

"Well, let's wait, then," replied Pan. "Wrap them up in tarps and lay them here in the shade."

The trapped wild horses, cracking their hoofs and whistling in the huge corrals, did not at the moment attract Pan or wean him away from the deep unsettled condition of mind. As he passed the corral on the way to the camp the horses moved with a trampling roar. The sound helped him toward gaining a hold on his normal self.

The hour now was near sunset and the heat of day had passed. A cool light breeze made soft low sound in the trees.

Pan found his father sitting with bandaged head beside the campfire, apparently recovering somewhat.

"Did you take a peep at our hosses?" he asked.

"No, not yet," replied Pan. "I reckon I will, though, before it gets dark."

"We've got a big job ahead."

"That depends, Dad. If we can sell them here we haven't any job to speak of. How about it, Blink?"

"How aboot what?" inquired the cowboy, who had just come up.

"Dad's worrying over what he thinks will be a big job. Handling the horses we've caught."

"Shore thet all depends. If we sell heah, fine an' dandy. The other fellar will have the hell. Reckon, though, we want to cut out a string of the best hosses fer ourselves. Thet's work, when you've got a big drove millin' round. Shore is lucky we built thet mile-round corral. There's water an' feed enough to last them broomies a week, or longer on a pinch."

While they were talking Gus and Charley Brown returned to camp. They were leading the horses that had been ridden by Hardman and Purcell.

"Turn them loose, boys," directed Pan, to whom they looked for instructions.

Presently Gus handed Pan a heavy leather wallet and a huge roll of greenbacks.

"Found the wallet on Purcell an' the roll on Hardman," said Gus.

"Wal, they shore was well heeled," drawled Blinky.

"But what'll I do with all this?" queried Pan blankly.

"Pan, as you seem to forget Hardman owed your dad money, reckon you might rustle an' hunt up Dick Hardman an' give it to him. Say, Dick'll own the Yellow Mine now. Gee! He would spend all this in his own joint."

"Dad, you never told me how much Hardman did you out of," said Pan.

"Ten thousand in cash, an' Lord only knows how many cattle."

"So much! I'd imagined. . . . Say, Dad, will you take this money?"

"Yes, if it's honest an' regular for me to do so," replied Smith stoutly.

"Regular? There's no law in Marco We've got to make our own laws. Let it be a matter of conscience. Boys, this man Hardman ruined my father. I heard that from a reliable source at Littleton before I ever got here. Don't you think it honest for Dad to take this money?"

"Shore, it's more than thet," replied Blinky. "I'd call it justice. If you turned thet money over to law in Marco it'd go to Matthews. An' you can bet your socks he'd keep it."

The consensus of opinion did not differ materially from Blinky's.

"Dad, it's a long trail that has no turning," said Pan, tossing both wallet and roll to his father. "Here's to your new ranch in Arizona!"

Lying Juan soon called them to supper. It was not the usual cheery meal, though Juan told an unusually atrocious lie, and Blinky made several attempts to be funny. The sudden terrible catastrophe of the day did not quickly release its somber grip.

After supper, however, there seemed to be a lessening of restraint, with the conversation turning to the corrals full of wild horses.

"Wal, let's go an' look 'em over," proposed Blinky.

Pan was glad to see his father able and eager to accompany them, but he did not go himself.

"Come on, you wild-hoss trapper," called Blinky. "We want to bet on how rich we are."

"I'll come, presently," replied Pan.

He did not join them, however, but made his way along the north slope to a high point where he could look down into the second corral. It was indeed a sight to fill his heart —that wide mile-round grassy pasture so colorful with its droves of wild horses. Black predominated, but there were countless whites, reds, bays, grays, pintos. He saw a blue roan that shone among the duller horses, too far away to enable Pan to judge of his other points. Pan gazed with stern restraint, trying to estimate the numbers without wild guess of enthusiasm.

"More than fifteen hundred," he soliloquized at last, breathing hard. "Too good to be true! Yet there they are. . . . If only that . . well, no matter. I didn't force it. I wasn't to blame . . . Maybe we can keep it from Mother and Lucy."

Pan did not start back to camp until after nightfall, when he heard Blinky call

"Say, you make a fellar nervous," declared Blinky, in relief, as Pan approached the bright campfire. "Wal, did you take a peep at 'em?"

"Yes. It's sure a roundup," replied Pan. "I'd say between fifteen and sixteen hundred head."

"Aw, you're just as locoed as any of us."

Whereupon they fell into a great argument about the

number of horses; and though Pan had little part in it he gradually conceived an idea that he had underestimated them.

"Say, fellows," he said, breaking up the discussion, "if Hardman's gang raises a row in Marco we'll know tomorrow."

"Shore, but I tell you they won't," returned Blinky doggedly.

"We'll look for trouble anyway. And meanwhile we'll go right on with our job. That'll be roping and hobbling the horses we want to keep. We'll turn them loose here, or build another corral. Hey, Blink?—How about a string for your ranch in Arizona?"

"Whoopee!" yelled the cowboy. Pan had heard Blinky yell that way before. He clapped his hands over his ears, for no more mighty pealing human sound than Blinky's famous yell ever rose to the skies. When Pan took his hands away from his ears he caught the clapping echoes, ringing, prolonged, back from bluff to slope, winding away, to mellow, to soften, to die in beautiful concatenation far up in the wild breaks of the hills.

Pan lay awake in his blankets. He had retired early leaving his companions continuing their arguments, their conjectures and speculations. The campfire flared up and died down, according to the addition of new fuel. The light flickered on the trees in fantastic and weird shadows. At length there was only a dull red glow left, and quiet reigned. The men had sought their beds.

Then the solemn wilderness shut down on Pan, with the loneliness and solitude and silence that he loved. But this night there were burdens. He could not sleep. He could not keep his eyes shut. What question shone down in the pitiless stars? Something strange and inscrutable weighed upon him. Was it a regurgitation of his early moods, when first he became victim to the wilderness of the ranges? Was it newborn conscience, stirred by his return to his mother, by his love for Lucy? He seemed to be haunted. Reason told him that it was well he had come to fight for his father. He could not be blamed for the machinations of evil men. He suffered no regret, no remorse. Yet there was something that he could not understand. It was a physical sensation

160

that gave him a chill creeping of his flesh. It was also a spiritual shrinking, a withdrawing from what he knew not. He had to succumb to a power of the unseen.

Other times he had felt the encroachment of this insidious thing, but vague and raw. Whisky had been a cure. Temptation was now strong upon him to seek his companions and dull his faculties with strong drink. But he could not yield to that. Not now, with Lucy's face like a wraith floating in the starlight. He was conscious of a larger growth. He had accepted responsibilities that long ago he should have taken up. He now dreamed of love, home, children. Yet beautiful as was that dream it could not be realized in these days without the deadly spirit and violence to which he had just answered. That was the bitter anomaly.

Next morning, in the sweet cedar-tanged air and the rosy-gold of the sunrise, Pan was himself again, keen for the day.

"Pard, you get first pick of the wild hosses," announced Blinky.

"No, we'll share even," declared Pan.

"Say, boy, reckon we'd not had any hosses this mawnin' but fer you," rejoined his comrade. "An' some of us might not hev been so lively an' full of joy. Look at your dad! Shore you'd never think thet yestiddy he had his haid broke an' his heart, too. Now just would you?"

"Well, Blink, now you call my attention to it, Dad does look quite chipper," observed Pan calmly. But he felt a deep gladness for this fact he so lightly mentioned.

Blinky bent to his ear: "Pard, it was the money thet perked him up," whispered the cowboy.

Pan reflected that his father's loss and continued poverty had certainly weakened him, dragged him down.

"Listen, Blink," said Pan earnestly. "I don't want to be a kill-joy. Things do look wonderful for us. But I haven't dared yet to let myself go. You're a happy-go-lucky devil and Dad is past the age of fight. It won't stay before his mind. But I *feel* fight. And I can't be gay because something tells me the fight isn't over."

"Wal, pard," drawled Blinky, with his rare grin, "the way I feel aboot fight is thet I ain't worryin' none if you're around. . . . All the same, old pard, I'll take your hunch, an' you can bet your life I'll be watchin' like a hawk till we shake the dirty dust of Marco."

"Good, Blinky, that will help me. We'll both keep our eyes open today so we can't be surprised by anybody."

Pan's father approached briskly, his face shining. He was indeed a different man. "Boys, are we goin' to loaf round camp all day?"

"No, Dad, we're going to rope the best of the broomtails. I'll get a chance to see you sling a lasso."

"Say, I'd tackle it at that," laughed his father.

"Blinky, trapping these wild horses and handling them are two different things," remarked Pan thoughtfully. "Reckon I'll have to pass the buck to you."

"Wal, pard, I'm shore there. We'll chase all the hosses into the big corral. Then we'll pick out one at a time, an' if we cain't rope him without scarin' the bunch too bad we'll chase him into the small corral."

"Ah-huh! All right. But I'll miss my guess if we don't have a hot dusty old time," replied Pan.

"Fellars," called Blinky, "come ararin' now, an' don't any of you fergit your guns."

"How about hobbles?" inquired Pan.

"I've got a lot of soft rope, an' some burlap strips."

Gus and Brown brought in the saddle horses, and soon the men were riding down to the corrals. This was a most satisfactory incident for all concerned, and there were none not keen and excited to see the wild horses, to pick and choose, and begin the day's work.

Upon their entrance to the first and smaller corral a string of lean, ragged, wild-eyed mustangs trooped with a clattering roar back into the larger corral.

"Wal, boys, the show begins," drawled Blinky. "Mr. Smith, you an' Charley take your stands by the gate, to open it when you see us comin' with a broomie we want to rope. An' Pan, you an' me an' Gus will ride around easy like, not pushin' the herd at all. They'll scatter an' mill around till they're tired. Then they'll bunch. When we see one we want we'll cut him out, an' shore rope him if we get close enough. But I reckon it'd be better to drive the one we want into the small corral, rope an' hobble him, an' turn him out into the pasture."

162

The larger corral was not by any means round or level, and it was so big that the mass of horses in a far corner did not appear to cover a hundredth part of the whole space. There were horses all over the corral, along the fences especially, but the main bunch were as far away as they could get from their captors, and all faced forward, wild and expectant.

It was a magnificent sight. Whether or not there was much fine stock among them or even any, the fact remained that hundreds of wild horses together in one drove, captive and knowing it, were collected in this great trap. The intense vitality of them, the vivid coloring, the beautiful action of many and the statuesque immobility of the majority, were thrilling and all satisfying to the hearts of the captors.

Pan and Blinky and Gus spread out to trot their mounts across the intervening space. The wild horses moved away along the fence, and halted to face about again. They let the riders approach to a hundred yards, then, with a trampling roar, they burst into action. Wild pointed noses, ears, heads, manes and flying hoofs and tails seemed to spread from a dark compact mass.

They ran to the other side of the corral, where the horsemen leisurely followed them. Again they broke into mighty concerted action and into thunder of hoofs. They performed this maneuver several times before the riders succeeded in scattering them all over the pasture. Then with wild horses running, trotting, walking, standing everywhere it was easy to distinguish one from another.

"Regular lot of broomtails," yelled Blinky to Pan. "Ain't seen any yet I'd give two bits fer. Reckon, as always, the good hosses got away."

But Pan inclined to the opinion that among so many there were surely a few fine animals. And so it proved. Pan's first choice was a blue roan, a rare combination of color, build and speed. The horse was a mare and had a good head. She had a brand on her left flank. Pan rode around after her, here, there, all over the field, but without help he could not turn her where he wished.

He had to watch her closely to keep from losing sight of her among so many moving horses, and he expected any moment that the boys would come to his assistance. But they did not. Whereupon Pan faced about, just in time to see a wonderful-looking animal shoot through the open gate into the smaller corral. Blinky and Gus rode after him.

The gate was closed, and then began a chase round the corral. The wild horse was at a disadvantage. He could not break through the solid fence or leap over it, and presently two lassoes caught him at once, one round his neck, the other his feet. As he went down, Pan heard the piercing shriek. The two cowboys were out of their saddles in a twinkling, and while Gus held the horse down Blinky hobbled his front feet. Then they let him get up. Charley Brown ran to open another gate, that led out into the unfenced pasture. This animal was a big chestnut, with tawny mane. He leaped prodigiously, though fettered by the hobbles. Then he plunged and fell and rolled over. He got up to try again. He was savage, grotesque, awkward. The boys drove him through the gate.

"*Whoopee!*" pealed out Blinky's yell.

"Reckon those boys know their business," soliloquized Pan, and then he yelled for them to come and help him.

It took some time for Pan to find his roan, but when he espied her, and pointed her out to Blinky and Gus the chase began. It was a leisurely performance. Pan did not run Sorrel once. They headed the roan off, hedged her in a triangle, cut her out from the other horses, and toward the open gate. When the mare saw this avenue of escape she bolted through it.

Pan, being the farthest from the gate, was the last to follow. And when he rode in, to head off the furiously running roan, Gus made a beautiful throw with his lasso, a whirling wide loop that seemed to shoot perpendicularly across in front of her. She ran into it, and the violent check brought her down. Blinky was almost waiting to kneel on her head. And Gus, leaping off, hobbled her front feet. Snorting wildly she got up and tried to leap. But she only fell. The boys roped her again and dragged her out into the pasture.

"Aw, I don't know," sang Blinky, happily. "Two horses in two minutes! We ain't so bad, fer cowboys out of a job."

Warming to the work they went back among the circling animals. But it was an hour before they cut out the next choice, a dark bay horse, inconspicuous among so many, but one that proved on close inspection to be the best yet. Gus had the credit of first espying this one.

After that the picked horses came faster, until by noon they had ten hobbled in the open pasture. Two of these were Pan's. He had been hard to please.

"Wal, we'll rest the hosses an' go get some chuck," suggested Blinky.

Early afternoon found them again hard at their task. The wild horses had not only grown tired from trooping around the corral, but also somewhat used to the riders. That made choosing and driving and cutting out considerably easier. Pan helped the boys with their choices, but he had bad luck with his own. He had espied several beautiful horses only to lose them in the throng of moving beasts. Sometimes, among a large bunch of galloping horses, the dust made vision difficult. But at length, more by good luck than management, Pan found one of those he wanted badly. It was a black stallion, medium size, with white face, and splendid proportions. Then he had to chase him, and do some hard riding to keep track of him. No doubt about his speed! Without heading him off or tricking him, not one of the riders could stay near him.

"Aw, I'm sick eatin' his dust," shouted Blinky, savagely.

Whereupon both Pan and Gus, inspired by Blinky, cut loose in dead earnest. They drove him, they relayed him, they cornered him, and then as he bolted to get between Gus and Pan, Blinky wheeled his horse and by a mighty effort headed him with a lasso. That time both wild stallion and lassoer bit the dust. Gus was on the spot in a twinkling, and as the animal heaved to his feet, it was only to fall into another loop. Then the relentless cowboys stretched him out and hobbled him.

"Heah, now, you fire-eyed—air-pawin' hoss—go an' get gentle," panted Blinky.

By the time the hunters had caught three others, which achievement was more a matter of patience than violence, the herd had become pretty well wearied and tamed. They crowded into a mass and moved in a mass. It took some clever riding at considerable risk to spread them. Fine horses were few and far between.

"Let's call it off," shouted Pan. "I'm satisfied if you are."

"Aw, just one more, pard," implored Blinky. "I've had my eye on a little bay mare with four white feet. She's got a V bar brand, and she's not so wild."

They had to break up the bunch a dozen times before they could locate the horse Blinky desired. And when Pan espied the bay he did not blame Blinky, and from that moment, as the chase went on, he grew more and more covetous. What a horse for Lucy! Pan had been satisfied with the blue roan for her but after he saw the little bay he changed his mind.

The little animal was cunning. She relied more on crowding in among the other horses than in running free, and therefore she was hard to get out into the open. Blinky's mount went lame; Gus's grew so weary that he could not keep up; but Pan's Sorrel showed wonderful powers of endurance. In fact he got better all the time. It began to dawn upon Pan what a treasure he had in Sorrel.

"Aw, let the darn little smart filly go," exclaimed Blinky, giving up in disgust. "I never wanted her nohow."

"Cowboy, she's been my horse ever since you showed her to me," replied Pan. "But you didn't know it."

"Wal, you hoss-stealin' son-of-a-gun!" ejaculated Blinky with pleasure. "If you want her, we shore will run her legs off."

In the end they got Little Bay—as Pan had already named her—into the roping corral, along with two other horses that ran in with her. And there Pan chased her into a corner and threw a noose round her neck. She reared and snorted, but did not bolt.

"Hey, pard," called Blinky, who was close behind. "Shore as you're born she knows what a rope is. See! She ain't fightin' it. I'll bet you my shirt she's not been loose long. Thet bar V brand now. New outfit on me. Get off an' haul up to her."

Pan did not need a second suggestion. He was enraptured with the beauty of the little bay. She was glossy in spite of long hair and dust and sweat. Her nostrils were distended, her eyes wild, but she did not impress Pan as being ready to kill him. He took time. He talked to her. With infinite patience he closed up on her, inch by inch. And at last he got a hand on her neck. She flinched, she appeared about to plunge, but Pan's gentle hand, his soothing voice kept her still. The brand on her flank was old. Pan had no way to guess how long she had been free, but he concluded not a great while, because she was not wild. He loosened the noose of his lasso on her neck. It required more patience and dexterity to hobble her.

"Pard, this little bay is fer your gurl, huh?" queried Blinky, leaning in his saddle.

"You guessed right, Blink," answered Pan. "Little Bay! that's her name."

"Wal, now you got thet off your chest s'pose you climb on your hoss an' look heah," added Blinky.

The tone of his voice, the way he pointed over the cedar fence to the slope, caused Pan to leap into his saddle. In a moment his sweeping gaze caught horsemen and pack animals zigzagging down the trail.

"If it's Hardman's outfit, by Gawd, they're comin' back with nerve," said Blinky. "But I never figgered they'd come."

Pan cursed under his breath. How maddening to have his happy thoughts so rudely broken! In a flash he was hard and stern.

"Ride, Blink," he replied briefly.

They called the others and hurriedly got out of the corral into the open.

"Reckon camp's the best place to meet thet outfit, if they're goin' to meet us," declared Blinky.

Pan's father exploded in amazed fury.

"Cool off, Dad," advised Pan. "No good to cuss. We're in for something. And whatever it is, let's be ready."

They made their way back to camp with eyes ever on the zigzag trail, where in openings among the cedars the horsemen could occasionally be seen.

"Looks like a long string," muttered Pan.

"Shore, but they're stretched out," added Gus. " 'Pears to me if they meant bad for us they wouldn't come pilin' right down thet way."

"Depends on how many in the outfit and what they know," said Pan. "Hardman's men sure knew we weren't well heeled for a shooting scrape."

"Pard, are you goin' to let them ride right into camp?" queried Blinky, hard faced and keen.

"I guess not," replied Pan bluntly. "Rifle shot is near enough. They might pretend to be friendly till they got to us. But we'll sure fool them."

Not much more was spoken until the approaching horsemen emerged from the cedars at the foot of the slope. They rode straight toward the camp.

"How many?" asked Pan. "I count six riders."

"Seven fer me, an' aboot as many pack horses. . . . Wal, I'll be damned! Thet's all of them."

"Mebbe there's a bunch up on the slope," suggested Charley Brown.

After a long interval fraught with anxiety and suspense, during which the horsemen approached steadily, growing more distinct, Blinky suddenly burst out: "Fellars, shore as you're born it's Wiggate."

"The horse dealer from St. Louis!" ejaculated Pan in tremendous relief. "Blink, I believe you're right. I never saw one of those men before, or the horses either."

"It's Wiggate, son," corroborated Pan's father. "I met him once. He's a broad heavy man with a thin gray chin beard. That's him."

"Aw, hell!" exclaimed Blinky, regretfully. "There won't be any fight after all."

The approaching horsemen halted within earshot.

"Hi, there, camp," called the leader, whose appearance tallied with Smith's description.

"Hello," replied Pan, striding out.

"Who's boss here?"

"Reckon I am."

"My name's Wiggate," replied the other loudly.

"All right, Mr. Wiggate," returned Pan just as loud voiced. "What's your business?"

"Friendly. Give my word. I want to talk horses."

"Come on up, then."

Whereupon the group of horsemen advanced, and presently rode in under the trees into camp. The foremost was a large man, rather florid, with deep-set eyes and scant gray beard. His skin, sunburned red instead of brown, did not suggest the westerner.

"Are you the younger Smith?" he asked, rather nervously eyeing Pan.

"Yes, sir."

"And you're in charge here?"

Pan nodded shortly. He sensed antagonism at least, in this man's bluff front, but it might not have been animosity.

"Word come to me this morning that you'd trapped a large number of horses," went on Wiggate. "I see that's a fact. It's a wonderful sight. Of course you expect to make a deal for them?"

"Yes. No trading. No percentage. I want cash. They're a shade better stock then you've been buying around Marco. Better grass here, and they've not been chased lean."

"How many?"

"I don't know. We disagree as to numbers. But I say close to fifteen hundred head."

"Good Lord!" boomed the big man. "It's a haul indeed. . . . I'll give you our regular price, twelve fifty, delivered in Marco."

"No, thanks," replied Pan.

"Thirteen."

Pan shook his head.

"Well, young man, that's the best offer made so far. What do you want?"

"I'll sell for ten dollars a head, cash, and count and deliver them here tomorrow."

"Sold!" snapped out Wiggate. "I can pay you tomorrow, but it'll take another day to get my men out here."

"Thank you—Mr. Wiggate," replied Pan, suddenly rather halting in speech. "That'll suit us."

"May we pitch camp here?"

"Sure. Get down and come in. Plenty of water and wood. Turn your horses loose. They can't get out."

Pan had to get away then for a while from his father and the exuberant Blinky. How could they forget the dead men over there still unburied? Pan had read in Wiggate's look and speech and in the faces of his men, that they had been told of the killing, and surely to the discredit of Pan and his followers. Pan vowed he would put Wiggate in possession of the facts. He gave himself some tasks, all the while trying to realize the truth. Fortune had smiled upon him and Blinky. Rich in one drive—at one fell swoop! It was unbelievable. The retrieving of his father's losses, the new ranches in sunny Arizona, comfort and happiness for his mother, for Bobby and Alice—and for Lucy all that any reasonable woman could desire—these beautiful and sweet dreams had become possibilities. All the loneliness and privation of his hard life on the ranges had been made up for in a few short days. Pan's eyes dimmed, and for a moment he was not quite sure of himself.

Later he mingled again with the men round the campfire. Some of the restraint had disappeared, at least in regard to Wiggate and his men toward everybody except Pan. That nettled him and at an opportune moment he confronted the horse buyer.

"How'd you learn about this drive of ours?" he asked, briefly.

"Hardman's men rode in to Marco this morning," replied Wiggate, coldly.

"Ah-huh! And they told a cock-and-bull story about what happened out here!" flashed Pan hotly.

"It placed you in a bad light, young man."

"I reckon. Well, if you or any of your outfit or anybody else calls me a horse thief he wants to go for his gun. Do you understand that?"

"It's pretty plain English," replied Wiggate, manifestly concerned.

"And here's some more. Jard Hardman *was* a horse thief," went on Pan in rising passion. "He was a low-down yellow horse thief. He hired men to steal for him. And by God, he wasn't half as white as the outlaw who killed him!"

"Outlaw? I declare—we—I—Do you mean you're an—" floundered Wiggate. "We understood you killed Hardman."

"Hell, no!" shouted Blinky, aflame with fury, bursting into the argument. "We was all there. We saw—"

"Blink, you keep out of this till I ask you to talk," ordered Pan.

"Smith, I'd like to hear what he has to say."

"Wiggate, you listen to me first," rejoined Pan, with no lessening of his intensity. "There are three dead men across

170

the field, not yet buried. Hardman, his man Purcell, and the outlaw Mac New. He called himself Hurd. He was one of Hardman's jailers there in Marco. But I knew Hurd as Mac New, back in Montana. I saved him from being hanged."

Pan moistened lips too dry and too hot for his swift utterance, and then he told in stern brevity the true details of that triple killing. After concluding, with white face and sharp gesture, he indicated to his men that they were to corroborate his statement.

"Mr. Wiggate, it's God's truth," spoke up Pan's father, earnestly. "It was just retribution. Hardman robbed me years ago."

"Wal, Mr. Wiggate, my say is thet it'll be damned onhealthy fer anybody who doesn't believe my pard," added Blinky, in slow dark menace.

Gus stepped forward without any show of the excitement that characterized the others.

"If you need evidence other than our word, it's easy to find," he said. "Mac New's gun was not the same caliber as Pan's. An' as the bullet thet killed Hardman is still in his body it can be found."

"Gentlemen, that isn't necessary," replied Wiggate, hastily, with a shudder. "Not for me. But my men can substantiate it. That might sound well in Marco. For I believe that your young leader—Panhandle Smith, they call him—is not so black as he has been painted."

15

❖

THE following morning, while Pan was away for a few hours deer hunting, Wiggate's men, accompanied by Blinky, attended to the gruesome detail of burying the dead men.

Upon Pan's return he learned of this and experienced

relief that Wiggate had taken the responsibility. Wiggate had addressed him several times, civilly enough, but there was a restraint that Pan sensed often in his encounter with men. They were usually men who did not understand westerners like himself.

Wiggate had all his men, except the one he had sent back to Marco, with several of Pan's engaged in counting the captured wild horses. It was a difficult task and could hardly be accurate in short time.

"Anxious to get back to Marco?" queried Wiggate, not unkindly as he saw Pan's restlessness.

"Yes, I am, now the job's done," replied Pan heartily.

"Well, I wouldn't be in any hurry, if I were you," said the horse dealer, bluntly.

"What do you mean?" queried Pan.

"Young Hardman is to be reckoned with."

"Bah!" burst out Pan in a scorn that was rude, though he meant it for Hardman. "That pop-eyed skunk! What do I care for him?"

"Excuse me, I would not presume to advise you," returned Wiggate stiffly.

"Aw, I beg your pardon, Mr. Wiggate," apologized Pan. "I know you mean well. And I sure thank you."

Wiggate did not answer, but he took something from his vest pocket. It was a lead bullet slightly flattened.

"Let me see your gun?" he asked.

Pan handed the weapon to him, butt first. Wiggate took it gingerly, and tried to fit the bullet in a chamber of the cylinder, and then in the barrel. It was too large to go in.

"This is the bullet that killed Hardman," said Wiggate gravely. "It was never fired from your gun. I shall take pains to make this evident in Marco."

"I don't know that it matters but I'm sure much obliged," returned Pan with warmth.

"Well, I'll do it anyhow. I've been fooled by Hardman and, if you want to know it, cheated too. That's why I broke with him."

"Hope you didn't have any other association with him—besides this horse buying."

"No, but I'm lucky I didn't."

"Hardman had his finger in a lot of things in Marco. I

172

wonder who'll take them up. Say, for instance, some of the gold claims he jumped."

"Well! I knew Hardman had mining interests, but I thought they were legitimate. It's such a queer mixed-up business, this locating, working, and selling claims. I want none of it."

"Hardman's men, either at his instigation or Dick's, deliberately ran two of my men out of their claims. They'll tell you so."

"I'm astonished. I certainly am astonished," replied Wiggate, and he looked it.

"Marco is the hardest town I ever rode into," declared Pan. "And I thought some of the prairie towns were bad. But I see now that a few wild cowboys, going on a spree, and shooting up a saloon, or shooting each other occasionally, was tame beside Marco."

"You're right. Marco is a hard place, and getting worse. There's considerable gold. The new Eldorado idea, you know. It draws lawless men and women from places that are beginning to wake up. And they prey upon honest men."

"Did the Yellow Mine belong to Hardman?" asked Pan curiously.

"Him and Matthews. Young Hardman claims it. He's already clashed with Matthews, so I heard."

"He'll do more than clash with Matthews, if he isn't careful. He'll *cash!*" declared Pan grimly. "Matthews is a four-flush sheriff. He wouldn't face a dangerous man. But he'd make short work of Dick Hardman."

"If I'm not inquisitive in asking—would you mind telling me, do you mean to *meet* Matthews and young Hardman?" inquired Wiggate, hesitatingly.

"I'll avoid them if possible," rejoined Pan. "Dad and I will get out of Marco pretty pronto. We're going to Arizona and homestead."

"That's sensible. You'll have money enough to start ranching. I wish you luck. I shall make this my last horse deal out here. It's profitable, but Marco is a little too—too raw for my blood."

According to figures that the counters agreed upon there were fourteen hundred and eighty-six wild horses in the trap.

173

Wiggate paid cash upon the spot. He had some bills of large denomination, but most of the money was in rather small bills. Pan made haste to get rid of all except his share. He doubled the wages of those who had been hired. Then he divided what was left with Blinky.

"My—Gawd!" gasped that worthy, gazing with distended eyes at the enormous roll of bills. "My Gawd! . . . How much heah?"

"Count it, you wild-eyed cowpuncher," replied Pan happily. "It's your half."

"But, pard, it's too much," appealed Blinky. "Shore I'm robbin' you. This was your drive."

"Yes, and it was your outfit," returned Pan. "You furnished the packs, horses, location, and I furnished the execution. Looks like a square deal, share and share alike."

"All right, pard," replied Blinky, swallowing hard. "If you reckon thet way. . . . But will you keep this heah roll fer me?"

"Keep it yourself, you Indian."

"But, pard, I'll get drunk an' go on a tear. An' you know how bad I am when I get lickered up."

"Blink, you're not going to drink, unless in that one deal I hinted about," said Pan meaningly. "Hope we can avoid it."

"Aw, we're turnin' over a new leaf, huh?" queried the cowboy in the strangest voice.

"You are, Blink," replied Pan with a frank, serious smile. "I've been a respectable sober cowboy for some time. You've been terrible bad."

"Who said so?" retorted Blinky, aggressively.

"I heard it at the Yellow Mine."

That name, and the implication conveyed by Pan made Blinky drop his head. But his somber shame quickly fled.

"Wal, pard, I'll stay sober as long as you. Shake on it."

Pan made his plans to leave next morning as early as the wild horses they had hobbled could be gotten into shape to travel. Wiggate expected the riders he had sent for to arrive before noon the next day; and it was his opinion that he would have all the horses he had purchased out of there in a week. Pan and Blinky did not share this opinion.

Wiggate and his men were invited to try one of Lying

174

Juan's suppers, which was so good that Juan had the offer of a new job. Upon being urged by Pan to accept it, he did so.

"I can recommend Lying Juan as the best cook and most truthful man I ever knew," remarked Pan.

Blinky rolled on the ground.

"Haw! Haw! Wait till Lyin' Juan tells you one of his whoppers."

"*Lying Juan!* I see. I was wondering about such a queer name for a most honest man," replied Wiggate. "I know he's a capital cook. And I guess I can risk the rest."

After supper Pan and Blinky took great pains cutting and fixing the ropes which they intended to use on the wild horses that were to be taken along with them.

"Wal, now thet's done, an' I reckon I'd write to my sweetheart, only I don't know nothin' to write aboot," said Blinky.

"Go to bed," ordered Pan. "We've got to be up and at those horses by daylight. You ought to know that tieing the feet of wild horses is sure enough work."

Next morning it was not yet daylight when Blinky drawled: "Wal, cowboys, we've rolled out, wrangled the hosses, swallered some chuck, an' now fer the hell!"

In the gray of dawn when the kindling east had begun to dwarf the glory of the morning star, the cowboys drove all the hobbled horses into the smaller corral. There they roped off a corner and hung a white tarpaulin over the rope. This was an improvised second corral where they would put the horses, one by one, as they tied up their feet.

Blinky and Gus made one unit to work together, and Pan, his father, and Brown constituted another.

Blinky, as usual, got in the first throw, and the hungry loop of his lasso circled the front feet of the plunging roan. He stood on his head, fell on his side, and struggled vainly to get up. But he was in the iron hands of masters of horses. Every time the roan half rose, Blinky would jerk him down. Presently Gus flopped down on his head and, while the horse gave up for a moment, Blinky slipped the noose off one foot and tied the other foot up with it. They let the roan rise. On three feet he gave a wonderful exhibition of bucking. When he slowed down they drove him behind the rope corral.

"The night's gone, the day's come, the work's begun," sang out Blinky. "Eat dust, you buckaroos."

Pan chose the little bay to tie up first. But after he had roped her and got up to her there did not appear to be any urgent reason for such stringent measure. Little Bay was spirited, frightened, but not wild.

"I'll risk it," said Pan, and led her to the rope corral.

The sun rose hot and, likewise, the dust. The cowboys did not slacken their pace! It took two hours of exceedingly strenuous labor to tie up all the wild horses. Each horse had presented a new fight. Then came the quick job of packing their outfits, which Juan had gotten together. Everyone of the men had been kicked, pulled, knocked down, and so coated with sweat and dust that they now resembled Negroes. Their hands were fairly cooked from the hot ropes' sizzling when the horses plunged. And at nine o'clock they were ready for the momentous twenty-five mile drive to Marco.

"All ready for the parade!" yelled Blinky. "Go ahaid, you fellars. Open the gate, an' leave it fer me to close."

Pan and the others were to ride in front, while Blinky drove the horses. The need for men was in front, not behind. As they started down the wing of the trap to open the gate the roped wild horses began a terrific plunging, kicking, bucking and falling down. Some of them bit the rope on their feet. But little by little Blinky drove them out into the open. Pan and his father dropped back to each side, keeping the horses in a close bunch. That left Gus and Brown in front to run down those that tried to escape. The white-footed stallion was the first to make a break. He ran almost as well on three feet as on four, and it took hard riding to catch him, turn him and get him back in the bunch. The next was Pan's roan. He gave a great deal of trouble.

"Haw! Haw! Thet's Pan's hoss. Kill him! I guess mebbe Pan cain't pick out the runners."

When the wild horses got out of the narrow gateway between bluff and slope they tried to scatter. The riders had their hands full. Riding, shooting, yelling, swinging their ropes, they moved the horses forward and kept them together. They were learning to run on three feet and tried hard to escape. Just when the melee grew worst they

176

reached the cedar fence, only half of which had been burned by the resentful Hardman outfit, and this obstruction was of signal help to the riders. Once more in a compact bunch, the wild horses grew less difficult to handle.

As Pan rode up the ridge leading out of the valley he turned to have a last look at this memorable place. To his amaze and delight he saw almost as many wild horses as before the drive.

"Gee, I'm greedy," he muttered. "Lucky as I've been, I want to stay and make another drive."

"Wal, pard, I'm readin' your mind," drawled Blinky. "But don't feel bad. If we tried thet drive again we might ketch a few. But you cain't fool them broomies twice the same way."

Another difficulty soon presented itself. Several of the wild horses could not learn to travel well on three feet.

"Reckon they've had long enough trial. We gotta cut them loose," said Blinky.

"We'll lose them sure," complained Pan.

"Mebbe so. But we cain't do nothin' else. It's mighty strange, the difference in hosses. Same as people, come to think aboot it. Some hosses learn quick, an' now an' then there's one like thet stallion. He can run like hell. Most wild hosses fight an' worry themselves, an' quick as they learn to get along on three feet they make the best of it. Some have to be cut loose. Fact is, pard, we've got a mighty fine bunch, an' we're comin' along better'n I expected. . . . Loose your lasso now, cowboy, for you'll shore need it."

The need of that scarcely had to be dwelt on, for the instant Gus and Blinky cut loose a poor traveler, he made a wild dash for liberty. But he ran right into a hateful lasso. This one let out a piercing whistle.

All the time the riders were moving the bunch forward down into flat country between gray brushy hills. Evidently this wide pass opened into a larger valley. The travel was mostly over level ground, which facilitated the progress.

It took two men to lasso a horse, hold his ears, cut the rope round his legs, release the noose on his neck and let him go. They could not afford to lose any precious second over this job. Time was too badly needed.

The parade, as Blinky had called it, made only a few

miles an hour, and sometimes this advance was not wholly in the right direction. Nevertheless the hours seemed to fly. There was no rest for horses or men. The afternoon had begun to wane before the horses had all made up their minds that fighting and plunging were of no avail. Weary, exhausted, suffering from the bound up legs, they at last surrendered. Whereupon Blinky and Gus cut their feet loose. Sometimes the whole bunch would have to be held up for one horse that, upon release, could not use his freed foot. Pan had an idea the horses did not want that tried on them twice. They showed intelligence. This method was not breeding the horses for saddle and bridle, which was of course the main consideration to come, but it certainly tamed them. It was a little too cruel for Pan to favor.

"Wal, we'll shore be lucky if we make Snyder's pasture tonight," remarked Blinky. "No hope of makin' Marco."

Pan had never expected to do so, and therefore was not disappointed. His heart seemed so full and buoyant that he would not have minded more delay. Indeed he rode in the clouds.

The pass proved to be longer than it looked, but at last the drove of horses was headed into the wide flat country toward the west. And soon trail grew into road. The sunset dusk mantled the sweeping prairielike valley, and soon night fell, cool and windy. The wild horses slowed to a walk and had to be driven to do that. Pan felt that he shared their thirst.

When at about ten o'clock, Blinky espied through the gloom landmarks that indicated the pasture he was seeking, it was none too soon for Pan.

"Water an' grass heah, but no firewood handy," announced Blinky, as they turned the horses into the pasture. "Fellar named Snyder used to ranch heah. It didn't pay. This little pasture is lucky fer us. I was heah not long ago. Good fence, an' we can round up the bunch easy in the mawnin'."

The weary riders unpacked the outfit, took a long deep drink of the cold water, and unrolling their tarps went supperless to bed. Pan's eyes closed as if with glue and his thoughts wavered, faded.

Pan's father was the first to get up, but already the sun

178

was before him. Pan saw him limp around, and leave the pasture to return with an armful of firewood.

"Pile out!" he yelled. "It's Siccane, Arizona, or bust!"

One by one the boys rolled from their beds. Pan was the only one who had to pull on his boots. Somebody found soap and towel, which they fought over. The towel had not been clean before this onslaught. Afterward it was unrecognizable. Gus cooked breakfast which, judged from the attack upon it, was creditable to him.

"Wal, our hosses are heah," said Blinky, cheerfully. "Reckon I was afeared they'd jump the fence. We may have a little hell on the start."

"Blink, you don't aim to tie up their feet again, do you?" inquired Pan anxiously.

"Nope. They had all they wanted of thet. Mebbe they'll try to bust away first off. But our hosses are fresh, too. I'm gamblin' in three hours we'll have them in your dad's corral."

"Then we don't have to drive through Marco?"

"Shore not. We're on the main road thet passes your dad's. Reckon it's aboot eight miles or so."

"Say, Blink, do we take this road on our way south to Siccane?"

"Yep. It's the only road. You come in on it by stage. It runs north and south. Not very good road this way out of Marco."

"Then, by golly, we can leave our new horses here," exclaimed Pan gladly.

"Wal, I'll be goldarned. Where's my haid? Shore we can. It's a first-rate pasture, plenty of water, an' fair grass. But I'll have to go in town, thet's damn shore, you know. An' we cain't leave these hosses heah unguarded."

"Gus, will you and Brown stay here? We'll leave grub and outfit."

Brown had to refuse, and explained that he was keen to get back to his mining claim, which he believed now he would be able to work.

"I'll stay," said Gus. "It's a good idee. Workin' with these hosses a day or two will get 'em fit to travel. An' I reckon I'd like a job with you, far as Siccane anyway."

179

"You've got it, and after we reach Siccane, too, if you want one," replied Pan quickly.

The deal was settled to the satisfaction of all concerned.

"How aboot our pack hosses?" asked Blinky. "Course Charley will have to take his, but will we need ours? I mean will we have to pack them from heah?"

"No, all that stuff can go in the wagons," replied Pan. "We'll need three wagons anyhow. Maybe more. Dad, how much of an outfit have you at home?"

"You saw it, son," said Smith, with a laugh. "Mine would go in a saddlebag. But I reckon the women folks will have a wagon load."

"Rustle. I'm ararin' to go," yelled Pan, striding out into the pasture to catch his horse. In the exuberance of the moment Pan would have liked to try conclusions with the white-footed stallion or the blue roan, but he could not spare the time. He led Sorrel back to camp and saddled him. Blinky and Pan's father were also saddling their mounts.

"I'll take it easy," explained Charley Brown, who had made no move. "My claim is over here in the hills not very far."

"Brown, I'm sorry you won't go south with us," said Pan warmly, as he shook hands with the miner. "You've sure been a help. And I'm glad we've—well, had something to do with removing the claim jumpers."

As Pan rode out that morning on the sorrel, to face north on the road to Marco, he found it hard to contain himself. This hour was the very first in which he could let himself think of the glorious fulfillment of his dream.

His father was too lame to ride fast and Pan, much as he longed to rush, did not want to leave him behind. But it was utterly impossible for Pan to enter into the animated conversation carried on by his father and Blinky. They were talking wagons, teams, harness, grain, homesteads and what not. Pan rode alone, a little ahead of them.

Almost, he loved this wild and rugged land. But that was the ecstasy of the moment. This iron country was too cut up by mountains, with valleys too bare and waterless, to suit Pan. Not to include the rough and violent element of men attracted by gold!

Nevertheless on this bright autumn morning there was a

glamour over valley and ridge, black slope and snowy peak, and the dim distant ranges. The sky was as blue as the inside of a columbine, a rich and beautiful light of gold gilded the wall of rock that boldly cropped out of the mountainside; and the wide sweeping expanse of sage lost itself in a deep purple horizon. Ravens and magpies crossed Pan's glad eyesight. Jack rabbits bounded down the aisles between the sage bushes. Far out on the plain he descried antelope, moving away with their telltale white rumps. The air was sweet, intoxicating, full of cedar fragrance and the cool breath from off the heights.

While he saw and felt all this his mind scintillated with thoughts of Lucy Blake. He would see her presently, have the joy of surprising her into betrayal of love. He fancied her wide eyes of changing dark blue, and the swift flame of scarlet that so readily stained her neck and cheek.

He would tell her about the great good fortune that had befallen him; and about the beautiful mare, Little Bay, he had captured for her; and now they could talk and plan endlessly, all the way down to Siccane.

When would Lucy marry him? That was a staggering question. His heart swelled to bursting. Had he the courage to ask her at once? He tried to see the matter from Lucy's point of view, but without much success.

Dreaming thus, Pan rode along without being aware of the time or distance.

"Hey, pard," called Blinky, in loud banter. "Are you goin' to ride past where your gurl lives?"

With a violent start Pan wheeled his horse. He saw that he had indeed ridden beyond the entrance to a farm, which upon second look he recognized. It was, however, an angle with which he had not been familiar. The corrals and barn and house were hidden in trees.

"I'm loco, all right," he replied with a little laugh.

Through gate and lane they galloped, on to the corral, and round that to the barn. This was only a short distance to the house. Pan leaped from his horse and ran.

With an uplift of his heart that was almost pain, he rushed round the corner of the house to the vine-covered porch.

The door was shut. Stealthily he tiptoed across the porch

to knock. No answer! He tried the door. Locked! A quiver ran through him.

"Strange," he muttered, "not home this early."

He peered through the window, to see on floor and table ample evidence of recent packing. That gave check to a creeping blankness which was benumbing Pan. He went on to look into his mother's bedroom. The bed looked as if it had been used during the night and had not been made up. Perhaps his mother and Lucy had gone into Marco to purchase necessities.

"But—didn't I tell Lucy not to go?" he queried, in bewilderment.

Resolutely he cast out doubtful speculations. There could hardly be anything wrong. He returned to the barn.

"Wal, I'll tell you," Blinky was holding forth blandly, "this heah grubbin' around without a home an' a woman ain't no good. I'm shore through. I'm agoin'—"

"Nobody home," interrupted Pan.

"Well, that's nothin' to make you pale round the gills," returned his father. "They're gone to town. Mother had a lot of buyin' to do."

"But I particularly told Lucy to stay here."

"S'pose you did," interposed Blinky. "Thet's nothin'. You don't expect this heah gurl to mind you."

"No time for joking, Blink," said Pan curtly. "It just doesn't set right on my chest. I've got to find Lucy pronto. But where to go!"

With a single step he reached his stirrup and swung into his saddle.

"Pan, Lucy an' the wife will be in one of the stores. Don't worry about them. Why, they did all our buyin'."

"I tell you I don't like it," snapped Pan. "It's not what I think, but what I feel. All the same, wherever they are it doesn't change our plans. I'll sure find them, and tell them we're packing to leave pronto. . . . Now, Dad, buy three wagons and teams, grain, grub, and whatever else we need for two weeks or more on the road. Soon as I find Lucy and Mother I'll meet you and help you with the buying."

"I ought to talk it over with Ma before I buy grub," replied his father, perplexedly scratching his head. "I wish they was home."

182

"Come on, Blink," called Pan, as he rode out.

Blinky joined him out in the road.

"Pard, I don't get your hunch, but I can see you're oneasy."

"I'm just loco, that's all," returned Pan, forcing himself. "It's—such—such a disappointment not to see—her. . . . Made me nervous. Makes me think how anything might happen. I never trusted Jim Blake. And Lucy is only a kid in years."

"Ahuh," said Blinky, quietly. "Reckon I savvy. You wouldn't feel thet way fer nothin'."

"Blink, I'm damn glad you're with me," rejoined Pan feelingly, turning to face his comrade. "No use to bluff with you. I wish to heaven I could say otherwise, but I'm afraid there's something wrong."

"Shore. Wal, we'll find out pronto," replied Blinky, with his cool hard spirit, "an' if there is, we'll damn soon make it right."

They rode rapidly until they reached the outskirts of town, when Blinky called Pan to a halt.

"Reckon you'd better not ride through Main Street," he said significantly.

They tied their horses behind a clump of trees between two deserted shacks. Pan removed his ragged chaps, more however to be freer of movement than because they were disreputable.

"Now, Blink, we'll know pronto if the town is friendly to us," he said seriously.

"Huh! I ain't carin' a whoop, but I'll gamble we could own the town. This fake minin', ranchin', hoss-dealin' Hardman was a hunk of bad cheese. Pard, are you goin' to deny you killed him? Fer shore they've been told thet."

"No. Wiggate can do the telling. All I want is to find Lucy and send her back home, then buy our outfit and rustle."

"Sounds pretty. But I begin to feel hunchy myself. Let's have a drink, Pan."

"We're not drinking, cowboy," retorted Pan.

"Ain't we? Excuse me. Shore I figgered a good stiff drink would help some. I tell you I've begun to get hunches."

"What kind?"

"No kind at all. Just feel that all's not goin' the way we hope. But it's your fault. It's the look you got. I'd hate to see you hurt deep, pard."

They passed the wagon shop where Pan's father had been employed, then a vacant lot on one side of the street and framed tents on the other. Presently they could see down the whole of Main Street. It presented the usual morning atmosphere and color, though Pan fancied there was more activity than usual. That might have been owing to the fact that both the incoming and outgoing stages were visible far up at the end of the street.

Pan strained his eyes at people near and far, seeking first some sign of Lucy, and secondly someone he could interrogate. Soon he would reach the first store. But before he got there he saw his mother emerge, dragging Bobby, who evidently wanted to stay. Then Alice followed. Both she and her mother were carrying bundles. Pan's heart made ready for a second and greater leap—in anticipation of Lucy's appearance. But she did not come.

"Hello, heah's your folks, pard, figgerin' from looks," said Blinky. "What a cute kid! . . . Look there!"

Pan, striding ahead of Blinky saw his mother turn white and reel as if about to faint. Pan got to her in time.

"Mother! Why, Mother," he cried, in mingled gladness and distress. "It's me. I'm all right. What'd you think? . . . Hello, Bobby, old dirty face . . . Alice, don't stare at me. I'm here in the flesh."

His mother clung to him with hands like steel. Her face and eyes were both terrible and wonderful to see. "Pan! Pan! You're alive? Oh, thank God! They told us you'd been shot."

"Me? Well, I guess not. I'm better than ever, and full of good news," went on Pan hurriedly. "Brace up, Mother. People are looking. There . . . Dad is out home. We've got a lot to do. Where's Lucy?"

"Oh, God—my son, my son!" cried Mrs. Smith, her eyes rolling.

"Hush!" burst out Pan, with a shock as if a blade had pierced his heart. He shook her not gently. *"Where* is Lucy?"

His mother seemed impelled by his spirit, and she wheeled to point up the street.

"Lucy! There—in that stage—leaving Marco!"

"For God's—sake!" gasped Pan. "What's this? Lucy! Where's she going?"

"Ask her yourself," she cried passionately.

Something terrible seemed to crash inside Pan. Catastrophe! It was here. His mother's dark eyes held love, pity, and passion, which last was not for him.

"Mother, go home at once," he said swiftly. "Tell Dad to rush buying those wagons. You and Alice pack. We shake the dust of this damned town. Don't worry. Lucy will leave with *us!*"

Then Pan broke into long springy strides, almost a run. Indeed Blinky had to run to keep up with him. "I told you, pard," said his comrade, huskily. "Hell to pay! —— —— the luck!"

Pan had only one conscious thought—to see Lucy. All else seemed damming behind flood gates.

People rushed into the street to get out of the way of the cowboys. Others stared and made gestures. Booted men on the porch of the Yellow Mine stamped noisily as they trooped to get inside. Voices of alarm and mirth rang out. Pan took only a fleeting glance into the wide doorway. He saw nothing, thought nothing. His stride quickened as he passed Black's store, where more men crowded to get inside.

"Save your—wind, pard," warned Blinky. You might—need it."

They reached the end of the street and across the wide square stood the outgoing stage, before the express office. There was no driver on the front seat. Smith, the agent, was emerging from the office with mailbags.

"Slow up, pard," whispered Blinky, at Pan's elbow.

Pan did as he was advised, though his stride still retained speed. Impossible to go slowly! There were passengers in the stagecoach. When Pan reached the middle of the street he saw the gleam of golden hair that he knew. Lucy! Her back was turned to him. And as he recognized her, realized he had found her, there burst forth in his mind a thundering clamor of questioning voices.

185

A few more strides took him round the stage. Men backed away from him. The door was open.

"Lucy!" he called, and his voice seemed to come piercingly from a far-off place.

She turned a strange face, but he knew her eyes, saw the swift transition, the darkening, widening. How white she turned! What was this? Agony in recognition! A swift unuttered blaze of joy that changed to terror. He saw her lips frame his name, but no sound came.

"Lucy!" he cried. "What does this mean? Where are you going?"

She could not speak. But under her pallor the red of shame began to burn. Pan saw it, and he recognized it. Mutely he gazed at the girl as her head slowly sank. Then he asked hoarsely: "What's it mean?"

"Pard, take a peep round heah," drawled Blinky in slow cool speech that seemed somehow to carry menace.

Pan wheeled. He had the shock of his life. He received it before his whirling thoughts recorded the reason. It was as if he had to look twice. Dick Hardman! Fashionably and wonderfully attired! Pan got no farther than sight of the frock coat, elaborate vest, flowing tie, and high hat. Then for a second he went blind.

When the red film cleared he saw Hardman pass him, saw the pallor of his cheek, the quivering of muscle, the strained protruding of his eye.

He got one foot on the stage step when Pan found release for his voice.

"Hardman!"

That halted the youth, as if it had been a rope, but he never turned his head. The shuffling of feet inside the coach hinted of more than restlessness. There was a scattering of men from behind Pan.

He leaped at Hardman and spun him round.

"Where are you going?"

"Frisco, if it's—any of your business," replied Hardman incoherently.

"Looks like I'll make it my business," returned Pan menacingly He could not be himself here. The shock had been too great. His mind seemed stultified.

186

"Hardman—do you mean—do you think—you're taking *her*—away?" queried Pan, as if strangling.

"Ha!" returned Hardman with an upfling of head, arrogant, vain for all his fear. "I know it. . . . She's my wife!"

16

❖

DESTRUCTION, death itself seemed to overthrow Panhandle Smith's intensity of life. He reeled on his feet. For a moment all seemed opaque, with blurred images. There was a crash, crash, crash of something beating at his ears.

How long this terrible oblivion possessed Pan he did not know. But at Hardman's move to enter the stage, he came back a million times more alive than ever he had been—possessed of devils.

With one powerful lunge he jerked Hardman back and flung him sprawling into the dust.

"There! Once more! . . ." cried Pan, panting. "Remember—the schoolhouse? That fight over Lucy Blake! Damn your skunk soul! . . . Get up, *if* you've got a gun!"

Hardman leaned on his hand. His high hat had rolled away. His broadcloth suit was covered with dust. But he did not note these details of his abasement. Like a craven thing fascinated by a snake he had his starting eyes fixed upon Pan, and his face was something no man could bear to see.

"Get up—*if* you've got a gun!" ordered Pan.

"I've no—gun—" he replied, in husky accents.

"Talk, then. Maybe I can keep from killing you."

"For God's sake—don't shoot me. I'll tell you anything."

"Hardman, you say you—you *married* my—this girl?" rasped out Pan, choking over his words as if they were poison, unable to speak of Lucy as he had thought of her all his life.

187

"Yes—I married her."

"*Who* married you?"

"A parson from Salt Lake. Matthews got him here."

"Ah-huh!—Matthews. *How* did you force her?"

"I swear to God she was willing," went on Hardman. "Her father wanted her to."

"What? Jim Blake left here for Arizona. I sent him away."

"But he never went—I—I mean he got caught—put in jail again. Matthews sent for the officers. They came. And they said they'd put Blake away for ten years. But I got him off . . . Then Lucy was willing to marry me—and she did. There's no help for it now . . . too late."

"*Liar!*" hissed Pan. "You frightened her—tortured her."

"No, I—I didn't do anything. It was her father. He persuaded her."

"Drove her, you mean. And you paid him. Admit it or I'll—" Pan's move was threatening.

"Yes—yes, I did," jerked out Hardman in a hoarser, lower voice. Something about his lifelong foe appalled him. He was abject. No confession of his guilt was needed.

"Go get yourself a gun. You'll have to kill me before you start out on your honeymoon. Reckon I think you're going to hell. . . . Get up. . . . Go get yourself a gun. . . ."

Hardman staggered to his feet, brushing the dirt from his person while he gazed strickenly at Pan.

"My God, I can't fight you," he said. "You won't murder me in cold blood . . . Smith, I'm Lucy's husband . . . She's my wife."

"And what is Louise Melliss?" whipped out Pan. "What does *she* say about your marriage? You ruined her. You brought her here to Marco. You tired of her. You abandoned her to that hellhole owned by your father. He got his just deserts and you'll get yours."

Hardman had no answer. Like a dog under the lash he cringed at Pan's words.

"Get out of my sight," cried Pan, at the end of his endurance. "And remember the next time I see you, I'll begin to shoot."

Pan struck him, shoved him out into the street. Hardman staggered on, forgetting his high hat that lay in the dust. He got to going faster until he broke into an uneven half-run. He kept to the middle of the street until he reached the Yellow Mine, where he ran up the steps and disappeared.

Pan backed slowly, step by step. He was coming out of his clamped obsession. His movement was now that of a man gripped by terror. In reality Pan could have faced any peril, any horror, any physical rending of flesh far more easily than this girl who had ruined him.

She had left the stage and she stood alone. She spoke his name. In the single low word he divined fear. How long had she been that dog's wife? When had she married him? Yesterday, or the day before—a week, what did it matter?

"You—you!" he burst out helplessly in the grip of deadly hate and agony. He hated her then—hated her beauty—and the betrayal of her fear for him. What was life to him now? Oh, the insupportable bitterness!

"Go back to my mother," he ordered harshly, and averted his face.

Then he seemed to forget her. He saw Blinky close to him, deeply shaken, yet composed and grim. He heard the movement of many feet, the stamping of hoofs.

"All aboard for Salt Lake," called the stage driver. Smith the agent passed Pan with more mailbags. The strain all about him had broken.

"Pard," Pan said, laying a hand on Blinky. "Go with her—take her to my mother. . . . And leave me alone."

"No, by Gawd!" replied Blinky sullenly. "You forget this heah is my deal too. There's Louise. . . . An' Lucy took her bag an' hurried away. There, she's runnin' past the Yellow Mine."

"Blink, did she hear what I said to Hardman about Louise?" asked Pan bitterly.

"Reckon not. She'd keeled over aboot then. I shore kept my eye on her. An' I tell you, pard—"

"Never mind," interrupted Pan. "What's the difference? Hell's fire! Whisky! Let's get a drink. It's whisky I want."

"Shore. I told you thet a while back. Come on, pard. It's red-eye fer us!"

They crossed to the corner saloon, a low dive kept by a Chinaman and frequented by Mexicans and Indians. These poured out pellmell as the cowboys jangled up to the bar.

Jard Hardman's outfit coming to town had prepared the way for this.

"Howdy," was Blinky's greeting to the black bottle that was thumped upon the counter. "You look mighty natural . . . heah's to Panhandle Smith!"

Pan drank. The fiery liquor burned down to meet and coalesce round the gnawing knot in his internals. It augmented while it soothed. It burned as it cooled. It inflamed, but did not intoxicate.

"Pard, heah's to the old Cimarron," said Blinky, as they drank again.

Pan had no response. Memory of the Cimarron only guided his flying mind over the ranges to Las Animas. They drank and drank. Blinky's tongue grew looser.

"Hold your tongue, damn you," said Pan.

"Imposshiblity. Lesh have another."

"One more then. You're drunk, cowboy."

"Me drunk? No shir, pard. I'm just tongue-tied. . . . Now, by Gawd, heah's to Louise Melliss!"

"I drink to that," flashed Pan, as he drained his glass.

The afternoon had waned. Matthews lay dead in the street. He lay in front of the Yellow Mine, from which he had been driven by men who would no longer stand the strain.

The street was deserted except for that black figure, lying face down with a gun in his right hand. His black sombrero lay flat. The wind had blown a high hat down the street until it had stopped near the sombrero. Those who peeped out from behind doors or from windows espied these sinister objects.

Pan had patrolled the street. He had made a house-to-house canvass, searching for Jim Blake. He had entered every place except the Yellow Mine. That he reserved for the last. But he did not find Blake. He encountered, however, a slight pale man in clerical garb.

"Are you the parson Matthews brought to Marco?" demanded Pan harshly.

"Yes, sir," came the reply.

"Did you marry young Hardman to—to—" Pan could not end the query.

The minister likewise found speech difficult, but his affirmative was not necessary.

"Man, you may be innocent of evil intent. But you've ruined my—girl . . . and me! You've sent me to hell, I ought to kill you."

"Pard, shore we mushn't kill thish heah parson just yet," drawled Blinky, thickly. "He'll come in handy."

"Ahuh! Right you are, Blinky," returned Pan, with a ghastly pretense of gaiety. "Parson, stay right here till we come for you. Maybe you can make up a little for the wrong you did one girl."

The Yellow Mine stood with glass uplifted and card unplayed.

Pan had entered from the dance hall entrance. Blinky, unsteady on his feet, came in from the street. After a tense moment the poker players went on with their game, and the drinkers emptied their glasses. But voices were low, glances were furtive.

Pan had seen every man there before he had been seen himself. Only one interested him—that was Jim Blake. What to do to this man or with him Pan found it hard to decide. Blake had indeed fallen low. But Pan gave him the benefit of one doubt—that he had been wholly dominated by Hardman. Yet there was the matter of accepting money for his part in forcing Lucy to marry Dick.

The nearer end of the bar had almost imperceptibly been vacated by drinkers sliding down toward the other rear end. Pan took the foremost end of the vacated position. He called for a drink. As fast as he had drunk, the fiery effects had as swiftly passed away. Yet each drink for the moment kept up that unnatural stimulus.

Pan beckoned for Blinky. That worthy caused a stir, then a silence, by going round about the tables, so as not to come between Pan and any men there.

"Blink, do you know where Louise's room is?" queried Pan.

"Shore. Down thish hall—third door on left," replied Blinky.

"Well, you go over there to Blake and tell him I want to talk to him. Then you go to Louise's room. I'll follow directly."

191

Blake received the message, but he did not act promptly. Pan caught his suspicious eye, baleful, gleaming. Possibly the man was worse than weak. Presently he left the poker game which he had been watching and shuffled up to Pan. He appeared to be enough under the influence of liquor to be leeringly bold.

"Howdy," he said.

"Blake, today I got from Hardman the truth about the deal you gave me and Lucy," returned Pan, and then in cold deliberate tones he called the man every infamous name known to the ranges. Under this onslaught, Blake sank into something akin to abasement.

"Reckon you think," concluded Pan, "that because you're Lucy's father I can't take a shot at you. Don't fool yourself. You've killed her soul—and mine. So why shouldn't I kill you? . . . Well, there isn't any reason except that away from Hardman's influence you might brace up. I'll take the chance. You're done in Marco. Jard Hardman is dead and Dick's chances of seeing the sun rise are damn thin. . . . Now you rustle out that door and out of Marco. When you make a man of yourself come to Siccane, Arizona."

Blake lurched himself erect, and met Pan's glance with astonished bewildered eyes; then he wheeled to march out of the saloon.

Pan turned into the hallway leading into the hotel part of the building, and soon encountered Blinky leaning against the wall.

"Blink, isn't she in?" asked Pan, low voiced and eager.

"Shore, but she won't open the door," replied Blinky dejectedly.

Pan knocked and called low: "Louise, let us in."

There was a long wait, then came a low voice: "No."

"Please, it's very important."

"Who are you?"

"It's Panhandle Smith," replied Pan.

"That cowboy's drunk and I—no—I'm sorry."

"Louise, I'm not drunk, but I am in bad temper. I ask as a friend. Don't cross me here. I can easy shove in this door."

He heard soft steps. a breathless exclamation, then a key turned in the lock, and the door opened. The lamplight was not bright, Louise stood there half dressed, her bare arms and bosom gleaming. Pan entered, dragging Blinky with him, and closed the door all but tight.

"Louise, it wasn't kind of you to do that," said Pan reproachfully. "Have you any better friends than Blinky or me?"

"God knows—I haven't," faltered the girl. "But I've been ill—in bed—and am just getting out. I—I—heard about you—today—and Blink being with you—drunk."

Pan stepped to the red-shaped lamp on a small table beside the bed, and turned up the light. The room had more comfort and color than any Pan had seen for many a day.

He bent searching eyes upon Louise. She did look ill——white, with great dark shadows under her eyes, but she seemed really beautiful. What a tragic face it was, betrayed now by lack of paint! Pan had never seen her like this. If he had needed it, this would have warmed his heart to her.

"What do you want of me?" she asked, with a nervous twisting of hands she tried to hide.

Pan took her hands and pulled her a little toward him.

"Louise, you like me, don't you, as a friend or brother?" he asked gently.

"Yes, when I'm sober," she replied wanly.

"And you like Blinky, here, don't you—like him a lot?"

"I did. I couldn't help it, the damn faithful little cowboy," she returned. "But I hate him when he's drunk, and he hates me when I'm drunk."

"Blink, go out and fetch back a bottle—presently. We'll all get drunk."

The cowboy stared like a solemn owl, then very quietly went out.

"Louise, put something over your shoulders. You'll catch cold. Here," said Pan and he picked a robe off the bed and wrapped it round her. "I didn't know you were so pretty. No wonder poor Blink worships you."

She drew away from him and sat upon the bed, dark eyes questioning, suspicious. Yet she seemed fascinated. Pan caught a slight quivering of her frame. Where was the audacity, the boldness of this girl? But he did not know her, and he had her word that drink alone enabled her to carry on. He had surprised her. Yet could that account for something different, something quite beyond his power to grasp? Surely this girl could not fear him. Suddenly he remembered that Hardman had fled to this house—was hidden there now. Pan's nerves tautened.

"Louise," he began, taking her hand again, and launching directly into the reason for this interview he had sought, "we've had a great drive. Blink and I have had luck. Oh, such luck! We sold over fifteen hundred horses. . . . Well, we're going to Arizona, to a sunny open country, not like this. . . . Now Blink and I want you to go with us."

"What! Go away with you? How, in God's name?" she gasped in utter amaze.

"Why, as Blink's wife, of course. And I'll be your big brother," replied Pan, not without agitation. It was a pregnant moment. She stared a second, white and still, with great solemn searching eyes on his. Pan felt strangely embarrassed, yet somehow happy that he had dared to approach her with such a proposition.

Suddenly she kissed him, she clung to him, she buried her face on his shoulder and he heard her murmur incoherently something about "honest-to-God men."

"What do you say, little girl?" he went on. "It's a chance for you to be good again. It'll save that wild cowboy, who never had a decent ambition till he met you. He loves you. He worships you. He hates what you have to suffer here. He—"

"So this is Panhandle Smith?" she interrupted, looking up at him with eyes like dark stars. "No! No! No! I wouldn't degrade even a worthless cowboy."

"You're wrong. He'll *not* be worthless, if you repay his faith. Louise, don't turn your back on hope, on love, on a home."

"No!" she flashed, passionately.

"Why?" he returned, in sharp appeal.

"Because he's too good for me. Because I don't deserve your friendship. But so help me God I'll love you both all the rest of my miserable life—which won't be long."

He took her in his arms, as if to add force to argument. "But, you poor child, this is no place for you. You'll only go to hell—commit suicide or be killed in a drunken brawl."

"Panhandle, I may end even worse," she replied, in bitter

mockery. "I might marry Dick Hardman. He talks of it—when he's drunk."

Pan released her, and leaned back to see her face. "*Marry* you! Dick Hardman talks of that?" he burst out incredulously.

"Yes, he does. And I might let him when I'm drunk. I'd do anything then."

At that moment the door opened noiselessly and Blinky entered carrying a bottle and glasses.

"Good, Blink, old pard," said Pan, breathing heavily. "Louise and I have just made up our minds to get drunk together. Blink, you stay sober."

"I cain't stay what I ain't," retorted Blinky. "An' I won't stay heah, either, to see her drink. I hate her then."

She poured the dark red liquor out into the glasses. "Boy, I want you to hate me. I'll make you hate me . . . Here's to Panhandle Smith!"

While she drank Blinky moved backwards to the door, eyes glinting brightly into Pan's and then he was gone.

In the mood under which Pan labored, liquor had no effect upon him but to act as fire to body and mind. The girl, however, was transformed into another creature. Bright red spots glowed in her cheeks, her eyes danced and dilated, her whole body answered to the stimulus. One drink led to another. She could not resist the insidious appetite thus created. She did not see whether Pan drank or not. She grew funny, then sentimental, and finally lost herself in that stage of unnatural abandon for which, when sober, she frankly confessed she drank.

Pan decided that presently he would wrap a blanket around her, pick her up and pack her out. Blinky would shoot out the lights in the saloon, and the rest would be easy. If she knew that Hardman was in the house, as Pan had suspected, she had now no memory of it.

"You big handsome devil," she called Pan. "I told you—to keep away from me."

"Louise, don't make love to me," replied Pan.

"Why not? Men are all alike."

"No, you're wrong. You forget what you said a little while ago. I've lost my sweetheart, and my heart is broken."

She leered at him, and offered him another drink. Pan

took the glass away from her. It was possible he might over-
do his part.

"So you're liable to marry young Hardman?" he asked
deliberately.

The question, the name, gave her pause, as if they had
startled her memory.

"Sure I am."

"But, Louise, how can you marry Hardman when he
already has a wife?" asked Pan.

She grasped that import only slowly, by degrees.

"You lie, you gun-slinging cowboy!" she cried.

"No, Louise. He told me so himself."

"He did! . . . When?" she whispered, very low.

"Today. He was at the stage office. He meant to leave today. He was all togged up, frock coat, high hat. . . . Oh,
God—Louise, I know, I *know*, because it—was—my—
sweetheart—he married."

Pan ended gaspingly. What agony to speak that
aloud—to make his own soul hear that aloud!

"*Your* sweetheart? . . . Little Lucy—of your
boyhood—you told me about?"

Pan was confronted now by something terrible. He had
sought to make this girl betray herself, if she had anything to
betray. But this Medusa face! Those awful eyes!

"Yes, Lucy, I told you," he said, reaching for her. "He
forced her to marry him. They had Lucy's father in jail.
Dick got him out. Oh, it was all a scheme to work on the
poor girl. She thought it was to save her father. . . . Why,
Dick paid her father. I made him tell me . . . yes, Dick
Hardman in his frock coat and high hat! But when I drove
him out to get his gun, he forgot that high hat."

"Ah! His high hat!"

"Yes, it's out in the street now. The wind blew it over
where I killed Matthews. Funny! . . . And Louise, I'm going
to kill Dick Hardman, too."

"Like hell you are!" she hissed, and leaped swiftly to
snatch something from under the pillow.

Pan started back, thinking that she meant to attack him.
How tigerishly she bounded! Her white arm swept aside red
curtains. They hid a shallow closet. It seemed her white
shape flashed in and out. A hard choking gasp! Could that

196

have come from her? Pan did not see her drawn lips move. Something hard dropped to the floor with metallic sound.

The hall door opened with a single sweep. Blinky stood framed there, wild eyed. And the next instant Dick Hardman staggered from that closet. He had both hands pressed to his abdomen. Blood poured out in a stream. Pan heard strange watery sounds. Hardman reeled out into the hall, groaning. He slipped along the wall. Pan leaped, to see him slide down into a widening pool of blood.

It was a paralyzing moment. But Pan recovered first. The girl swayed with naked arms outstretched against the wall. On her white wrist showed a crimson blot. Pan looked no more. Snatching a blanket off the bed he threw it round her, wrapped it tight, and lifted her in his arms.

"Blink, go ahead," he whispered, as he went into the hall. "Hurry! Shoot out the lights! Go through the dance hall!"

The cowboy seemed galvanized into action. He leaped over Hardman's body, huddled and lax, and down the hall, pulling his guns.

Pan edged round the body on the floor. He saw a ghastly face—protruding eyes. And on the instant, like lightning, came the thought that Lucy was free. Almost immediately thundering shots filled the saloon. Crash! Crash! Crash! The lights faded, darkened, went out. Yells and scraping chairs and overturned tables, breaking glass, pounding boots merged in a pandemonium of sound.

Pan hurried through the dance hall, where the windows gave dim light, found the doorway, gained the side entrance to the street. Blinky waited there, smoking guns in his hands.

"Heah—this—way," he directed in a panting whisper, as he sheathed the guns, and took the lead. Pan followed in the shadow of the houses.

17

◆

THE street down that way was dark, with but few lights showing. Blinky kept looking back in the direction of the slowly subsiding tumult. Pan carried Louise at rapid pace, as if she made no burden at all. In the middle of the next block Blinky slowed up, carefully scrutinizing the entrances to the buildings. They came to an open hallway, dimly lighted. Pan read a sign he remembered. This was the lodging house.

"Go in, Blink," directed Pan quickly. "If you find our parson chase everybody but him and call me pronto."

Blinky ran into the place. Pan let Louise down on her feet. She could not stand alone.

"Cowboy—smozzer me," she giggled, pulling at the fold of blanket round her face.

Pan rearranged the blanket over her bare shoulders, and folded it round more like a coat. He feared she might collapse before they could accomplish their design. The plight of this girl struck deeply into his heart.

"Whaz—mazzer, cowboy?" she asked. "Somebody's raid us?"

"Hush, Louie," whispered Pan shaking her. "There'll be a gang after us."

"Hell with gang. . . . Shay, Pan, whaz become of Dick?"

She was so drunk she did not remember. Pan thanked God for that. How white the tragic face. Her big eyes resembled bottomless gulfs. Her hair hung disheveled round her.

A low whistle made Pan jump. Blinky stood inside in a

flare of light from an open door. He beckoned. Pan lifted the girl and carried her in.

Five minutes later they came out, one on each side of Louise, trying to keep her quiet. She was gay, maudlin. But once outside again, the rush of cold mountain air aided them. They hurried down the dark street, almost carrying the girl between them. A few people passed, fortunately on the other side. These pedestrians were hurrying in the other direction. Some excitement uptown, Pan thought grimly! Soon they passed the outskirts of Marco and gained the open country. Pan cast off what seemed a weight of responsibility for Blinky and Louise. Once he got them out of town they were safe.

Suddenly Blinky reached behind the girl and gave Pan a punch. Turning, Pan saw his comrade point back. A dull red flare lighted up the sky. Fire! Pan's heart gave a leap. The Yellow Mine was burning. The crowd of drinkers and gamblers had fled before Blinky's guns. Pan was hoping that only he and Blinky would ever know who had killed Dick Hardman.

From time to time Pan glanced back over his shoulder. The flare of red light grew brighter and higher. One corner of Marco would surely be wiped out.

The road curved. Soon a dark patch of trees, and a flickering light, told Pan they had reached his father's place. It gave him a shock. He had forgotten his parents. They entered the lane and cut off through the dew-wet grass of the orchard to the barn. Pan caught the round pale gleam of canvas-covered wagons.

"Good! Dad sure rustled," said Pan with satisfaction. "If he got the horses, too, we can leave tomorrow."

"Shore, we will anyhow," replied Blinky, who was now sober and serious.

They found three large wagons and one smaller, with a square canvas top.

"Blink, hold her, till I get some hay," said Pan.

He hurried into the open side of the barn. It was fairly dark but he knew where to go. He heard horses munching grain. That meant his father had bought the teams. Pan got

199

an armful of hay, and carrying it out to the wagon, he threw it in, and spread it out for a bed.

"Reckon we'd better put Louise here," said Pan, stepping down off the wheel. "I'll get some blankets from Dad."

Blinky was standing there in the starlight holding the girl in his arms. His head was bowed over her wan face.

They lifted Louise into the wagon and laid her down upon the hay.

"Whish you—gennelmanz my hushband?" she asked thickly.

Pan had to laugh at that, but Blinky stood gazing intently down upon the pale gleam of face. Pan left him there and strode toward the house. Though the distance was short, he ran the whole gamut of emotions before he stopped at a lighted window. He heard his father's voice.

"Dad," he called, tapping on the window. Then he saw his mother and Alice. They had started up from packing. One glance at the suffering expressed in his mother's face was enough to steady Pan. The door opened with a jerk.

"That you—Pan?" called his father, with agitation.

"Nobody else, Dad," replied Pan, trying to calm his voice. "Tell Mother I'm here safe and sound."

His mother heard and answered with a low cry of relief.

"Dad, come out. . . . Shut the door," returned Pan sharply.

Once outside his father saw the great flare of light above the town.

"Look! What's that? Must be fire!" he burst out.

"Reckon it is fire," returned Pan shortly. "Blinky shot out the lamps in the Yellow Mine. Fire must have caught from that."

"Yellow Mine!" echoed Smith, staring in momentary stupefaction.

Pan laid a heavy hand on him. It was involuntary, an expression of a sudden passion rising in Pan. He had a question to put that almost stifled him.

"Lucy! . . . Did she—come home?" he forced out.

"Sure. Didn't you know? She was home when I got here at noon. Son, I bought all our outfit in no time."

"What did Lucy tell you?"

"Nothin' much," replied his father, in earnest wonder.

200

"She was in an awful state. Said she couldn't go because you were *not* dead . . . poor girl! She had hysterics. But Mother got her quieted down by suppertime."

"Where is she now?"

"In bed, I reckon. Leastways she's in her room."

"Dad, does she know? But of course she couldn't . . . nor could you!"

"Son, I know aplenty," replied his father, solemnly. "Lucy told Mother when she saw you come to the stagecoach that it nearly killed her. They believed you dead—Mother an' Lucy. . . . She told how you threw Hardman out of the stage on to the street. Said she almost fainted then. But she came to in time to see you kick him—drive him off."

"Is that all she knows?" queried Pan.

"Reckon it is. I know more, but I didn't tell her," replied Smith, lowering his voice to a whisper. "I heard about them drivin' Matthews out to meet you. . . . McCormick told me you hadn't lost any friends."

"Ah-huh!" ejaculated Pan somberly. "Well, better tell Lucy at once. . . . Reckon that's best—the sooner the better."

"Tell Lucy what?" asked Smith anxiously.

"That she's a widow."

"It—is Dick Hardman dead—too?" gasped out Smith.

"Yes."

"My God! Son—did—did you—"

"Dad, I didn't kill him," interrupted Pan. "Dick Hardman was—was knocked out—just before Blinky shot out the lights. Reckon it's a good bet no one will ever know. He sure was burned up in that fire."

"*Alive?*" whispered Smith.

"He might still have been alive, but he was far gone—unconscious when I passed him in the hall. You needn't tell Lucy that. Just tell her Hardman is dead and that *I* didn't kill him."

"All right, I'll go right an' do it," replied his father huskily.

"Before you do it fetch me a roll of blankets. We haven't any beds. And Blinky's wife is with us."

201

"Wife? I didn't know Blinky had one. Fetch her in. We'll make room somewhere."

"No, we've already fixed a place for her in that wagon with the square top," went on Pan. "She's been sick. Rustle, Dad. Fetch me the blankets."

"Got them right inside. We bought new ones," said Smith, opening the door to hurry in.

"Mother," called Pan, "everything's all right. We'll be leaving early tomorrow."

Then his father reappeared with a roll of blankets. Pan found Blinky exactly as he had left him, leaning over the wagon.

"Blink, put a couple of these blankets over her," directed Pan.

"She went right off, asleep, like she was daid," whispered the cowboy, and he took the blankets and stepped up on the wheel hub to lay the blankets softly over the quiet form Pan saw dimly in the starlight.

"Come here, cowboy," called Pan.

And when Blinky got down and approached, Pan laid hold of him with powerful hand.

"Listen, pard," he began, in low voice. "We're playing a deep game, and by God, it's an honest game, even though we have to lie. . . . Louise will never remember she cut that traitor's heart out. She was too crazy. If it half returns to her we'll lie—you understand—*lie*. . . . Nobody will ever know who did kill Hardman, I'll gamble. I intended to, and all Marco must have known that. If he burned up they can't ever be sure. Anyway, that doesn't matter. It's our women folks we've got to think of. I told Dad you'd brought your wife—that she'd been sick. He'll tell Mother and Lucy. They don't know, and they never will know what kind of a girl Louise has been. . . . Savvy, pard?"

"Reckon I do," replied Blinky, in hoarse trembling accents. "But won't we have hell with Louise—when she wakes up sober?"

"Cowboy, you bet we will," returned Pan grimly "But we'll be far on our way when she wakes up. You can drive this wagon. We'll keep watch on her. And, well—leave it to me, Blink."

"Pan, we feel the same aboot Louie? Shore I don't mean thet you love her. Reckon it's hard fer me to find words."

"I understand, Blink," replied Pan, earnestly, hoping to dispel the groping and doubt of his comrade's soul. "For you and me Louie's past is dead. We're gambling on life. And whatever way you put it, whatever the future brings, we're better for what happened tonight."

Pan strode off in the starlight, across the orchard, down along the murmuring stream to the cottonwood tree with the bench.

It was useless for him to try to sleep. To and fro he paced in the starlight. Alone now, with the urgent activities past for the time, he reverted to the grim and hateful introspection that had haunted his mind.

This once, however, the sinister strife in his soul, that strange icy clutch on his senses—the aftermath of instinctive horror following the death of a man by his hand—wore away before the mounting of a passion that had only waited.

It did not leap upon him unawares, like an enemy out of ambush. It grew as he walked, as his whirling thoughts straightened in a single line to—Lucy. She had betrayed him. She had broken his heart. What if she had thought him dead—sacrificed herself to save her father?—She had given herself to that dog Hardman. The thought was insupportable. "I hate her," he whispered. "She's made me hate her."

The hours passed, the stars moved across the heavens, the night wind ceased, the crickets grew silent, and the murmuring stream flowed on at Pan's feet. Spent and beaten he sat upon the bench. His love for Lucy had not been killed. It lived, it had grown, it was tremendous—and both pity and reason clamored that he be above jealousy and hate. After all there was excuse for Lucy. She was young, she had been driven by grief over his supposed death and fear for her father. But oh! The pity of it—of this hard truth against the sweetness and purity of his dream! Life and love were not what he had dreamed them as he had ridden the lonely ranges. He must suffer because he had left Lucy to fight her battles.

203

"I'll try to forget," he whispered huskily. "I've got to. But not yet. I can't do it yet. . . . We'll leave this country far behind. And some day we can go on with—with all we planned."

Pan went back to the barn and threw himself upon the hay, where exhausted brain and body sank to sleep and rest. It seemed that a voice and a rude hand tore away the sweet oblivion.

"Pard, are you daid?" came Blinky's voice, keen and full with newer note. "Sunup an' time to rustle. Your dad's heah an' he says breakfast is waitin'."

Pan rose and stretched. His muscles ached as though he had been beaten. How bright the sun! Night was gone and with it something dreadful.

"Pan, shore you're a tough-lookin' cowboy this mawnin'," said Blinky. "Wash an' shave yourself like I did. Heah's my razor. There's a basin an' water up under the kitchen porch."

"Howdy, bridegroom," returned Pan with appreciative eyes on Blinky's shiny face and slick hair. "How's your wife?"

"Daid to the world," whispered Blinky, blushing red as a rose. "I took a peep. Gee! Pard, I hope she sleeps all day an' all night. Shore I'm scared fer her to wake."

"I don't blame you, cowboy. It'll be funny when she finds out she's got a boss."

"Pard, if we was away from this heah town I'd be happy, I swear. Wouldn't you?" returned Blinky shyly.

"Why, Blink, I believe I would," said Pan, and strode off toward the house.

He made himself presentable before anyone saw him. Then he waited for his father and Blinky, whom he heard talking. When they came up he joined them. Wild horses could not have dragged him into the house alone. As they entered the kitchen Bobby let out a yell and made for him. That loosened a strain for Pan and he picked up the lad. When he faced his mother it was with composure that belied the state of his feelings. She appeared to be in a blaze of excitement, and at once he realized that all she had needed was his return, safe and sound. Then he heard Alice's voice and Lucy's in reply. As he set Bobby down, thrilling all over, the girls entered the kitchen. Alice's reply to his greeting was at once bright and shy. Lucy halted in the doorway, with a hand on her breast. Her smile, slow and wistful, seemed to blot out traces of havoc in her face. But her eyes were dark purple, a sign of strong emotion. Pan's slight inclination, unaccompanied by word of greeting, was as black a pretense as he had ever been guilty of. Sight of her had shot him through and through with pangs of bitter mocking joy. But he gave no sign. During the meal he did not look at her again.

"Dad, have you got everything we'll need?" queried Pan presently.

"I guess so," replied Smith. "You can start loadin' the wagons. An' by the time two of them are done we'll have everythin' packed."

"Blink can drive one wagon, you another, and I'll take the third till we get out to Snyder's. Then we'll need another driver, for it'll take two of us to handle the wild horses."

"No, we won't," replied his father. "Your mother an' Lucy can drive as well as I. Son, I reckon we don't want anybody except our own outfit."

"I'd like that myself," admitted Pan thoughtfully. "If you've got good gentle teams maybe Mother an' Lucy can take turns. We'll try it, anyhow."

"I'll help you hitch up," said Smith, following Pan out. "Son, do you look for any trouble this mornin'?"

"Lord no. I'm not looking for trouble," replied Pan. "I've sure had enough."

"Huh!" ejaculated Blinky. "Your dad means any backfire from Marco. Wal, I say there'll be nothin'. All the same we want to move pronto."

"I'd like to hear what happened after we left," said Pan.

"Somebody will tell us," returned Smith.

They had reached the end of the arbor when Lucy's voice called after them: "Pan—please wait."

He turned to see her coming, twisting her apron in nervous hands. Pan's father and Blinky kept on toward the barn. Lucy came hurriedly, unevenly, pale, with parted lips, and eyes that held him.

"Mother said you knew but—I must tell you—myself,"

she said brokenly, as she halted close to him. "Day before yesterday—those men brought word you'd been—killed in a fight over wild horses. It broke my heart. . . . I'd have taken my own life but for my father. I didn't care what happened. . . . Dick pressed me hard. Father begged me to save him from prison. . . . So I—I married Dick."

"Yes, I know—I figured it out that way," returned Pan in strange thick utterance. "You didn't need to tell me."

"Why, Pan, you—you seem *different*," she said, as if bewildered. "Your look—your voice . . . oh, dear. I know yesterday was awful. It must have driven you mad."

"By heaven, it did!" muttered Pan under his breath.

"But you—you forgive me?" she faltered, reaching to touch him with a shaking hand. The gesture, so supplicating, so tender, the dark soft hunger of her eyes, the sweetness of her then roused a tumult in him. How could she look at him like that? How dared she have such love light in her eyes?

"Forgive you for—" he cried in fierce passion. But he could not put into words what she had done. "I meant to kill that dog, Dick Hardman. But I didn't. . . . Forgive you—" he broke off, unable to go on.

She was slow to grasp his intimation, though not his fury. Suddenly her eyes dilated in horror. Then a great wave of scarlet blood swept over her white neck and face. Pan saw in it the emblem of her shame. With a rending of his heart he swung away and left her.

He plunged into the work at hand, and during the next couple of hours recovered from the shock of resisting Lucy's appeal. He hated himself for the passion he could not subdue. When, however, it had slunk away for the time being, he began to wonder at her innocence and simplicity. He could not understand her.

Presently his father and Blinky hunted him up with news of strong purport plain in their faces.

"Son, Marco is with you to a man!"

"Pard, I guess mebbe I didn't hev them hombres figgered?"

"What happened? Out with it," replied Pan sharply.

"Evans drove out bringin' stuff I bought yesterday," returned his father. "He was full as a tick of news. By some miracle, only the Yellow Mine burned. It was gutted, but the bucket brigade saved the houses on each side. . . . Hardman's body was found burned to a crisp. It was identified by a ring. An' his dance-hall girl was found dead too, burned most as bad as he. . . . Accordin' to Evans most everybody in Marco wants to shake hands with Panhandle Smith."

The covered wagons wound slowly down the hill toward Snyder's pasture. Pan, leading Blink's horse, held to the rear. The day, in some respects, had been as torturing to him as yesterday—but with Marco far behind and the open road ahead, calling, beckoning, the strain began to lessen.

At the pasture gate the drivers halted the wagon teams, waiting for Pan to come up. Gus had opened the wide-barred gate, and now stood there with a grin of relief and gladness.

"Drive in," shouted Pan from behind. "We'll camp here tonight."

"Howdy thar, you ole wild-hoss night wrangler," yelled Blinky to Gus.

"Howdy, yourself," was the reply. "You can bet your roll that I never expected to see you again. What'd you do to Marco?"

They drove in along the west fence, where a row of trees shaded the still hot sun.

"Gus, I see our wild horses are still keeping you company," remarked Pan, as he loosened the cinch of his saddle.

"Shore. But they ain't so wild no more. I've fooled around with them for two days now," replied Gus.

Pan smacked Sorrel on the flank: "There! Go take a look at your rival, Whitefoot." But the sorrel hung around camp. He had been spoiled by an occasional nose bag of grain. Pan lent a hand all around, and took note of the fact that Blinky lingered long around his wagon. Pan peeped over the wagon side. Louise lay on her side with face exposed. It was pale, with eyelids tight. In sleep her features betrayed how life had wronged her.

"Reckon you're wise, Blink, to keep your wagon away

from the others like this," said Pan. "Because when your wife wakes up there's liable to be hell. Call me pronto."

"Pard, you're shore she ain't in a stupor or somethin'?" queried Blinky, apprehensively.

"Blink, you know she was ill for ten days. Then she drank a lot. Reckon she's knocked out. But there's nothing to worry about, except she'll jump the traces when she comes to."

"You mean when she finds out—I—she—we're married?"

"That's what, Pard Blink. I wish you didn't have to tell her."

"Me? My Gawd, I cain't tell her," replied Blinky, in consternation. "Shore you gotta do that."

"All right, Blink. I'll save what little hair you have left," returned Pan, good humoredly.

He walked out to take a look at the horses, which were scattered on the far side of the pasture. They could not be closely approached, yet were not nearly so wild as he had expected them to be. The saddle and wagon horses grazed among them. The blue roan looked vastly better for two days' rest. Whitefoot was a noble stallion. Sight of Little Bay brought keen pain to Pan. What boundless difference between his state of mind when he had caught that beautiful little horse and what it was now!

Pan went back to the campfire. Supper was in progress, with the capable Mrs. Smith bustling about. Lucy and Alice were assisting. Pan stole a glance at Lucy. Her face was flushed from the wind and sun; she wore a white apron; her sleeves were rolled up to show round strong arms. Bobby and his two puppies were much in the way.

"Pan, how is Mrs. Somers?" inquired his mother solicitously.

"Who?" queried Pan, puzzled.

"Why, your partner's wife."

"Oh, Blinky! . . . Gee, I'd clean forgot his right name," laughed Pan, mentally kicking himself. "She's still sound asleep. I told Blinky not to wake her. She looked white and worn out."

"But she'll starve," interposed Lucy, with questioning eyes on Pan. Indeed their meaning had no relation to her words. "You men don't know anything. Won't you let me wake her?"

"Thanks. Better let her alone till tomorrow," replied Pan briefly.

Presently there came the call to supper, which had been laid upon a new tarpaulin spread on the ground. The men flopped down, and sat crosslegged, each with silent or vociferous appreciation of that generous repast.

"Shades of the grub line!" ejaculated Blinky. "Am I ridin' or dreamin'?"

"Mother, this is heaven for a cowboy. And think, we'll be three weeks on the road," added Pan.

"But, son, our good things to eat won't last that long," she replied, much gratified by his compliment.

"Aw, the good Lord shore remembered me when he throwed me in with this outfit," declared the usually reticent Gus.

Pan observed that both Alice and his mother strictly avoided serving him with those things that had to be carried hot from the campfire. They let Lucy do it. Pan did not look up at her, and murmured his thanks in monosyllables. Once her hand touched his and the contact was like a galvanizing current. For the moment he could not go on eating.

During the sunset hour Pan helped grease the wagon wheels, something that had been neglected, and had retarded their progress. Other tasks used up the time until dark. Bobby got himself spanked by falling out of the wagon after he had been put to bed.

It was after nightfall when Pan heard Blinky's call. He hurried over to the wagon, where he found his comrade tremendously excited.

"Pard, she's waked up," he whispered.

Pan strode to the wagon. There was enough light for him to see the girl sitting up, with hands pressed to her head.

"Hello, Louie," he said gently.

"Where the hell am I?" she replied huskily, dropping her hands to stare at him.

"On the way to Arizona."

"Well, if it isn't handsome Panhandle . . . and Blinky!"

"Howdy—Louie," said Blinky fearfully.

"I've been drunk?" she queried.

"Reckon you have—a little," replied Pan.

"And you boys have kidnapped me?" she went on.

"I'm afraid that's so, Louie."

"Get me a drink. *Not* water! My head's bursting. And help me out of this haymow."

She threw aside the blanket that partially covered her and got to her knees. Pan lifted her out of the wagon. Then he ran off toward camp to get a flask. Upon returning he found Blinky trying to put a blanket round Louise's shoulders. She threw it off.

"Wait till I cool off," she said. "Panhandle, did you get it? I'm shaky, all right. . . . Thanks. Someday I'll take my last drink."

"Louie, I hope that will be soon," rejoined Pan.

"You know I hate whisky. . . . Oh, my head! And my legs are cramped. Let me walk a little."

Pan drew Blinky aside in the gloom. "She hasn't begun to think yet. Reckon you'd better stay away from her. Let her come back to the wagon."

"Pard, shore she took our kidnappin' her all right," whispered Blinky, hopefully.

"Blink, I'll bet a million she'll be glad—after it all comes out," responded Pan.

Presently Louise interrupted their whispered colloquy. "Help me up. I'm sick—and weak."

They lifted her back into the wagon and covered her. In the pale starlight her eyes looked unnaturally big and black.

"No use—to lie," she said drowsily, her head rolling. "I'm glad to leave—Marco. . . . Take me anywhere."

Then her eyes closed. Again Pan drew Blinky away into the gloom.

"It's the way I figured," whispered Pan swiftly. "She'll never remember what happened."

"Thank Gawd fer thet," breathed Blinky.

They found the campfire deserted except for Gus and Pan's father. Evidently Pan's advent interrupted a story that had been most exciting to Gus.

"Son, I—I was just tellin' Gus all I know about what come off yesterday," explained Smith, frankly, though with some haste. "But there are some points I'd sure like cleared up for myself."

Pan had expected this, and had fortified himself against the inevitable.

"Well, get it over then once and for all," he replied, not too civilly.

"You come damn near buttin' right into the weddin'!" ejaculated Smith, with a sense of what dramatic possibility had just been missed.

Pan, whose back had been turned to the campfire light, suddenly whirled as if on a pivot.

"What?" he cried. Then there seemed to be a cessation of all his faculties.

"Why, son, you needn't jump out of your boots," returned the father, somewhat offended. "Lucy was married to Hardman in the stage office just before you got there. Fact was, she'd just walked out to get in the stage when you came. . . . Now, I was only sayin' how funny it'd been if you got there sooner."

"Who—told—you—that?"

"Lucy told me. An' she said tonight she didn't believe you knew," returned his father.

There was a blank silence. Pan slowly turned away from the light.

"No. I had an idea—she'd been married—days," replied Pan in a queer strangled voice.

"You should have asked some questions," said Smith bluntly. "It was a damn unfortunate affair, but it mustn't be made worse for Lucy than it actually was. . . . She was Dick Hardman's wife for less than five minutes before you arrived."

Without another word Pan stalked away into the darkness. He heard his father say: "Bet that's what ailed him—the darned idiot!"

Pan gained the pasture fence under the dark trees, and he grasped it tightly as if his hold on life had been shaken. The shock of incredulous amaze passed away, leaving him in the grip of joy and gratitude and remorse. How vastly different was this vigil under the stars!

18

◇

IT was Pan who routed out the campers next morning when the first rose of dawn flushed the clear-cut horizon line.

He had the firewood collected, and the saddle horses in for their grain before Blinky presented himself. Wild eyed, indeed, was the cowboy.

"Pard," he whispered, huskily, dragging Pan aside some paces, "the cyclone's busted."

"Yes?" queried Pan in both mirth and concern.

"I was pullin' on my boots when Louise pokes her head above the wagon an' says: 'Hey, you bow-legged gurl snatcher, where's my clothes?'

"'What clothes?' I answers. An' she snaps out, 'Mine. Didn't you fetch my clothes?'

"'Louie,' I says, 'we shore forgot them an' they burned up with all the rest of the Yellow Mine. An' if you want to know, my dear, I'm darn glad of it.'

"Then, Pan, she began to cuss me, an' I jumps up mad, but right dignified an' says, 'Mrs. Somers, I'll require you to stop usin' profanity.'

"'Mrs. Somers!' she whispers, her eyes poppin'. 'Are you crazy?' An' I told her I shore wasn't crazy an' I shore was sober. An' thet my name wasn't Moran, but Somers.

"She gave a gasp an' fell back in the wagon. An' you bet I run fer you. Now, pard, for Gawd's sake, what'll I do?" finished Blinky with a groan.

"Cowboy, you've done noble," replied Pan in great satisfaction.

"Wha-at!—Say, Pan, you look queer this mawnin'. Sort

of shiny eyed an' light-footed. You don't look drunk or loco. So what ails you?"

"Blink, I'm as crazy as you," responded Pan, almost hugging his friend. "But don't worry another minute. I swear I can fix it up with Louise. I swear I can fix *anything.*"

With that, Pan strode across the dew-wet grass to the trees under which stood Blinky's wagon. There was no sign of the girl. Pan breasted the wagon side to look down. She was there, wide-eyed, with arms under her head, staring at the colored leaves.

"Morning, Louie, how are you?" he began cheerfully, smiling down upon her.

"I don't know," she replied.

"Well, you look better, that's sure."

"Pan, am I that cowboy's wife?" she queried gravely.

"Yes," he replied, just as gravely.

"Did he force me to marry him when I was drunk?"

" No. Blink is innocent of all except loving you, Louie," answered Pan, deliberately choosing his words. He had planned all he meant to say. Last night under the trees, in the dark, many truths had come to him. "It was *I* who forced you to marry him."

She covered her eyes with her hands and pressed hard as if to make clear her bewildering thoughts. "Oh, I—I can't remember."

"Louie, don't distress yourself," he said, soothingly. "You bet *I* can remember, and I'll tell you."

"Wait. I want to get up. But you forgot my clothes. I can't go round in a blanket."

"By golly, I never thought of that. But we didn't have much time. . . . See here, Louise, I can fix it. You're about the same height as Lucy. I'll borrow some of her clothes for you."

"Lucy?" she echoed, staring at him.

"Yes, Lucy," he replied, easily. "And while I'm at it, I'll fetch a basin of hot water—and everything."

Whereupon he hurried over to the campfire, where he found Mrs. Smith busy and cheerful. "Lucy up yet?" he asked briskly.

"Yes, Pan," she replied with hurried glad smile. "She's brushing her hair there, by the wagon."

Pan strode up to Lucy where she stood before the wagon, a mass of golden hair hanging down her back, to which she was vigorously applying a brush.

"Hello, Lucy," he said coolly.

"Oh—how you startled—me!" she exclaimed, turning with a blush.

"Say, wont you help us out?" he went on, not so coolly. "The other night, in the excitement we forgot to fetch Louise's clothes. . . . Fact is, we grabbed her up out of a sick bed, with only a dressing gown and a blanket. Won't you lend her some clothes, shoes, stockings—and—everything?"

"Indeed I will," responded Lucy and with alacrity she climbed into the covered wagon.

Pan waited, and presently began to pace to and fro. He was restless, eager, buoyant. He could not stand still. His thoughts whirled away from the issue at hand, back to Lucy and the glory that had been restored to him.

"Here, Pan," called Lucy, reappearing with a large bundle. "Here's all she'll need, I think. Lucky I bought some new things. Alice and I can get along with one mirror, brush and comb."

"Thanks," he said. "It was lucky. . . . Sure our luck has changed."

"Don't forget some warm water," added Lucy practically, calling after him.

Thus burdened, Pan hurried back to Louise's wagon and deposited the basin on the seat, and the bundle beside her. "There you are, pioneer girl," he said cheerily, and with swift hands he let down the canvas curtains of the wagon, shutting her in.

"Come on, Blink," he called to the cowboy watching from behind the trees. "Let's wrangle the teams."

"Gus an' your dad are comin' in with them now," replied Blinky, joining him and presently, when they got away from the wagon he whispered: "How aboot it?"

"Blink, I swear it'll go through fine," declared Pan earnestly. "She knows she's your wife—that I got her drunk and forced her into it. She doesn't remember. I'm hoping she'll not remember anything, but even if she does I'll fix it."

"Shore—you're Panhandle Smith—all right," returned Blinky unsteadily.

214

At this juncture they were called to breakfast. Pan needed only one glance at his father, his mother and Lucy to gather that bewilderment and worry had vanished. They knew that he knew. It seemed to Pan that the bursting sun knew the dark world had been transformed to a shining one. Yet he played with his happiness like a cat with a mouse.

"Mrs. Smith," begged Blinky presently, "please fix me up some breakfast fer Louise. She's better this mawnin' an' I reckon in a day or so will be helpin' you an' Lucy."

Pan set himself some camp tasks for the moment, and annoyed his mother and embarrassed Lucy by plunging into duties they considered theirs.

"Mother, don't you and Lucy realize we are going to a far country?" he queried. "We must rustle. . . . There's the open road. Ho for Siccane—for sunny Arizonaland!"

When he presented himself before Louise he scarcely recognized her in the prim, comely change of apparel. The atmosphere of the Yellow Mine had vanished. She had managed to eat some breakfast. Blinky discreetly found a task that took him away.

"We've a little time to talk now, Louie," said Pan. "They'll be packing the wagons."

He led her under the cottonwoods to the pasture fence where he found a seat for her.

"Pan, why did you do this thing?" she asked.

That was the very question he had hoped she would put first.

"Because my friend loves you and you told me you tried to keep him away from you—that if you didn't you would like him too well," answered Pan. "Blink had never been any good in the past. Just a wild reckless hard-drinking cowpuncher. But his heart was big. Then you were going straight to hell. You'd have been knifed or shot in some brawl, or have killed yourself with drink. A few more months of the Yellow Mine would have been your end. . . . Well, I thought, here's an opportunity to make a man out of my friend, and save the soul of a girl who hasn't had a chance I never hesitated about taking advantage of you. That was only a means to an end. So I planned it and did it "

"But, Pan—how impossible!" she replied brokenly.

"Why, I'd like to know?"

215

"I am—degraded."

"No! I've a different notion. You were *not* when you were sober. But even so, *that* is past."

"Blink might have been what you said, but still I—I'm no fit wife for him."

"You *can* be," went on Pan with strong feeling. "Just blot out the past. Begin now. Blink will make a good man, a successful rancher. He has money enough to start with. He'll never drink again. No matter what you call yourself, you're the only girl he ever loved. You're the only one who can make him earnest. Blink saw as well as I the pity of it—your miserable existence there in that gambling hell."

"Pan, you talk—like—oh, you make me think of what might have been," she cried. "But I'll not consent. I'll not give men the right to point their fingers at Blink. . . . I'll run away—or—or kill myself."

"Louie, that is silly talk," censured Pan sharply. "Don't make me regret my interest in you—my affection. You are judging this thing with your mind on the past. You're not considering the rough wild raw life we cowboys have lived. We must make way for the pioneers and become pioneers ourselves. In fifty years, when the West is settled, who will ever recall such as you and Blinky? These are hard days. You can do as much for the future of the West as *any* woman, Louise Melliss!"

"Pan, I understand—I—I could—I know, if I dared to bury it all. But I want to play square."

"Could you come to love my friend—in time—I mean? That's the great thing."

"I believe I love him now," she murmured. "That's why I *can't* risk it. Someone who knew me would turn up. To disgrace my husband—and—and children, if I had any."

"Not one chance in a million," flashed Pan, feeling that she could not withstand him. "We're going far—into another country. . . . Besides, everyone in Marco believes you lost your life in the fire."

"What—fire?"

"The Yellow Mine burned. It must have caught—when we shot out the lamps . . . Dick Hardman was burned, and a girl they took for you."

Suddenly Louise leaped up, ghastly pale.

"I remember now . . . Blink came to my room," she said hoarsely. "I wouldn't let him in. Then you came . . . oh, I remember now. I let you in when all the time Dick Hardman was hiding in my closet."

"I knew you had him hidden," rejoined Pan.

"You meant to kill him! The yellow dog! . . . He came to me when I was sick in bed. He begged me to hide him. And I did. . . . Then you talked to me, as you're talking now . . . Blink came with the whisky. Oh, I see it all now!"

"Sure. And, Louie—what did I tell you about Hardman?" returned Pan, sure of his ground now and stern in his forcefulness.

"I don't remember."

"You told me Hardman said he'd marry you, and that someday when you were drunk you'd do it."

"Yes, he said that, and I might have agreed, but I don't remember telling you."

"Well, you did. And then I told you Hardman had forced my sweetheart, Lucy, to marry him."

"*What?* He did that?"

"Reckon he did. I got there too late. But I drove him off to get a gun. Then he hid there with you."

"So that was why?" she pondered, as if trying to penetrate the cloudiness of her mind. "Something comes like a horrible dream."

"Sure," he hurried on. "Let me get it over. . . . I told you he couldn't marry you when he already had a wife. You went crazy then. You betrayed Hardman. . . . He came rushing out of the closet. Pretty nasty, he was, Louie . . . well, I left him lying in the hall! I grabbed you—wrapped you in a blanket—and ran out. Blink was waiting. He shot out the lights in the saloon. We got away. The place burned up, with some girl they took for you—and Hardman—"

"My God! Burned alive?"

"No," replied Pan hoarsely.

"Pan—you—you avenged me—and your Lucy—you?" she whispered, clinging to him.

"Hush! Don't speak it! Don't ever *think* it again," he said sternly. "That's our secret. Rumor has it he fled from me to hide with you, and you were both burned up."

"But Lucy—your mother!" she cried.

"They know nothing except that you're my friend's wife—that you've been ill," he replied. "They're all kindness and sympathy. Dad never saw you, and Gus will keep his mouth shut. Play your part now, Louise. You and Blink make up your past. Just a few simple statements. . . . Then bury the past forever."

"Oh—I'm slipping—slipping—" she whispered, bursting into tears. "Help me—back to the wagon."

She walked a few rods with Pan's arm supporting her. Then she collapsed. He had to carry her to the wagon, where he deposited her, sobbing and limp behind the canvas curtains. Pan pitied her with all his heart, yet he was glad indeed she had broken down. It had been easier than he had anticipated.

Then he espied Blinky coming in manifest concern.

"Pard," said Pan in his ear, "you've a pat hand. Play it for all you're worth."

The wagons rolled down the long winding open road.

For the shortest, fullest eight hours Pan had ever experienced he matched his wits against the wild horses that he and Gus had to drive. It was a down grade and the wagons rolled thirty miles before Pan picked a camp site in the mouth of a little grassy canyon where the wild horses could be corralled. Jack rabbits, deer, coyotes ranged away from the noisy invasion of their solitude. It was wild country. Marco was distant forty miles up the sweeping ridges—far behind—gone into the past.

As the wagons rolled one by one up to the camping place, Pan observed that Blinky, the last to arrive, had a companion on the driver's seat beside him. Pan waved a glad hand. It was Louise who waved in return. Wind and sun had warmed the pallor out of her face.

Four days on the way to Siccane! The wild horses were no longer wild. The travelers to the far country had become like one big family. They all had their tasks. Even Bobby sat on his father's knee and drove the team down the open road toward the homestead where he was to grow into a pioneer lad.

So far Pan had carried on his pretense of aloofness from

218

Lucy, apparently blind to the wondering appeal in her eyes. Long ago he had forgiven her. Yet he waited, divining surely that some day or night when an opportune moment came, she would voice the question in her eyes. He thought he could hold out longer than she could.

That very evening when he went to fetch water she waylaid him, surprised him.

"Panhandle Smith, you are *killing* me!" she said with great eyes of accusation.

"How so?" he asked weakly.

"You know," she retorted. "And I won't stand it longer."

"What is it you won't stand?" teased Pan.

But suddenly Lucy broke down. "Don't. Don't keep it up," she cried desperately. "I know it was a terrible thing to do. But I told you why. . . . I *couldn't* have gone away with him—after I'd seen you."

"Well, I'm glad to hear that. I was mad enough to think you might—even care for him."

"Pan, I love only you. All my life it's been only you."

"Lucy! . . . Tomorrow we ride into Green River. Will you marry me there?"

"Yes—if you—love me," she whispered, going close to him.

Pan dropped both of the buckets, splashing water everywhere.

Arizonaland!

It was not only a far country attained, but another, strange and beautiful. Siccane lay a white and green dot far over the purple sage. The golden-walled mesas stood up, black fringed against the blue. In the bold notches burned the red of autumn foliage. Valleys spread between the tablelands. There was room for a hundred homesteads. Pan's keen eye sighted only a few and they were farther on, green squares in the gray. Down toward Siccane cattle made tiny specks on the vast expanse. Square miles of bleached grass contended with the surrounding slopes of sage, sweeping with slow graceful rise up to the bases of the walls and mesas.

"Water! Grass! No fences!" exclaimed Pan's father, with a glad note of renewed youth.

"Dad. Lucy. Look," replied Pan, pointing across the valley. "See that first big notch in the wall? Thick with bright green? There's water. And see the open canyon with the cedars scattered? What a place for a ranch. It has been waiting for us all these years . . . That's where we'll homestead."

"Wal, pard, an' you, Louie—look over heah aways," drawled Blinky, with long arm outstretched. "See the red circle wall, with the brook shinin' down like a ribbon. Lookin' to the south! Warm in winter—cool in summer. Shore's I was born in the West thet's the homestead fer me."

The wagons rolled on behind wild horses that needed little driving. Down the long winding open road across the valley! And so on into the rich grass where no wheel track showed—on into the sage toward the lonely beckoning walls.